Hell's Game

Teresa Lo

Also by Teresa Lo
The Red Lantern Scandals

This book is a work of fiction. Names, characters, places and incidents are either the product of the author's imagination or are used fictitiously. Any resemblance to actual persons, living or dead, business establishment, events, or locales is entirely coincidental.

ACKNOWLEDGMENTS

Thank you to Eric Smith, Rebecca Lo, Rebecca Bumgarner, and Lizette Clarke for the notes and feedback. Thank you to my family for your continued support, and to the readers who make this all worth it.

This book is dedicated to the victims of bullying.

PART ONE: HALLOWEEN NIGHT

Do not be afraid of those who kill the body but cannot kill the soul. Rather, be afraid of The One who can destroy both soul and body in Hell.

-Matthew 10:28

CHAPTER ONE

They shouldn't have been out that night.

It was Halloween in Deer Creek, Kansas, and everyone knew not to go out, at least not once it got dark. The stores sold costumes, candy, and decorations for the holiday, but because of the curfew, everyone in town who wanted to trick-or-treat or play dress up celebrated the evening before. The curfew stated that all Deer Creek citizens must not be out on October 31st once the sun set, and if anyone was found violating the curfew, then they could be fined or face jail time. No one really questioned the law because it had been around for decades. Staying in on the holiday was just what people did.

Until that night.

Jake Victor's black Mustang roared through town, its streets completely empty and the night chilly and smelling like autumn leaves and pumpkins.

Jake drove while staring straight ahead, deep in thought. Although he was not model-perfect, he was handsome. He had nice dark hair. Big brown eyes. An All-American look. He was incredibly popular even though he wasn't from a rich or influential family, but he was a terrific athlete and a nice, charismatic guy that everyone seemed to like.

Dressed as an angel, Jake's beautiful blonde girlfriend Ashley Gemini, rolled down the passenger window. She climbed halfway out, laughing at the freedom of being alone in public, laughing at rebelling from a stupid rule created by stupid old people.

"It's Halloween, bitches!" she screamed in the air as it whipped through her wavy hair. Her pretty blue eyes sparkled as she took in the sight of Deer Creek's Main Street. There were little Mom-and-Pop shops, a bakery, and a post office, and the storefronts were quaint and inviting, offering a picturesque view of small town, Midwestern life.

Jake glanced at Ashley, concerned. "Ashley, get down from there," he said. He felt awkward reprimanding his girlfriend, and sometimes he wondered how they had lasted two years as a couple. They were so different, personality-wise, which was the main reason they fought, but on the other hand, they were also incredibly attracted to each other. Ashley loved how he was the epitome of the tall, dark, and handsome leading man; and Jake liked her classic features, her blonde hair, and her crisp blue eyes.

Ashley ignored him and continued to let the wind play with her hair.

"You excited, Ronnie? We're going to see The Gateway to Hell!" Ashley's twin brother Ashton said from the backseat. He was tall and lithe. The definition of a blonde pretty boy. He sat with his arm wrapped around his girlfriend Kristin Grace, and she sat in between him and the redheaded dweeb Ronnie Smalls, who smiled nervously. Ronnie held a camera in his lap, and his nervous, sweaty palms soaked into the plastic of its exterior.

"What do you think the "Gateway to Hell" is exactly?" Kristin asked, and Ashton gazed at her warmly. Besides her sweet personality, he loved how unaware she was of her beauty. She had large, almond-shaped eyes, long black hair, thin limbs, and a smile that could put the tensest person at ease.

Ashton turned to Ronnie, and in a dramatic tone, he said, "I hear that the Gateway is where the Devil comes out to snatch the souls of the wicked."

Ronnie gulped, and Jake looked into the rearview mirror as Ashton winked at him.

"You're so full of it, man," Jake said. He smiled to show he was kidding, but inside, he was worried that he and Ashley were crossing the line with Ronnie. The poor kid was an outsider to the group who wanted so desperately to break into it.

"Oh, yeah?" Ashton asked before he took a swig from his can of beer. "What do you think it is?"

"There's no Gateway to Hell," Jake said. "That's just something old people say to scare us. My Mom said the real reason for the curfew is that a group of kids got hurt at the cemetery years ago. Mayor Hercules went berserk."

"Ugh, that guy," Ashton said, making a face. "Why's he always wearing suits, even in the summer? He looks like the ghost from *Poltergeist*."

Jake shrugged. "Well, he started the curfew. That's what my mom told me."

Ashley climbed back into the car, the adrenaline rush making her giddy. "Were you guys talking about Mayor Hercules?" she asked.

"We were talking about where this Gateway to Hell business started," Jake said.

"Ah, are you scared?" Ashley asked as she reached over to touch Jake's strong jaw in a flirty manner. "Don't be. I'll protect you from the demons."

Jake tried to suppress a smile, but Ashley always had a way with him.

"This whole curfew is set just to control everybody," Ashley continued. "The adults in charge take advantage of the fact that people here are like zombies. They don't think for themselves. Everyone in this town is such a stupid piece of shit!"

"Watch the language!" Ashton teased.

"It's true!" Ashley said. She looked to Ronnie. "I'm glad you're here to take pictures. We can show everyone how stupid this curfew really is."

Jake glanced in his rearview mirror at Ronnie, who was now blushing. He wore a letterman jacket like Jake and Ashton did despite not being on the varsity football or basketball team. Only the varsity players and the varsity cheerleaders were given jackets by the Booster Club, but Ronnie had gone to the store by himself and purchased his own. The jacket cost him over six months of wages from his part-time job working with his dad as a janitor at the hospital, but he thought it would be worth it. The store didn't have one in his size, so he bought a large, which engulfed him and made him look like he was ten-years-old.

Jake's vintage Mustang pulled into the cemetery's parking lot, and Ashley stopped looking at her beautiful reflection in the passenger mirror to squeal in delight. "We're heeeeere," she sang.

Ronnie walked slowly as the group moved closer to the church. He stared up at the cloudless sky, at the bright stars and the full moon that shone above him. The air smelled like dry grass and evergreen trees, most likely from the forest surrounding the cemetery. The temperature was cool, not too cold but slightly chilly from the night breeze. On any other evening, tonight would be quite beautiful, but tonight, it was eerie and silent. It was as if even the animals and the crickets knew better than to be around.

The cemetery had a four-acre spread of land, and the old church sat right in the middle. With its two empty windows and a heavy metal door between them, the front of the church looked like a sad face, begging them to walk away and leave it in peace.

"It doesn't look so bad," Ashton said. He stared upward at the church's pagan cross that rested on the frame of the roof.

"Let's go home," Kristin said, and Ashton put his arm around her. It surprised him to find that she was shaking.

"Awww, are you scared?" he asked.

"I don't think we should be here," she replied. "Something doesn't feel right."

"You should go down there and take pictures," Ashley said to Ronnie, motioning to the church. Jake shot her a warning glance.

"Really?" Ronnie asked with a tremble in his voice.

"Yes, really," she replied. "You're supposed to take pictures of everything so that we can show people how stupid the curfew is. How this cemetery isn't scary at all. So far you haven't been taking pictures of anything."

Ronnie awkwardly snapped a photo of Ashley, and she stared at him, annoyed.

"That's not what I asked you to do," she snapped, and his face reddened as bright as his hair.

After a few painful moments of watching Ashley scold Ronnie, Jake sighed. "This is stupid," he said. He really questioned why he had agreed to do this. What if the cemetery's groundskeeper appeared and threatened to call the police? Jake really couldn't afford to get into any trouble. He didn't want to ruin his future of getting a college scholarship and getting the hell out of Deer Creek.

"You're not taking tonight's rebellion seriously," Ashley barked.

"Let's go home," Jake said. "And stop trying to get Ronnie to go into the church. He doesn't want to."

"Yes, he does."

"No, he doesn't."

"Yes, he does. Ask him."

Ronnie stared at the two of them. He felt like he had to choose between his Mom and Dad in a divorce proceeding, and he didn't know what to say.

"You don't have to," Jake said, and Ronnie stared back at him, unsure if he was being tested. He looked to Ashley.

"Really?" Ronnie finally asked. Jake was annoyed that Ronnie only cared about receiving her approval. After all, it was Jake who had once been Ronnie's childhood best friend.

She stared back at Ronnie cruelly as Jake looked on. "You don't have to go inside the church, but if you don't—then bye, bye popular table."

Ronnie's shoulders deflated.

"Think of tonight as your initiation," she added.

"You don't have to do anything you don't want to do," Jake said, but Ronnie felt that he was lying. Maybe Jake would allow him to cower away, but Ashley wouldn't. It was bad enough if he lost the privilege of sitting at the table with them on Monday, but he knew that if he didn't go up to the church, she would also tell everyone what a coward he was. People would mock him even more than they already did, and he shuddered at the thought of that.

"Can we go?" Kristin asked. "My mom's probably realized by now that I'm not in my room."

Ashton and Ashley stared at Ronnie, hard. He looked so frustrated that he was about to cry.

"No one can be a part of this group without being initiated," Ashley said, hoping to give him a boost. "And this is your initiation. If you don't do everything I say tonight, then you're not in the group. I want my damn pictures, and you promised to give them to me."

Ronnie remained silent.

"Oh, come on…" Jake said. He was ready to go, and he had had enough of this nonsense. He pulled out his keys and turned to walk back to his car. If the others weren't going to follow him, then they could walk home for all he cared. "I'm leaving now. You're welcome to stay, but you'd better find your own way back."

The twins knew Jake would never be cruel enough to leave them, so they ignored his threat and focused on Ronnie.

Ashley looked like a snake about to devour, while Ashton appeared to be nothing more than her twin crony.

"We all were initiated in some way or the other," Ashley lied. She looked to her brother for confirmation. "Tell him, Ashton."

Ashton shrugged his shoulders. Why not? He'd play along because this all seemed harmless enough.

Ashley smiled. "Kristin agrees, too. Right, Kristin?"

Kristin looked to Ronnie and Jake and then to Ashley and Ashton. She didn't know what to say.

"Umm…" she said, trying to stall. She hated lying.

Ashley rolled her eyes. Kristin's conscience really annoyed her sometimes.

"I'm going!" Jake yelled as he held up his car keys, but he had only taken three steps before he stopped.

"Make a decision already, Pencil Dick," Ashley said.

"What did you call me?" Ronnie asked. His cheeks flushed bright red. He had heard exactly what she had said. She had called him the nickname that the bullies at school had branded him with, a name that filled him with shame. Every time he heard it, he thought about the day he had received it, that day when the bullies had attacked him in the locker room shower.

"Nothing," Ashley said with a cruel smile. "All I'm saying is that if you don't go into the church after eleven, then you can return to your old status and kiss being our friend goodbye. I don't need your stinking pictures. I'll take them myself."

She walked up to him and snatched the camera that hung on a breakable cord around his neck.

"This isn't so hard. Why do we need you?" Ashley said as she made a big show out of taking pictures of everything around her.

Jake couldn't believe he was still watching this. "Ashley, stop," he said.

"Jake's right, Ashley. Let's go," Kristin interjected.

"No, Ronnie wasted my time. I'm not happy," she said. "Thanks a lot, Ronnie, for wasting my time."

"I'm sorry, Ashley," Ronnie said, and Jake couldn't believe he was apologizing.

Ronnie stared at Ashley, the embodiment of high school cool. She was beautiful, rich, and popular. Everything he wanted to be. He then glanced at the church, the symbol of his initiation into their circle of popularity.

"Then go into the church," Ashley said as her eyes bore into him, "and I promise you that no one will ever call you Pencil Dick again." She returned the camera to him, then gazed into his eyes as she gently clasped the strap back around his neck. His cheeks flushed again, and he could feel an erection forming. Luckily, no one else noticed.

"Do you promise?" he asked, his voice choking where his words came out like a whisper.

"I promise," she lied.

"Okay, I'll do it," Ronnie finally said, and Ashley smiled.

Jake put his keys back into his pocket and stormed over, upset.

"Fine," Jake said. "Just one picture and let's go!"

Ronnie nodded and got his camera ready, and Jake watched as he took his first step towards the metal door. As Ronnie approached, it was as if a light came on inside of the building, which made the windows flicker like the eyes of a Jack-o'-lantern.

Something was wrong.

Panicked, Jake ran forward and screamed out, "Don't go in there!"

Ronnie stopped. "What?" he asked, confused. Just seconds ago, Jake had given his consent.

"You don't have to do it!" Jake replied.

"Of course I do…" Ronnie said, dropping his camera, letting it dangle from his neck.

Ashley glared at her boyfriend as Ashton and Kristin stared back, mesmerized by the scene.

"Tell him, Kristin," Jake said. "We were never initiated. This is all a mean trick created by Ashley. Ronnie, Ashley's not going to let you hang out with us just because you go into the church."

"Is that true?" Ronnie asked.

Ashley glared at Jake. "Jake's lying," she said. "All of us had to do something like this. It's a rite of passage. He's the only one telling you otherwise because he doesn't want you to hang out with us. He told me this afternoon how he felt sorry for you ever since you were kids. He thinks you're a wimpy baby, and I personally think you're better than that."

Ronnie's eyes grew wide. "Is that true?" he asked Jake. His eyes watered and a lump stuck in his throat.

"You don't have to go into that church," Jake said, avoiding the question.

"He thinks you're pathetic and weak," Ashley said.

Jake looked to the ground, and Ronnie noted that he didn't deny her claim.

"Is what she's saying true?" Ronnie repeated. "Do you feel sorry for me?"

Jake wasn't good at lying, but he should've lied then.

Instead, he stood quiet.

Ronnie's lip quivered. At first it seemed as if he was going to cry, but to everyone's surprise, he exploded with anger, the years of pent up frustration boiling over towards his former friend.

"I'll show you, Jake!" Ronnie screamed, and he marched up to the metal door of the church. He grabbed the heavy handle, a bar that rested across the door.

"Ronnie, don't!" Jake yelled as the eyes of the church glowed red. Ronnie's hands gripped the metal, and evil laughter echoed from inside.

"See?" Ronnie said, triumphant. "I did it! I'm the only one who was brave enough to touch the church."

"You're supposed to go inside and take pictures. Not touch the door handle, jackass!" Ashley said. Jake stared at both her and Ronnie in confusion. Was he the only one who heard the laughter?

Ronnie let go of the handle, and he looked at the sinister-looking building in front of him. His initial courage had vanished, and he felt his palms sweat. He wiped them against the sides of his jean pants.

"Are you going to move or what, Smalls?" Ashton said. Kristin clutched at his arm, and she stared at Ronnie. Her eyes said it was okay to not go in, but her mouth remained shut. She looked as if something was eating away at her.

Ronnie looked to Jake, who motioned for him to leave. "Come on, Ronnie," Jake said. "I'm going to take you home."

Jake started to walk away, and this bothered Ronnie. It was as if he just assumed that he would follow him like a dog. Ashley smirked as Ronnie's face returned to its defiant glare.

"So what's it going to be, Smalls?" she called out.

Ronnie turned his back to the group, and he put his hands on the handle. The laughter inside roared, and a fire erupted behind the windows. Kristin's eyes widened as she saw it.

"Oh my God," Kristin whispered as she and the rest of the group stepped back, appalled.

"What's happening?" Ashley said.

Ronnie whimpered as his hands tried to release the handle. He felt his flesh burning, and when he looked down, he saw they were sizzling like hamburger meat on a grill.

"What's that smell?" Ashton asked.

Ronnie screamed as smoke erupted from his hands. With all of his might, he tried to let go of the handle, but it was as if an unseen force was pushing them down onto the burning metal. Tears streamed from his eyes.

"Help me!" Ronnie begged. "Help me!"

Jake ran up to the church. As his body moved closer and closer, he suddenly found himself smacked up against something, an invisible force field. Ashley, Ashton, and Kristin watched, horrified, their jaws dropped, their bodies frozen.

The laughter became a sinister whisper, chanting words from a language that no one knew.

The grip on Ronnie's hands released, and the heavy metal door flew open. Before he could move, giant black hands that were as gnarled as tree trunks flew out from the church and yanked him inside, into a wild party of flames. He screamed as the door slammed shut.

"What have I done?" Ashley whispered as her eyes filled with tears. Behind her, Ashton held Kristin tight against him as she trembled, and Jake fell to his knees in shock.

Then, as if nothing had happened, the eyes of the church returned to nothingness.

CHAPTER TWO

Ever since Jake was a child, he felt sorry for Ronnie. The two boys grew up in the same neighborhood in the lower-class part of Deer Creek. Jake's dad, Steve Victor, was a mechanic, and he owned Victor's Auto Body Shop. His mom, Rosie, was a secretary at the elementary school, but she often took days off because she was sick with lupus, a chronic condition where her immune system attacked her own body's cells and tissues. Ronnie's dad, Harvey, was a janitor at the hospital, and his mom, Monica, was a waitress at a diner.

Jake and Ronnie used to play Cowboys and Indians in the park behind Jake's house. The game wasn't the most politically correct one out there, but it was a game passed on from their parents who didn't really know any better.

The park was a secluded area with an open field and a rusty swing set, and Jake, the Indian, used to run away from Ronnie, the Cowboy, who would chase after him while wielding his plastic gun.

"I'm going to get you!" Ronnie screamed.

"Not if you can't find me!" Jake yelled back. He ran past the swing set into the woods behind the park. His fit body moved quickly, outpacing Ronnie by several steps. The tiny Ronnie stopped to take a breather, and Jake disappeared, running deep into the woods. Once he realized that Ronnie was no longer chasing him, he paused to lean against a tree.

After a few seconds, Jake began to worry, wondering why he couldn't hear Ronnie.

"Ronnie?" Jake called.

There was no answer.

Jake wiped the sweat off of his brow, and he removed his plastic dollar store feather piece. As he held it, he heard Ronnie scream in the distance. The sound startled him so much that he dropped it on the ground.

"Ronnie!" Jake yelled.

"Help! Help!"

Jake ran towards Ronnie's pleas, and as he approached his location in the woods, he heard other voices, older boys from the neighborhood.

"What a faggot outfit!" Bradley said as he ripped Ronnie's plastic badge off of his shirt. The pimple-faced Bradley was in sixth grade, and so were his husky friends Dustin and Leo, who stood behind him and sneered.

Ronnie winced as Bradley smashed his toy gun into the dry earth. Jake watched as he carefully approached, grabbing a large stick that laid nearby.

"Leave him alone," Jake said.

The boys turned around. Bradley smirked with amusement. He was at least a foot taller than Jake, and his cronies Dustin and Leo had over fifty pounds each over him.

"Or what?" Bradley said. "You think you're such hot shit, don't you, Victor?"

"You should pick on someone your own size," Jake said. He held the stick as if it were a baseball bat.

Bradley gazed at the stick and smiled. "Why should I when picking on the little guy is so much more fun?"

Bradley stepped closer, and Jake stiffened. He wasn't sure what to do, but the adrenaline in his body told him there were only two options—flight or fight. He locked eyes with Ronnie for a brief second and he knew which option he had to choose.

He swung. The stick whacked Bradley in the face, and he went down. Dustin and Leo swarmed in from behind, and Jake swiveled his body and hit each bully in the face with such force that they cried out as the splinters hit their flesh.

"You'll be sorry about this, Victor," Bradley said as he covered his swelling eye and cheek with his hand.

"Ronnie, let's go," Jake said. Ronnie nodded, and they hurried out of the woods. They looked back as they ran, but the boys did not chase them.

Once at the swing set in the park, they stopped because Ronnie was tired and needed to breathe.

"Are you okay?" Jake asked.

Ronnie nodded. "How'd you learn to do that?" Ronnie asked.

"My dad taught me everything he learned in the army," Jake replied, and Ronnie remained quiet. He wished that his father knew how to fight.

They didn't say anything else for the rest of the day, and that was the last time that Ronnie ever asked Jake to play Cowboys and Indians with him.

**

Jake parked his Mustang on the street in front his house. The lights were off because his parents were asleep inside.

Killing the engine, Jake lowered his head onto the wheel and took several deep breaths. He had just dropped off Ashley, Ashton, and Kristin at their homes. The conversation that they had in his car still replayed in his mind. He had agreed to keep silent, and already that agreement was eating away at his soul.

Jake closed his eyes, wanting to cry, but the tears wouldn't come.

"Why, Ronnie?" Jake whispered into the air as if Ronnie were sitting next to him. "Why'd you want to be our friend so badly?"

The imaginary Ronnie looked at Jake with sad eyes before beginning his story. "Because…"

**

In junior high, the locker room had individual stalls, and all of the boys kept to themselves after gym class. They changed out of their dirty uniforms, took a quick shower, and got dressed before leaving. It was fast and simple, which is why Ronnie was surprised on his first day of high school gym class. He saw the boys from grades nine through twelve hang around once class was over, and the bigger boys, the jocks, would stare at the others, evaluating their bodies. The ones who were inferior were pointed at and mocked.

"Hey, faggot!" one of the seniors yelled at a scrawny sophomore with frizzy brown hair. The jock sat on a bench with nothing but his towel on, and his friends stood behind him, watching their leader, waiting for him to entertain them. The sophomore had tried to scurry to the showers, a giant room with five nozzles, but he hadn't successfully avoided their attention.

Ronnie, whose locker was in a corner, watched with fear. He wasn't sure how he too could run away, but he was thankful that the sophomore had diverted their attention.

"What?" the sophomore asked meekly.

"He answered to 'faggot!'" the senior yelled out, and his friends burst into laughter as if this was the comedy extravaganza of the season.

The sophomore weakly smiled as his face turned red, but he was glad that they left him at that. He hurried to the shower, and the group moved their attention to Ronnie, who had tried to change inconspicuously out of his soiled gym clothes and into his regular attire.

"Dude, that's gross!" the senior yelled, noticing Ronnie's sweaty hair and clothing. "You're going to have B.O. if you don't shower."

Ronnie didn't know how to respond. His eyes widened, and his posture deflated as if he were an animal about to be attacked by his prey. Smelling weakness, the leader of the bullies stood up and his three friends followed.

Ronnie's eyes darted from side to side. He wished that he could run away, but they were approaching.

"It's dirty to not shower," the leader said.

"Don't be gross, freshman," his crony said behind him.

"Why don't you want to shower?" the leader asked. "Coach told everyone they have to shower after class."

Ronnie couldn't come up with anything to say, and they were staring at him, hard. "I didn't want to…" he said.

The leader sneered. "We have a rebel, folks. Someone who thinks he's above the rules."

Ronnie's eyes widened as the rest of the boys revealed their smiles. They might as well have had fangs with the way they were going to tear into him.

"You know, Coach always told us that it was our responsibility to promote teamwork," the leader said. "What's your name, freshman?"

Ronnie didn't want to give it to them.

"What's your name?" the leader's friend repeated.

"It's Ronnie," he quietly answered.

"*Ronnie…*" the leader said in a mocking tone. He turned to his friends and for a moment, Ronnie thought that they had lost interest in him, just like they had lost interest in the sophomore.

He was wrong.

"To the showers, boys!" the leader said. Without any warning, the boys swarmed. They grabbed Ronnie and hoisted him into the air. He was still wearing his street clothes, and he tried to wiggle out of their grasp but it was futile. The sophomore was the only one in the shower, and when he saw the boys coming, his eyes revealed his shock as he jumped back out of view. The leader turned one of the showerheads on, and icy water blasted downwards. The bullies threw Ronnie onto the tiled floor, still dressed, and he winced at the impact and as the cold water hit his flesh like tiny needles.

"Please, stop it!" Ronnie said. He turned and made eye contact with the sophomore, who gazed back at him with sympathy. Ronnie hoped to use ESP to communicate with his fellow victim to run and get Coach, but instead, the sophomore turned off the shower and ran away. He obviously did not want to get involved.

The bullies tore off Ronnie's clothes, the way the bullies in the woods had torn off his Cowboy memorabilia when he was a child. Ronnie closed his eyes and prayed to God. "Why do you always let this happen to me?" he asked as the last of his clothes were ripped away.

The bullies threw his wet clothes onto the shower floor, then stepped away to admire their work. Ronnie curled up into the fetal position as the icy water hit his exposed flesh and his private parts, which were average-sized and covered with red hair.

"Look at that pencil dick," the leader said as his friends laughed.

"Guess it's true that the carpets match the drapes!" another boy quipped.

Ronnie ignored them, hoping that they would go away. He closed his eyes and turned his face to the floor. At least they weren't beating him.

"See you later, Pencil Dick," the leader said.

Ronnie breathed a sigh of relief, glad that the episode had not escalated further.

As the bullies departed, Ronnie hoped that that was the end, but to his dismay, the boys had told everyone at school about what had happened. The nickname had stuck even once those boys had graduated, and eventually the name had evolved into Pencil Dick Smalls. Every time Ronnie heard those three cruel words, he remembered that day in the shower and how violated he felt. He remembered how he never wanted to feel that way for the rest of his life.

CHAPTER THREE

Kristin sat on the edge of her bed, which was decorated with a lilac spread that looked more suitable for a little girl than a teenager. Her dark hair was set into sausage curls, and her mother, who had styled her, overdid her blush. She wore a puffy yellow dress and black Mary Janes, looking and feeling more foolish than cute.

"Kristin?" her mother, Susie, called from downstairs. She spoke with a glaring Chinese accent, which often caused Kristin to wince in public.

"Yeah, Ma?" Kristin yelled back.

"You coming down? I no want to be late for church!"

"Almost ready!"

Kristin sighed and got off of the bed. She stood in front of her full-length mirror and grimaced at her doll-like appearance before she clomped down the stairs. Her mother sat in the living room, smiling as she gazed at her daughter.

Susie was a small Chinese woman who had once been incredibly beautiful, but now half of her face was disfigured with raised brown scars. Despite her appearance, she smiled a lot and had a positive outlook on life, but Kristin was mortified that her mother sounded different from the other people in town and resembled Two-Face from the Batman comics. She hated herself for her shame, but she hated her mother more for embarrassing her.

"You look so pretty!" Susie exclaimed.

Kristin weakly smiled, but didn't return the compliment. "You ready?" Kristin asked.

It was Sunday, over a week since Halloween, and her mother had yet to ask her where she had been that night. It was a miracle, really, that Susie had not known or said anything about Kristin sneaking out; and to show her gratitude for that miracle, she had finally agreed to accompany her mother to church. It had been her first time going since she was a child.

"I ready," Susie replied with a smile.

Kristin watched as her mother covered her face with a floral scarf, the way actresses used to do in the old movies. Susie never wore scarves to church, but today Kristin was accompanying her to service and she didn't want to embarrass her only child.

**

Downtown, cars pulled up to the Holy Church of Christ, the largest church in town, a massive stone structure with gigantic stain-glassed windows. On the second floor, in her father's office, Ashley watched church-patrons arrive. She scowled before turning away in disgust. Everyone looked so pious on Sunday when they were jerks every other day of the week. The hypocrisy made her sick.

Ashley sat at her father's desk, a massive piece of oak with several large drawers. When she and Ashton were in elementary school, they used to play hide and seek in the church before her father's sermon, and Ashton's favorite place to hide was underneath the desk, which was cool and dark. Sitting here now, however, the beautiful Ashley looked cold and stoic, as she always became whenever she was forced to enter this building. It had taken her years before she could finally re-enter this office in particular, and once she had conquered her fear of the space, she had gathered all of her courage to finally be able to sit at her father's desk.

As she sat in his gigantic leather chair and felt the wood of the desk on her fingertips, she remembered that horrific day when she was nine. The memories caused her face to harden more.

"What are you doing?" a voice asked.

Ashley jumped. Ashton was standing in the doorway, wearing his Sunday best. He would have looked handsome and radiant if he didn't look so angry.

"I was just people-watching," Ashley said.

"I don't like how you hang out in here," Ashton said.

She shrugged. "Maybe I'm a glutton for punishment."

Ashton stared at his sister, unsure of what to say.

"Dad's sermon's going to start in ten minutes," he said.

"Let's go," she said. "We can sit next to Kristin and her mom."

"Kristin came?"

"Yeah, I saw her."

"I didn't see Jake," Ashton said.

"He can't avoid us forever," Ashley said before getting up and following her brother downstairs.

**

Jake laid in his bed, staring up at the popcorn ceiling. He had bags underneath his eyes, his hair was a mess, and his pajamas were soiled. He hadn't showered or left his house in eight days, and his parents were worried that he had was depressed, or worse, catatonic. After Halloween night, he had become withdrawn, tired, and moody, and he had lost the ability to sleep because his nightmares haunted him. All he could think about was Ronnie and how guilty he felt because of that night. If he hadn't have angered Ronnie, if he hadn't had made Ronnie feel as if he had something to prove, maybe They wouldn't have snatched him away.

After they had left the cemetery on Halloween, Ashley had whispered, "Nobody knows we were out with Ronnie tonight."

Jake's Mustang was the only car out on the roads. The shops were empty. The restaurants were closed. They were the only ones stupid enough to be out.

"I don't want to talk about this," Ashton said. Jake was grateful that Ashton had expressed this, because his own lips were unable to articulate any type of thought. His mind was too focused on those gnarled hands, the smell of Ronnie's flesh, and the sound of Ronnie's screams. Jake didn't want to think about what was happening to Ronnie's body or his soul, but he couldn't stop picturing the flames and those hands, scratching at Ronnie until the blood drained from his body.

"I don't want to talk about it either, dick breath, but we have to," Ashley said.

Ashton's jaw tightened, and his arm around Kristin pulled her closer. She clung to him and buried her face into his chest.

"Aren't you done with the names?" Jake said, but Ashley ignored him.

The car was eerily silent before Kristin spoke up. "We're next," she whispered.

Jake nodded, agreeing.

Ashton shifted uncomfortably, but he didn't argue.

Only Ashley seemed to be in denial.

"What are you talking about?!" she screeched.

"We're next," Kristin repeated.

"I heard you. What do you mean, 'We're next?' What kind of creepy bullshit is that?"

"We were there when They took Ronnie. They know we're the ones who made him do it. They're going to come for us and take us to Hell because it was our fault he was at the church tonight."

Ashley shook her head. "You're talking crazy, Kristin."

Ashton and Jake stared at Ashley. Was she really so in denial with the role she had played an hour ago?

"You're the one who made him do it," Kristin said. It was out of character for her to be defiant, but at the moment, she was too broken down to care anymore about Ashley's opinion.

"I didn't do anything. He wanted to."

"You pressured him into it."

"It was a joke!"

"You called him Pencil Dick."

"I didn't do anything!"

Ashley was crying now. Those in the car couldn't tell if it was because she was scared or because she felt guilty. Either way, no one felt sorry for her.

"What should we do?" Ashley finally asked. Her face was contorted as tears streamed down her cheeks.

"We need to call the police," Jake said.

Ashley shook her head. "They're going to blame us. We could go to jail."

"What would we go to jail for? *Demons* took Ronnie. Not us!"

Ashton took a deep breath as he contemplated what was at stake. He was angry at his sister for coming up with the prank on Ronnie, but he was angry with himself for going along with it. If he were to ask himself why he had followed her plan, why he had never talked her out of her scheme, he wouldn't have a real answer. All he could say was that it seemed "not that bad" at the time.

"She's right," Ashton said after a long pause.

"Don't tell me you're listening to her again," Jake muttered, and Ashley shot him a dirty look.

"She's right," Ashton continued. "We broke curfew on Halloween. That offense could put us in jail alone."

"What are you trying to say?"

"I'm saying we keep quiet."

This request visibly upset Jake and Kristin. Ashley, on the other hand, nodded as if none of this had been her idea in the first place.

"I think you're right," she said.

Jake glared at her. He couldn't believe how manipulative she was.

"What do you say, Kristin?" Ashley said.

"Please don't ask me," Kristin said.

"We didn't force Ronnie to go into that church. He wanted to prove himself to us."

"You shouldn't have asked him to," Kristin said.

"But don't you see? We only asked him. We only took him to the cemetery. Why should we all hurt ourselves when we can just keep quiet?"

"We didn't do it," Kristin said. "You did!"

Ashley growled, her sweet demeanor turning sour. "Fuck you, Kristin!"

"You're going to burn in Hell like he is," Kristin said.

Ashley removed her seatbelt, ready to jump into the backseat to fight her. "I'm going to kill you!"

Ashton shielded his girlfriend from his sister. "Girls! Stop fighting!" Ashley retreated and Kristin covered her chest with her crossed arms. "There's no point blaming each other when we're *all* going to Hell. You can sit here in denial, but you know it's true. Demons saw us tonight, and we're next…"

There was a hushed silence as Ashton's words sunk into their minds. He was right. They had all stood there and let Ronnie walk up to the church doors. Although Kristin had not goaded him like Ashley had, she hadn't said anything to stop him, either. Even Jake, who had tried to change Ronnie's mind, didn't act until the last moment. Why had he picked up the entire crew that night in his Mustang? What would have happened if he had stayed home like he was supposed to? Those who allow evil to happen are just as bad as those who conduct evil themselves.

"Let's take a vote," Ashton said. "If we keep quiet, raise your hand."

"I'm going to the police," Jake said.

"Get off your high horse, Victor!" Ashley seethed. "If you go to the police, you better only speak for yourself because if you come for us, we're going to say that it was all your idea."

Jake shook his head. Ashley really was the embodiment of teenage, human evil.

"You don't believe me?" Ashley said. "Let's take a vote. All those in favor of keeping quiet?"

She turned around and saw Ashton's hand up. She glared at Kristin, forgetting their tiff seconds before. Kristin lost her previous courage. One look from Ashley and her hand tentatively rose.

"If Jake here goes against us, we'll band together. Right?" Ashley said.

Jake turned to her. "You really are a jerk, you know."

Ashton looked at Jake with sympathy. "I'm sorry, Jake," he said. Ashton really wanted to do the right thing, but at the moment, his first instinct was only to protect himself and his sister, an instinct that had first come to fruition when he was a child.

"You with them too, Kristin?" Jake asked.

Kristin remained quiet and diverted her eyes.

"You're all unbelievable," he said.

The defeat in his voice made Ashley feel relieved and victorious. "So are you going to the police?" she asked.

Jake glared at her, but she already knew the answer.

**

"So are you going to the police?"

That question replayed in Jake's head as he lied in his bed and stared at the popcorn ceiling. Days had passed since Ronnie's disappearance, and Jake had yet to call the Deer Creek Police Department. What if Ashley were right? What if calling the police would bring nothing but trouble for those who had lived, who had witnessed what happened to Ronnie? Calling the police wouldn't bring Ronnie back, but would it bring Ronnie's parents peace to know where their son had gone? Would they hate Jake for letting Ronnie go out with them that night? Yes, Jake realized. Of course they would.

There was a knock on the door. Jake heard it but stayed mute. His mother Rosie entered, and she stared down at her son. There was something wrong, and she worried it was because Ronnie Smalls, his childhood friend, had gone missing. Since Friday, two days ago, the disappearance was all over the news.

"Jake?" Rosie asked.

He ignored her. He knew what she was going to ask, and he didn't want to talk about it.

"Are you okay?" she said.

"I'm fine, Mom."

"They're going to find Ronnie. I know it."

He glanced at her. Rosie was a short woman with thin arms and mousy brown hair, and she was so naïve, so wholesome, so warm and good. It pained Jake to shame her and his equally good father, which is why he chose instead to hide the truth from them. "How do you know?" he asked.

"Because I prayed for him," Rosie said with all sincerity.

**

Sitting in a pew next to her mother, Kristin looked up and saw Ashton and Ashley approaching. Standing next to one another, they looked more like a movie star couple than brother and sister.

"Hi, Susie, Kristin," Ashton said. It was strange for him to see his girlfriend for the first time in over a week. She had done everything she could to avoid him and Ashley since Halloween, and seeing her now felt like meeting a stranger. It was as if Kristin had put up a wall between them.

Kristin said nothing to him, but Susie smiled. "Hi, Ashton, Ashley."

"Hello, Susie," Ashley said. She touched Susie gently on the shoulder, and Susie smiled back at her. She had heard rumors about Ashley not being a nice girl, but to her, Ashley was nothing but sweet and kind.

"Do you mind if we sit with you?" Ashton said.

Kristin tensed, but Susie didn't notice. "No, no! Sit!" Susie said. Kristin watched Ashton as he sat next to her, Ashley sitting beside him.

"Hey," Ashton whispered in Kristin's ear.

She said nothing.

At that moment, the congregation hushed. Ashley stared at her father, who had walked to the front of the room. He wore an expensive gray suit, his salt and pepper hair was neatly trimmed. He closed his eyes, preparing to speak, but when he looked up, he refused to make eye contact with his children, even though they were close to the front. He preferred, instead, to stare at random spots in the back of the church. To those who didn't know what he was doing, it appeared as if he was scanning the crowd, speaking to them personally about the Word of God.

"Good morning, ladies and gentleman," Pastor Benedict Gemini said. Behind him, his wife Heather waited beside the table with the collection plates and take-away Bibles, beaming proudly at her husband.

"Good morning," the crowd murmured in reply. Kristin shifted uncomfortably in her seat when she felt Pastor Gemini look her way. He was only finding a random spot in the crowd to focus his eyes, but Kristin felt as if he was boring into her soul.

"As many of you know, over a week ago, October 31st struck our peaceful town once again," Pastor Gemini said. The mention of the holiday sent chills amongst the quiet crowd. "I'm noticing the fear in your eyes, and as many of you are aware, one of our young men, Ronnie Smalls, has disappeared."

The tears felt warm as they streamed down Kristin's face. Susie noticed, and immediately, she reached into her purse and pulled out some tissues. She handed them to her daughter and wrapped her arm around her. "My poor daughter," she thought. "She has so much love for her classmates…"

Kristin blew her nose, and the sound was obnoxiously loud. It echoed throughout the cavernous room with its high ceiling, and a few church-goers turned to look at her with sympathy. The noise also brought Kristin the attention of Pastor and Mrs. Gemini, who gazed at Kristin and then their children who sat beside her. "Our children must've been friends with that boy," Heather Gemini thought. "That's the kind of children we raised. Children who are not only beautiful and well-liked, but who also befriend those beneath them."

It took Pastor Gemini a second to regain his focus. "I'm sorry," he said. "I know that there are many of you here today who have loved Ronnie, and I urge everyone, whether or not you knew him, to keep him in your prayers."

"Excuse me, Pastor Gemini!" a voice said from the back of the crowd. People's heads turned, trying to find the speaker. Pastor Gemini scanned the room before he noticed the former mayor, Clarke Hercules, standing. Mayor Hercules was nearly ninety-years-old, thin with sunken cheeks and wrinkled skin.

"Yes, Mayor Hercules?"

Mayor Hercules stood and glared at Pastor Gemini, a man he hated for his unearned self-righteousness.

"Do you have anything else to say?" Pastor Gemini said. His tone implied that the answer had better be "no." Mayor Hercules felt judgmental eyes on him. He looked around at the other church-goers faces, seeing a mix of pity, anger, and annoyance.

"I want to say how tragic it is that Ronnie Smalls has disappeared, and I hope in the future that others will heed the warning and respect the curfew," Mayor Hercules said.

Before he sat down, he stared at Ashley, Ashton, and Kristin, as if aware of their secret. His gaze was so strong that it caused their breaths to stop.

"Now that we may continue, I would like to discuss with you all, The Triumph of Evil," Pastor Gemini said. "And how Evil wins because Good lets it."

He took a dramatic pause, and Kristin fought to pull herself together.

She looked up as Pastor Gemini began speaking once again, and saw the ominous shadows behind him. She gasps. There had been no change in light, and yet the shadows were there, growing, expanding. They started off as strange squares behind him, and then the shadows splintered as if they were alive.

"In Michael 4:17-17, it states, "Anyone, then, who knows the good he ought to do and doesn't do it, sins.""

Kristin's eyes widened as the shadow splinters became 3D, morphing into gnarled tree trunks.

"Oh, God," she whispered once she realized that the tree trunks were actually the gnarled hands from the Deer Creek Cemetery Church.

Pastor Gemini gazed around the congregation. "Look around you. Look inside of yourself. Are you guilty of evil? Have you asked God to forgive you for your sins, or are you too in denial of what you have done—or worse, what you have seen but did nothing about?"

The giant gnarled hands reached toward the ceiling, their fingers spread and arched forward, ready to attack, their claws dropped down. Kristin's mouth quivered in fear as the hands plunged down towards Pastor Gemini. She screamed before they could dig their nails into his flesh, and the entire congregation gasped.

"Is something wrong, Kristin?" Pastor Gemini asked.

Kristin uncovered her eyes to see her mother, Ashton, Ashley, and everyone else in the church staring at her. She slowly looked up at Pastor Gemini and to her amazement, there were no gnarled hands, no shadows, no evil presence. The only beings present at the front of the church were Pastor Gemini and his wife, both of whom stared at Kristin as if she had completely lost it.

"Excuse me," she said to no one in particular. She then stormed out of the room, unaware that Mayor Hercules was watching her with a strange curiosity.

CHAPTER FOUR

Ashton remembered the first time he had fought for Kristin. He and Jake were thirteen and running laps on the track for football practice. The cheerleaders were on the field, practicing "How Funky Is Your Chicken," and the afternoon was unbearably muggy. Ashton's t-shirt and shorts clung to his body, and Jake was equally sweaty. His dark hair matted to his face as he squinted to avoid the glare of the sun.

"What do you think of her?" Jake asked, pointing to a thin redhead with disproportionately large breasts.

"A seven," Ashton said. Jake chuckled, but didn't correct him. Their game of rating women was one they had been playing for months.

"What about her?" Jake asked, pointing at the captain of the team, a beautiful blonde who yelled at the others in an authoritative, precocious way. Ashton grimaced with disgust.

"That's gross!" Ashton said. Jake burst into laughter. The captain looked over and flashed a pearly smile.

"Hey, Jake!" Ashley said.

"Hey, Ashley," Jake replied with a flirty wave.

As other football players lapped them, Ashton glared at his running partner.

"What?" Jake asked, playing dumb.

"Are you really into my sister or are you messing with me?"

Jake ignored him. He loved making Ashton squirm, and he watched as Ashley showed a petite Asian girl the proper arm movements for a cheer.

"What about her?" Jake asked, pointing to Kristin.

"Kristin? That's my sister's best friend."

"She seems too nice to be Ashley's friend."

Ashton laughed in agreement. "We used to live next door to her. Back when we lived on Bumgarner Avenue."

"Oh, right. When you were a commoner," Jake joked.

Ashton laughed, although the joke made him slightly uncomfortable. His father had warned him never to talk about the family's money, nor their history of once scraping by and then suddenly having it all. People often mentioned things to Ashton, but he brushed them off, just like he was told.

Jake didn't notice Ashton's fakeness. Instead, he gazed at Kristin, who seemed to sparkle in the sunlight. "I'm thinking of asking her to the homecoming dance," Jake said.

"Really?" Ashton asked. He watched as Kristin replicated Ashley's moves, and he noted how agile her body was. How pretty her round, open face was. How shiny her straight, black hair was in the sunlight. Since Ashton had known Kristin as a child, he had always had a crush on her, but he was too chicken to admit it.

"What do you think? Should I?" Jake asked.

Ashton gazed at the other cheerleaders, and none of them sparked his interest like Kristin had. It worried him that Jake was about to take something that he had always wanted but was too afraid to admit to wanting.

"*I'm* going to ask her out," Ashton said.

Jake stopped running to stare at his friend in disbelief. "What? You weren't into her until I said I was!"

"That's not true."

"Yes, it is!"

Kristin, Ashley, and the rest of the cheerleaders looked over to watch Jake and Ashton yell at each other.

"I'm going to ask her!" Jake said.

"No, I am!" Ashton said just before shoving Jake.

The girls gasped. The other football players on the track stopped running to watch as Deer Creek Junior High's most popular students began to wrestle each other on to the ground.

"What do you think they're fighting about?" Ashley asked Kristin.

"I have no idea," she replied.

Ashley saw blood, and her jaw dropped. "Oh, no. They're really hurting each other," she said before she ran over to them. Kristin followed her to the scene where a teacher had broken up the fight and was now examining Ashton, who had a bloody nose. Ashley and Kristin walked up to Jake, who rubbed away the blood on his lip.

"Are you okay?" Ashley asked as she gazed deeply into Jake's eyes.

"Your brother has a mean right hook," Jake replied, but he smiled when he said it.

Kristin noticed Ashley was putting a lot of effort into making Jake want her, so she awkwardly stepped back, not wanting to intrude and unsure of what to do or say. She looked over at the teacher lifting Ashton's chin up, trying to look up his nose to see if it was broken.

Ashton noticed Kristin watching him, and despite the pain, his eyes sparkled when they met hers. Kristin looked away, embarrassed, but he continued to stare at her, happy that he had finally caught her attention.

**

On Monday afternoon, present day, Ashton pulled up in his white BMW in front of Kristin's house, a two-story colonial on a quiet street in the middle of town. He wore a pressed button-down shirt and brown slacks, and held a bouquet of sunflowers. As he walked up to the front door, his armpits felt sweaty and his heart raced. He hadn't remembered being this nervous in years—not since the last time he brought Kristin sunflowers.

**

It was three years ago, when he was thirteen. Days had passed since his skirmish with Jake on the track, and he had been suspended from school for two days because of it. He felt bad that he had shoved his best friend, but the thought of someone taking Kristin away from him brought a reaction within him that surprised him, a violent, angry reaction that he couldn't control. Now that he had time to cool down, he had to strategize about how to win Kristin's affections before his charismatic best friend had a chance to.

"What should I do?" Ashton had asked Ashley, who was annoyed that two boys were fighting over someone that wasn't her. They sat in her bedroom, overlooking their vast backyard, and she had a faraway look in her eyes.

"Go to her house and ask her out. I'm sure Jake's going to wait until you guys get back to school," she replied.

"When should I go?"

"Go now. I'm sure she's home with her mom… She's *always* with her mom."

Ashton didn't know what she was talking about. Ashley realized that she had to give him some backstory.

"Kristin's dad's *always* doing business in Asia, so he's never home. If you ask me, I wouldn't be surprised if he had another family over there. He's a creep."

Ashton shifted, not liking the way his sister was gossiping about Kristin's family.

"I don't know if I can do this…" Ashton said.

"Don't chicken out now," Ashley said. "When did my brother become such a wimp?"

He knew that she was trying to dig at him, but decided to ignore her.

Ashley hoped that Kristin would choose to go to the dance with her brother. After all, if Kristin went with Jake, who would Ashley go with? There were older boys who would take her, or she could find someone else from out of town, but it just seemed natural for her, the captain of the cheerleading team to go with the school's quarterback.

"You should bring her sunflowers," Ashley said.

"Why?" Ashton asked. He originally planned to just go to her house and ask. Bringing something had never crossed his mind.

"Kristin loves sunflowers, and all girls want a boy to bring her flowers."

Ashton nodded, but his hands and neck felt clammy. The confidence boost he had experienced had already evaporated.

"What if she says no?" Ashton asked.

"Go there now. Ask her first, and she won't say no."

"How am I supposed to get there?" Ashton asked. The twins were home alone and there wasn't anyone available to drive them into town.

"Take Dad's car," Ashley replied. "He won't notice."

"I don't know…"

Ashley rolled her eyes. "If you wait any longer, then Jake might get to her first."

Ashton hesitated, and Ashley stared at him. Her brother had never been this nervous before, which she found surprising. Perhaps he really *did* like Kristin.

"She's not going to say no," Ashley said softly. Ashton gazed into her eyes, wanting to see if she was telling the truth.

She was.

Even though he didn't have a license, Ashton drove to a nearby flower shop and bought a dozen sunflowers. He pulled up in front of the Grace home, and he stared at the blue house next door to it. The Gemini family had lived on this street until a few years ago, before they had upgraded to their giant house in the countryside.

Ashton nervously wiped his sweaty palms on his jeans before he got out of his dad's car and walked up to the front door. Little did he know, Ashley had already called Kristin while he was on his way.

"My brother's going over to ask you to the dance," Ashley said into the phone. "He likes you a lot."

"Really?" Kristin asked.

Ashley rolled her eyes. Kristin really was so clueless sometimes. "What are you going to say?" she asked.

Kristin wasn't even sure she was going to the dance in the first place. Her father was going to be out of town, and her mother hated to be left alone at night.

"I don't know…" Kristin said.

"I'm going with Jake Victor, and you should double date with us. Say yes."

"I didn't know Jake was going with you," Kristin replied. She hadn't heard the news yet, and she was certain that Ashley would have mentioned it earlier.

"Well, we are," Ashley lied. "So what do you say? A double date would be really fun. Maybe we can eat at McCue's beforehand."

Kristin bit her lip. "I'm sorry, Ashley. My mom's going to be alone…"

Ashley sighed loudly, annoyed. "She'll understand, Kristin. Just say yes to my brother, okay?"

"I don't know…"

"Come on, Kristin!"

Kristin felt tense. If she didn't do what Ashley said, then she would never hear the end of it. Ashley tapped her foot as she held the phone receiver next to her ear. She hated to wait.

"Okay," Kristin finally said. Ashley squealed with delight.

**

When Ashton had stood on Kristin's doorstep three years ago, he was relieved at how easy it was to ask her out. She came to the door as soon as he rang the doorbell, and after he spit out his rambling request for her to be his date to the Homecoming Dance, she immediately said yes.

Now at sixteen, standing on her doorstep, Ashton felt nervous again.

"Here goes," he said.

He pressed the doorbell and took a step back. As the seconds passed, he replayed in his mind what he wanted to say. "I'm sorry, Kristin. I miss you. I love you. I hope that we can look past what happened." But as he thought these words, he knew how stupid they would sound coming out of his mouth. How could "sorry" make up for what they had done, what they had seen, what had tainted their innocence?

The door finally opened and Susie appeared, her face uncovered. She smiled warmly when she saw Ashton.

"Back to see my daughter so soon?" Susie asked. Ashton made sure to look into her pretty brown eyes, not at her scars.

"We didn't get a chance to talk much at church, and she didn't come to school today."

"She still feel sick," Susie said before she stepped closer to Ashton. Then she whispered to him a secret. "I think she still sad about her friend. Kristin alway sensitive."

Ashton swallowed hard. He hoped that Susie couldn't see the guilt on his face. She noticed that something was wrong, but she wasn't sure what. Her eyes studied him, and he searched for something to say.

Finally, he said, "That's what I like about her."

Susie eyed the flowers, and her smile widened. Ashton really did love her daughter, and he was handsome, smart, and wealthy. Although Susie would have liked for Kristin to go to college, she also wouldn't have minded if she married Ashton and followed him with his sure-to-be promising future.

"Kristin out back in garden," Susie said, allowing Ashton inside.

He walked through the living room, which had two overstuffed couches and two La-Z-Boys. The room smelled like incense and dust, and it was cluttered with items: pictures of the family in mismatched frames, Chinese scrolls, old magazines, and knick knacks purchased by Bryan Grace from his travels around Asia. After that, he passed through the kitchen, which was just as cluttered as the living room, only with various kitchen appliances purchased from Wal-Mart and the Home Shopping Network.

Ashton then reached the glass sliding door that led to the backyard. Through the glass, he saw Kristin hanging from a tire swing, and the way she gazed off into the grass caused him alarm. She had a deadened look on her face, reminding him of the lobotomized mental patients he saw on TV.

Ashton stepped into the backyard, and as he approached Kristin, he extended the sunflowers.

"Hey," he said.

She looked up and stared at him, then at the flowers, and then back at him. There was no gratitude or joy on her face. He awkwardly lowered the flowers and stepped closer.

"Hi, Ashton," Kristin said.

"You weren't at school today."

"I didn't feel like going."

"A lot of people called in sick because of Ronnie's disappearance."

"So is that supposed to make me feel better?" Kristin snapped.

Ashton stared at her, sitting lazily in her swing. This encounter was not going well at all.

"I brought you sunflowers," he said. "Your favorite."

She stared at the yellow flowers once again. "Thank you," she said with no feeling.

Ashton was starting to get really fed up. "God damn it, Kristin. I'm sorry about what happened on Halloween. I really am."

"Sorry won't bring Ronnie back."

"I don't want you to hate me for what happened. We didn't know that the legend was true."

"We shouldn't have goaded him like that."

Ashton had tears in his eyes now. He wasn't sure what was worse: what he had seen and done, or the prospect of losing Kristin. "I can't change what happened. I'm sorry about what we did, but I don't want you to hate me."

Kristin shook her head. "I shouldn't have listened to you."

"I'm sorry."

"You shouldn't have asked me to go. You shouldn't have listened to Ashley. You *always* listen to Ashley!"

Ashton didn't believe her. "That's not true."

Kristin glared at him. Every nasty thought that had circulated in her head was bubbling inside of her, begging to be let out. "What if she hadn't decided to pick on Ronnie? What if she had wanted *me* to go into the church?"

Ashton was confused. His sister would never pressure Kristin to do that. "What are you talking about?"

"What if I wasn't your girlfriend? What if she thought it would be funny to *initiate* me instead? What if it was me who had to walk up to the church?"

"Ashley would never do that..."

"Are you really that blind to what your sister is? She's cruel and she's vicious, and she could turn on any one of us at any second. And you're no better. You've always just been her blind lackey."

"Why are you being so mean?"

She couldn't stop now. Her feelings exploded out of her like a flood bursting out of a crack of a dam. "I'm sorry that I was ever Ashley's friend, and I'm sorry that you can't see her for what she is."

Ashton was angry now. Where was this coming from? "I didn't come here to talk about Ashley. I came here to see if you were okay, to see if *we* were okay. I didn't think that you'd be so hysterical."

Kristin's eyes widened with disbelief.

"Of course I'm hysterical!" she said. "I saw a boy dragged to Hell! I was a part of a group that brought him to slaughter. I have every right to be hysterical, and you have no right to act as if nothing happened!"

Ashton threw the sunflowers onto the ground.

"Don't talk to me like what we did isn't hurting me! I may not be a sad sack like you, Kristin, but don't tell me I'm not just as broken inside about what happened as you are! I can't sleep at night without seeing those gnarled hands. I can't brush my teeth without hearing Ronnie's screams in my head. I can't eat without smelling his burning flesh." Ashton was full on sobbing now. "I'm scared. I'm scared that we're going to face the Devil soon for what we did."

Kristin got off of the swing and hurried to comfort him. His body convulsed against hers, and he buried his face into her hair.

"I'm sorry," she whispered. "I'm scared, too."

"I need you," he said. "Don't leave me. I can't face this alone."

Kristin tensed, but she didn't let go. As he continued to let out his cries, she looked to the ground and saw the sunflowers lying in the grass. She gasped as the bright yellow petals withered suddenly into ugly gray leaves.

"What?" Ashton said. He stepped away, and Kristin looked at the blood dripping from his temple. She covered her mouth in horror and shock. "What?" he repeated, alarmed.

Kristin felt like gagging, but she had to know whether or not what she was seeing was real. Without a word, she slowly approached the confused Ashton, gingerly touching the side of his head where blood poured out of a gunshot wound. His blonde hair was soaked with blood, bits of brain oozing from the giant hole.

"What are you doing?" Ashton asked.

Kristin pulled her hand away, looking at the thick chunk of blood on her fingertips. How was he still alive?

"Kristin, are you okay?"

Kristin looked up, and to her surprise, Ashton was normal again, as if the hole in his head had never existed. She glanced at her hand and saw the blood was gone.

"I can't see you anymore," she said, and he flinched. "This is too hard for me. I need some time."

Ashton's voice quivered. "This is hard for all of us. We need to stick together."

Kristin shook her head. Nearby her, the sunflowers laid on the ground, just as Ashton had left them.

Ashton stepped forward and grabbed her hands. "I love you," he said, and it was true.

She shook her head again. Tears streamed down her face. "Being with you means being around your sister. I can't ask you to choose, and if I did, I know you'd pick her." Kristin dropped his hands and began walking back to the house.

"Kristin, wait!" Ashton said.

She turned. "I'm sorry, Ashton," she whispered. "But it's over."

**

Five miles outside of town, Ashton's BMW raced down the country road, the fallen red and gold tree leaves fluttering from his speed.

Inside the car, Ashton drank from a bottle of vodka that he had stashed in his glove compartment. His eyes glistened with tears.

"Stupid bitch," he said, wiping the snot from his nose.

With his foot still on the accelerator, he closed his eyes, wondering what would happen if he swerved sharply, letting his car run into the field of trees. He imagined the smash of the metal into the wood, the way his nose would crack as it hit the steering wheel, the blood that would gush from his face as the glass cut it to pieces.

He wondered if anyone would miss him if he were gone.

Ashton re-focused his attention on driving, noticing a gravel road coming up on his right. He took another sip of his vodka as he slowed to make the turn. The gravel made it hard for him to drive fast, and as he lowered his speed, he felt the bumps of the rocks.

He drove until he reached the road's end, just at the edge of a field. He parked his car and stepped out, bringing his vodka with him.

The sun set, filling the sky with oranges and pinks. Ashton's watery eyes took in the beauty around him, but his legs moved as if they were tied with hundred-pound weights. He walked through the tall grass of the field until he reached a clearing of dirt. Without thinking, he plopped down onto the ground and closed his eyes.

"Stupid bitch," he whispered again as visions of his sister filled his mind. He imagined what it would have been like if she were never born, and as he closed his eyes and fell asleep, he smiled at the thought of it.

**

Dead silence.

"Where are you, Ashton?" Ashley asked into the phone. She had been calling Ashton's cell for the past hour, but he hadn't answered. She stared outside, at the moonlight and the stars, worrying about her brother's disappearance. She knew that he had gone to see Kristin, and she had figured it would go poorly. After all, she felt the tension in church, even before Kristin had her breakdown. She wanted to talk to Kristin about what had happened on Halloween night, too, but it wasn't time yet. Ashton, on the other hand, couldn't go a day without Kristin's affection. His constant need for her love really bothered his sister.

She dialed the Grace home next. With each ring, her impatience grew. She knew Kristin and her mother were screening her call.

"I know you're there…" she said.

Finally, after the third attempt, she slammed the phone down into the cradle. She paced around her bedroom, painted pink and white, and decorated with photographs of her with Jake, her brother, and Kristin. Above her bed was a giant painting of a white horse, her favorite animal since she was a little girl.

Ashley's grandparents on her mother's side lived outside of
Kansas City, on a massive estate with a pond, tennis court, and a
stable. Every Thanksgiving, the Geminis would stay there for the
weekend, and Ashley would always sneak away to see the horses.
Her favorite was Angela, a white mare with golden hair. Ashley
loved to brush Angela's hair, and while she did so, she would sing
a song that only she knew:

"*I'll take care of you, until the end of the time. I'll always love you,
but I can't make you mine...*

"*I'm sorry we can't be together, pretty girl, but I promise through the
darkness that I will guide you to the light...*"

"What are you singing?" Ashton asked one evening,
startling Ashley out of her song. The twins were eleven-years-old
at the time.

"Nothing," Ashley said.

"Where'd you hear that song? It's not on the radio..."

"I don't know. Someone sang it to me."

"Who? Was it Mom?"

Both of them knew that question was preposterous. Their
mother Heather only showed them attention at church when
other people were watching.

"A man sang it to me," Ashley said.

"Who?" Ashton asked.

"I don't know..."

Ashton stared at her as if she were crazy, and Ashley
decided then and there to never mention the song to him ever
again.

**

Ashley thought about Angela and the song even though angry
music was blasting from her car stereo as she sped down the road
to Kristin's house. When she arrived at her destination, she
slammed her car door shut and strode to the front door in a rage.

She pressed the doorbell. She heard the familiar *ding-dong* chime reverberate throughout the house, but no one was answering.

"I know you're home, you jerk," Ashley said. She stepped away from the door and looked upwards, where lights were on. She pressed again, four times incessantly, but still no answer. "Open the door, Kristin!" Ashley yelled as she pounded against the wood.

Inside the house, Susie stared at her daughter, waiting for her to tell her what to do. Kristin sat across from her in the kitchen, her skin pale and her eyes lifeless. She felt as drained as she looked. All she wanted was to be left alone.

"You should speak to her, Kristin," Susie said quietly.

They stared towards the front door, where the pounding continued.

"I don't want to talk to her, Ma," Kristin replied.

"She won't go away unless you do."

Kristin looked into her mother's eyes, and she knew she was right. She sighed before trudging towards the door. With each step she took, her body filled with dread.

"Open this door!" Ashley yelled, as if she knew Kristin was only a few feet away. Kristin unlocked the door, and it flew open, just as Ashley was about to strike again.

"Finally!" Ashley said.

"What do you want?" Kristin asked, her arms crossed.

"Where's my brother?"

Kristin stared at Ashley, whose wild eyes and tense body revealed that she truly was worried. Kristin thought about her afternoon conversation with Ashton. He had been upset when he left, but would he go missing? What if demons had snatched him away?

"Kristin!" Ashley said, seeing her former friend's faraway gaze and wanting her to snap out of it. "Where is he?"

"I don't know. He left hours ago."

"Was he okay? Did you say something to upset him?"

Kristin glared at Ashley. Of course she would manipulate things to make it *her* fault.

"I told him that I didn't want to be with him anymore," Kristin said. "I don't want anything to do with him, or you either."

Ashley gaped at her with her mouth hanging open.

"Why the hell would you do that? You know how sensitive my brother is!"

Kristin's jaw tightened with anger. It took every bit of willpower inside of her not to slam the door in Ashley's face.

"Ashton's not here. I'm sorry," Kristin said. She was about to shut the door when Ashley pushed it back open.

"Well, he didn't come home," Ashley said. "I need you to help me find him."

Kristin and Ashley were now in a standoff, but no matter what ill will existed between them, Kristin still cared about Ashton.

She sighed, succumbing to Ashley once again. "Fine," she said begrudgingly. "I'll go with you to look for him."

**

In the car, while Ashley blasted her angry music again, Kristin rubbed at her ears. She had hoped to not have to speak to Ashley at all, for fear she would twist her words around—but the music was jarring and it was giving her a headache.

"Can we turn this off, please?" Kristin asked.

"This is the only CD I have," Ashley said.

"Fine. What about the radio?"

Ashley sighed, making sure Kristin knew how much of a chore turning the dial was for her. She groaned when sedated music emerged. "Gross," Ashley said. She tried to change the channel but all the stations were also playing slow, sad music. It reminded her of the secret song she liked when she was a child.

"We don't need this," she griped as she turned the music off, leaving her and Kristin to sit in awkward silence. Ashley glanced over at Kristin, who stared straight ahead.

"Are you going to ignore me?" Ashley asked.

Kristin glanced over without saying anything.

Ashley rolled her eyes. "It's not my fault, you know."

Kristin stared at Ashley in disbelief. Was she seriously trying to have this conversation?

"Don't look at me like that. You were there, too."

"It wasn't my idea, Ashley!" Kristin said. She regretted opening her mouth, but she wasn't going to be a pushover either. Not anymore.

"I didn't think the legend was real, okay? Nobody did. Admit it."

Kristin agreed with her there, and it killed her to admit it to herself.

"You're not going to say anything, are you?" Ashley asked.

"Is that what this is about? You're worried we're going to nark? Is Ashton even missing?"

"Yes, he's missing! I wouldn't lie about that."

"With you, I never know…"

"I just mentioned the other stuff because there's nothing we can do. The only people who need to know what we did are each other and God. Nobody else in this town needs to be involved."

Kristin folded her arms and stared ahead. "You really are a piece of work."

"So you promise not to say anything?"

Kristin was fed up. "I just want to find Ashton and go home," she said. "Stop talking about Halloween!"

Ashley was satisfied by this answer. Even though Kristin was frustrated, she was willing to keep their secret, and that's all that mattered. "Maybe he's with Jake," Ashley said. She knew perfectly well that her brother wasn't with him, but she wanted to see her boyfriend—if he still *was* even her boyfriend. He had been in hiding since Halloween, and she really wanted to talk to him, to hear his voice.

"I doubt he's with Jake," Kristin said.

"What if he is?"

"He's not."

"How would you know?" Ashley glared at Kristin suspiciously. "Have you talked to him?"

"No, I haven't," Kristin replied. She knew that Ashley was jealous of her and Jake, though she found it flabbergasting. She and Jake never spent time together unless Ashley or Ashton was around, and it wasn't as though Jake had ever expressed any feelings for her.

"Then how do you know?" Ashley asked.

"I just have a feeling."

"But we've tried everywhere else."

"He's not with Jake."

"Then what if he's dead, Kristin?!"

The tension in the car increased ten-fold. Kristin balled up her fists angrily, upset that Ashley had played that card. It was Ashley now who stared straight ahead, thinking of the ominous words she had spit out. She had said them without thinking, just to get her way, but as the words hung in the air, she wondered if they were true.

"Let's see if he's with Jake," Ashley said. Kristin didn't argue as Ashley turned towards Jake's part of town.

**

The Victor family lived on the east part of town, where the lower-middle class homes were located. Their street was quiet in comparison to the others nearby, but Ashley hated to visit the area. She always felt like people were staring outside their windows, watching her and waiting for her to leave her car unattended or her doors unlocked.

"I doubt Jake's home," Kristin said.

Ashley gazed at the Victor home, a small bungalow with flowers lining the walkway to the front porch. There weren't any lights on inside, but Jake's Mustang was parked on the street and his Dad's truck sat in the driveway.

"We'll see about that," Ashley replied.

"Ashton's car isn't here either…" Kristin said, but by then, Ashley had already exited the car. As she headed up towards the porch, Kristin scrambled out of her seat.

"You better not knock on their door the way you did to mine," Kristin said.

"I'm not knocking," Ashley said. She bent down to search underneath the porch bench, where she found a key taped to the wood. "Gotcha," she said as she put the key into the doorknob. Kristin watched with amazement as Ashley stepped inside.

"Come on," Ashley said, leaving Kristin with no choice but to follow.

The living room was dark and smelled stale. Light seeped through the cracks in the blinds, and Kristin could see a few pieces of furniture that reminded her of the ones in her own home. She was so entranced by the unfamiliar space that she bumped her leg into a side table. She groaned, wincing from the sharp pain.

"Shhhh!" Ashley said. "We have to get upstairs."

Kristin shot Ashley a dirty look, but she obediently followed her up the old wooden steps, creaky and noisy underneath their feet.

"Shit," Ashley whispered.

"Let's walk slower," Kristin said.

They slowed their movements to lessen the sound, but it didn't matter. With each step, the wood wailed, and the girls grimaced as their eyes darted from side to side.

"We're going to get caught!" Kristin said.

"Fuck it. Run," Ashley said. They bolted upwards, and once they reached the landing, Ashley took a left turn. She hurried towards a closed door at the end of the hallway and without hesitation, turned the knob to Jake's room.

When the door flew open, she stopped dead in her tracks. Though she came specifically to see Jake, she was still shocked by the sight of him.

Jake laid on his bed, wearing the same clothing he wore on Halloween night. His old jeans. A white t-shirt underneath a plaid button-down shirt. He stared up at the popcorn ceiling, wishing that he had been a man before Halloween. He wished that he had stopped the prank before it even got to the cemetery. He wished that he had the courage and the strength to have stood up for what was right. Yet, now it was too late.

"Jake," Ashley said.

He heard her, but he chose to close his eyes instead.

"Jake, come on," she said.

He took deep breaths, hoping to meditate and drown her out, but this was Ashley, after all. There was no way to get rid of her besides giving her what she wanted.

"Jake," she said. "Get up. We need you."

"I don't want you using the key anymore," Jake said, referring to her break-in.

"Stop being like that and get up. Ashton's missing."

Jake opened his eyes and looked over at her. When he saw Kristin standing in the doorway, he turned his body towards the door. Ashley noticed that his attention was focused on her friend and not her, and she was not pleased.

"You came with her?" Jake asked. The way he gazed at Kristin caused her to blush with embarrassment.

"What if They took Ashton, too?" Kristin asked. Her soft voice irritated Ashley at that moment. Now was not the time for weakness. It was the time to hurry up and go.

Jake returned his attention to the popcorn ceiling.

He sighed.

"Then They're coming for all of us," he said.

Ashley glared at him. His defeatist attitude was not only annoying, but very unlike the proud Jake she knew. She marched over to him and pinched his nipple through his shirt. He howled before slapping her hand away.

"What's wrong with you?" he asked.

"What's wrong with *you*? The Jake Victor I know wouldn't lie around like a sad sack. The Jake Victor I know wouldn't let two girls roam a demonic town looking for his friend. The Jake Victor I know would get up and help!"

"I haven't given up," Jake said.

"Then why have you been in your room all this time? Why haven't you been to school or church?"

"I've been soul searching."

Ashley stared at him, incredulous.

"I let people down," Jake said. "You wouldn't know what that feels like because you don't care about anyone but yourself."

Ashley glared at him. How would he know what she felt?

"Are you going to help us?" she asked.

"You said you've searched everywhere," Jake said. "Why do you need me?"

Ashley stared down into his eyes. "Because we searched everywhere but one place," she said.

Jake knew exactly where she was talking about.

**

The crickets were out that night, loud and inescapable, and through the fog, Jake saw a deer leap over a grave marker. He, Kristin, and Ashley walked slowly through the cemetery, the fear and anticipation they felt on Halloween resurfacing in their bodies. Jake tried to hide his fear, but he saw Kristin shiver. He noticed the goose bumps on her bare arms, and it amazed him that she hadn't worn a jacket.

"Are you cold?" he asked.

"I'm scared," she said.

"Here," he said, removing his jacket. Before she could protest, he wrapped it around her shoulders.

Ashley looked on, livid. "I'm cold too!" she said.

"You have a jacket," Jake said. Ashley only pouted.

The trio walked past gravestones of various sizes. Some were large and covered with text; others were simple and bare. A name, a year of birth, a year of death, and nothing more.

"Ashton!" Ashley screamed, hoping he would respond.

"I don't think he's here…" Kristin said.

"We looked everywhere else!" Ashley snapped.

Jake's eyes searched around, but the fog blocked his vision. Though they were wandering throughout the markers, they had yet to approach the church.

"There's one place we haven't checked yet," Jake said.

Ashley and Kristin stared at him. He was right, but no one wanted to relive Halloween night. Besides, what if Ashton wasn't even there? What if they approached and the hands popped out, ready to grab them? Or even worse, what if there were other people at the church? Demon-worshippers who were looking for children to sacrifice? Witches who were there to cast spells on their enemies? Pagans who had come to dance in the moonlight? After Halloween, they all had come to expect the unexpected.

"What if it's a trap?" Kristin asked.

"What if They have Ashton?" Ashley asked.

"The church is the reason we're here right now," Jake said. "I don't want to go over there either, but we have to."

At that moment, the fog began to disappear, creating an eerie, clear path to the church, now visible and only a short distance away. It stared back at them with its sleepy expression, a stare that sent ice to down their spines.

"It's beckoning us," Jake said.

Kristin stared at it, her body frozen, but Jake took the first step towards it. The girls followed suit, with Ashley calling out, "Ashton! Ashton, where are you?!"

As Ashley called out her brother's name, Jake and Kristin stared at the front of the church. Even without the Gateway to Hell inside, the structure intimidated them with its cold, gray bricks and its face-like structure.

Kristin shivered and Jake looked over at her. "Are you still cold?" he asked.

"I'm fine," she said.

"Here, you should try warming your shoulders," he said. He approached her from behind and rubbed at her arms.

Ashley couldn't watch anymore. "What are you doing?"

"She's cold," Jake said.

"You shouldn't be touching her!"

"Ashley, chill out. Kristin's cold."

"You're my boyfriend, Jake. Stop feeling up my best friend!"

He gaped at Ashley, not understanding how she could be so stupid. "I'm not feeling Kristin up...but for the record, I am *not* your boyfriend anymore."

"What?" Ashley shrieked.

Kristin pulled Jake's jacket around her body and looked away.

"Is this because of her?" Ashley asked. Anger pulsated throughout her blood vessels, and she wanted to swing at something so badly.

Instead, she screamed. Even if the Gateway wasn't open, the demons in Hell surely could hear her.

"Arrrrrrggghhhh!!!!"

Kristin and Jake stared at her, unsure of what to do.

Once Ashley let the anger out of her system, she took a deep breath, and the way she heaved, it appeared as if she had just finished exorcising a demon from her body. She glanced at Kristin and Jake lookin at her with their jaws hanging open, and she suddenly realized that she had let her guard down. She bristled, trying to gain her composure.

"Ashton!" she yelled out, returning to the task at hand. "Ashton!"

**

He heard her.

The moonlight broke through the trees and illuminated Officer Eric Whitehorse's handsome face which was like that of an angel's. He had smooth skin, metallic blue eyes, and dark hair, and his athletic body moved quickly through the forest behind Deer Creek Cemetery. Although he looked twenty, no one was really sure of his age. He had moved to town a year ago, with no wife or children. He never dated, mostly keeping to himself. All he seemed to be interested in was work.

He often ran through the woods on cool evenings to clear his head. Although there was not a lot of crime reported in Deer Creek, he knew that there were a lot of evil things happening. Children being neglected. Wives being hit. Drugs being used. The town only had a population of 10,000, but there was plenty of corruption and it disturbed him. Tonight, he felt extra troubled as he thought about the disappearance of Ronnie Smalls.

"Ashton!" he heard a young female voice call out, startling him. He momentarily lost his focus. Just as he was about to run towards the girl, his foot landed upon a snake. He jumped back in alarm. The snake twisted violently, but Eric took off before it could have a chance to orient itself. As he ran away, he grew distracted, unaware of the figure in his path until it let out a low *snarl*.

"What the…" he said as he looked up and made eye contact with a gigantic wolf with piercing green eyes. The wolf appeared as though it had a purpose, and Eric hoped that the purpose wasn't to take a bite.

The wolf broke its stare and pointed its head to the left, as if signaling for him to follow. Eric did as he was asked, no questions, no hesitation, and the wolf led him further into the woods. Eric heard crickets and twigs snap as the wolf led him to a giant tree. Its trunk was the size of a bedroom. If it were hollowed out, a family of four could easily live inside of it. Its bark was gnarled and greenish-brown, forming a pattern that reached up to its branches, crazy and shattered like a crack across glass.

The wolf walked up to a hole at the foot of the tree, waiting for Eric to slowly approach. Once the wolf knew that Eric was where it wanted him to be, it departed.

Eric's eyes widened when he saw a bone glisten in the moonlight.

His nose wrinkled at the putrid smell, but he was a police officer and it was his duty to investigate. He reached into his pocket and pulled out a latex glove, something he kept on hand for times like these. He bent down closer to the bone, and as he got closer, rats scurried out of the tree trunk.

"Oh!" Eric grunted as he fell back into the tree's fallen leaves. His foot kicked forward and hit the bone, and the leaves on top of it cleared away to reveal frayed pant legs. The bone was only exposed because animals had eaten away at the leg's flesh, but the rest of the body was there.

Eric regained his footing, and he cleared away more leaves to reveal jeans and a letterman jacket. He said nothing as he carefully flipped the body over, but he knew who he was looking at before he read the name "Smalls" stitched onto the back.

PART TWO: TWO YEARS LATER...

The righteous perish, and no one ponders in his heart;
Devout men are taken away, and no one understands that
the righteous are taken away to be spared from evil.
Those who walk uprightly enter into peace; they find rest as
they lie in death.

-Isaiah 57:1-2

CHAPTER FIVE

"Jake Victor," a voice called.

Sitting on a hard cot against the concrete wall, Jake looked up. His hair was buzzed short, he wore a gray uniform that looked like scrubs, and his once boyishly-handsome face had hardened into that of a tired man. In the Kansas State Juvenile Detention Facility he had been sentenced to nearly two years ago, he had aged far beyond his eighteen years.

"You're up," Sharonda Judge said. She was a larger woman with maroon braids, dark skin, and a kind face. Unlike the other detention facility officers, Sharonda was respected by the confined teenage boys. They liked her because she treated them like adults, not criminals; and she also provided them a maternal figure that they needed, although some didn't like to admit that.

"Did you hear me, Jake?" she said.

Although Sharonda was staring at him, Jake didn't move. Today was his eighteenth birthday, which meant that he was up for release if the review board approved of it. Although his parents were excited and hopeful that he would be freed, he felt conflicted. Part of him wanted to continue to suffer for what he had done to Ronnie, while the other part of him wanted to experience life on earth before dying and joining Ronnie in Hell. Either way, Jake's soul was sentenced to eternal suffering, and knowing this made his view of life very bleak.

After changing from his uniform to an ill-fitted brown suit, Jake followed Sharonda down the hall, which had windows on either side. That afternoon, the sun shone brightly, causing the white walls of the room to appear illuminated, as if Jake were walking down a heavenly pathway. This hallway led to the exit of the facility along with the conference room and administrative office. Jake had only walked through this hallway once, when he had first come to the facility, and more than likely, this would be the last time.

Jake was escorted into the main conference room, where he sat across from three stern-looking adults in suits.

"Good afternoon, Jake," the woman in the middle said. It was Marcia Longbottom, the chairwoman of the review board. Jake had met her last year during his annual review and found her cold, but fair.

"Hi," Jake said as he sat down. Sharonda stood guard by the door. On the walk over, she had prepped him to sit up straight, speak from the heart to show them his remorse, and to not smile or show any type of glib behavior. Jake had appeared to take in everything that she had said, which is why she was surprised to see him slumped back in his chair, his legs out and open, his arm callously dangling over the back of his chair.

Marcia and one of the men on the board to hide their shock, but Jake could see what they were feeling. When he stepped into the room, he could see how sympathetic they were to him. They had felt sorry for the poor boy with the once promising future, and he knew that they had every intention of freeing him. However, Jake didn't like that. He wanted to be able to fully plea his case before an unbiased jury, and he wanted them to tell him what he had already concluded—that he was guilty for what had happened to Ronnie. He wanted them to tell him to stay in detention to think about his crime further. He wanted them to make him face the Smalls family. Jake was not interested in getting off easy, and when he saw that it was about to happen, he made the last minute decision to sabotage himself.

"How are you, Jake?" the fat man to Marcia's left asked.
"Fine."

"Our files state that you have spent the last year being a model citizen," Marcia said. "You go to church services every Sunday and in your spare time you read or exercise. You've never once been written up, and you keep to yourself."

Jake knew this was an opportunity to talk about how good he had been, but he said nothing. The fat man bristled.

Marcia continued. "We're really impressed by your track record. Sharonda has testified that she believes you have displayed remorse for your crime, and she has recommended that you be released."

Jake looked at Sharonda, who pled with her eyes for him to speak up for himself. He remained quiet. Instead, he focused his attention on the young, handsome man to Marcia's right, recognizing him as the policeman from Deer Creek, the one who had found Ronnie's body and testified at the trial—Eric Whitehorse. Jake wondered what he was doing there.

"Do you have anything you'd like to say?" the fat man asked. He and Marcia were extremely sympathetic to Jake's case. It had been clear that the trial had been biased, that Jake had been set up by the Geminis' and Graces' lawyers—a tragedy, really, to see the rich and powerful destroy the future of a good-hearted, poor boy. The fat man and Marcia wanted to do their part in giving him a second chance, but they really needed Jake to speak, to say something positive about himself for the record, but Jake shook his head no. He had nothing to say. He stared at the floor. The lines in the tile reminded him of the hands that dragged Ronnie to Hell.

Eric leaned forward and cleared his throat.

"Do you want to talk to us about Ronnie Smalls?" Eric asked.

Jake stiffened. The adults in the room noted this change, relieved that Jake had finally given up the cool, uncaring criminal act and had finally shown that he was human. It was as if his childhood memories and guilt had suddenly returned to him just at the sound of Ronnie's name.

There was a long pause as the adults stared at Jake, waiting. All they wanted was for him to say one positive thing about himself, and they would sign his release papers. That was it. One thing. All he had to say was one thing.

"Jake?" Marcia said, and Jake looked into her eyes. "Did you hear Eric's question? Do you want to talk a little bit about what happened? Maybe something about what you feel now?"

Jake stared at her, then the fat man, then Eric. Finally he looked to Sharonda, who mouthed, "Please." Jake closed his eyes, knowing it was selfish to sabotage himself when his mother and father were waiting for him at home.

"Breathe," Jake whispered. He had never thought of himself as someone who gave up easily, not until Halloween. But after he had seen what had happened to Ronnie, something inside of him broke. His lost his faith in himself, his belief in the protection of a higher power, and the point of living. After Ronnie was taken away, one question burned in his mind.

"What's the point?"

It was that question that dragged him down, and it was that question that he struggled with at this very moment.

"Can we have a moment?" a voice called out, and Jake looked over to see Sharonda marching towards him.

"Of course," Marcia said with relief as Jake and Sharonda stepped out of the room.

Once the door shut behind them, Sharonda shoved her finger into Jake's chest. "What the hell is wrong with you, Jake?"

Jake's eyes widened. He had never seen her act this way.

"Don't you care about yourself? Your family? Get it together and stop acting like a spoiled brat. This is your chance to fight back the people who put you here."

"I put myself here," Jake said. He winced when Sharonda slapped him across his face.

"If you don't want out of here, fine, but do it for your family. For the people who love you. Do it for me, because damn it, Jake. I don't want to see you here anymore."

He stared into her big brown eyes, seeing a need there that he didn't feel within himself, but when he saw it within her, he looked away in guilt. Sharonda gently pushed his face towards hers again. She wanted him to look at her.

"Do you understand me, Jake?" she said. "Don't ever give up."

He swallowed hard as she backed away and reached for the door. He watched as she entered the room, leaving him in the hallway. He took a deep breath, dizzy with the confusion of what just happened, before finally composing himself and walking inside.

When he entered, it felt as if everything had changed to slow-motion. He felt his legs moving, but his mind seemed to exit his body, watching him from a distance. He saw the fat man, Marcia, and Eric staring at him, their faces filled with anticipation.

Jake sat in his chair and stared at his three judges, whose faces meant nothing to him.

Then Jake looked over at Sharonda, who stared back at him like a proud watchman. He nodded at her, letting her know that things would be okay. She stared back, waiting.

Jake sat up straight, becoming the reformed man that everyone had wanted him to be. He couldn't see from where he was facing, but Sharonda was smiling.

"I apologize for how I was acting earlier," Jake said. "I was overwhelmed and nervous. Can I start over?"

The adults breathed a quiet sigh of relief. Marcia smiled. "Of course, Jake. Of course."

**

Kristin stared at the old Victorian, which looked like it had come straight out of a horror novel. From its structure, she could tell it was once a grand house. It had a wraparound porch, a dark roof with textured shingles, and stained-glass windows, but now it looked gray and run-down. She walked up to the front porch and nearly ran into a cobweb. Screaming, she jumped back.

Ever since she was little, spiders scared her.

She dusted off the web that had caught on the back of her arm and in her metal jewelry. She glanced back at the web's remains and saw its maker, a black spider that didn't look too happy to see her.

"Gross," Kristin said.

She looked around and found a twig in the grass. She used it to swat the web to the porch's floor, and before the spider could escape, she stomped it to death, its body goo covering the bottom of her shoe.

"Careful, Kristin," an old voice said. "Karma can be a bitch."

She looked up to find Mayor Hercules staring at her with his piercing gray eyes. She found it surprising how much the shape of them up close reminded her of a cat's.

"Hello, Mayor Hercules," she said. He must have opened the front door when she was killing the spider, but his stealth alarmed her and she didn't like the way he was studying her.

Yet, he couldn't help but stare. It amazed him how much Kristin had changed in the two years since the trial. Gone were the long locks and innocent, wide-eyed expressions. Now she had a boyish cut and wore heavy make-up. She dressed in masculine dark clothing, a black scarf around her neck, and punk jewelry that made her unrecognizable from the sweet, submissive girl she was at sixteen.

"Come inside," Mayor Hercules said.

He stepped back, allowing Kristin to enter his home for the first time. She wiped the spider's carcass off of her shoe before she stepped into the house, and immediately, she was in awe of his gigantic space, lit from the sunlight pouring through the stained glass. However, despite all of the architectural beauty, she was equally frightened by the stuffed crows that permeated throughout on bookshelves, the chandelier, even on the stair rail.

"Thank you for seeing me," Kristin said.

"Thank you for coming. I wasn't sure you would."

After the trial two years earlier, Mayor Hercules had reached out to Kristin. He had come to her house, unannounced in the middle of a Saturday afternoon, and though she was frightened by his appearance, he stood before her on the porch, wearing a faded blue suit and holding an antique book with a black cover.

"I want you to read this," he had said. "If any of this applies to you, I want you to call me."

She had accepted the book from him, but after flipping through the pages filled with scary drawings of demons and angels, she hid it in her closet. The book reminded her too much of Halloween. She almost wanted to dispose of it all together, but worried that it would somehow find its way back to her, as if it had a life of its own.

In the end, the book remained in her closet, underneath her sweatshirts and undershirts where it had collected dust for two years, never to be touched. It would've stayed unread if Kristin had never received her ominous invitation.

"It's quite warm today, even for September," Mayor Hercules said, bringing Kristin back to the present. Mayor Hercules seemed completely comfortable with the temperature compared to Kristin, whose face was already shiny with sweat.

"It's no big deal," she said. "I mostly stay indoors anyway."

"Do you go to school?" he asked.

"No."

"Are you working?"

"No."

He gazed at her, unsure of what else to ask. From their small talk, it appeared as if Kristin had chosen to do nothing with her life.

Mayor Hercules led her into his study, a room with gothic maroon wallpaper, velvet-lined chairs, and black furniture. "Sit," Mayor Hercules said, and Kristin sat in a chair next to an end table with a Tiffany lamp and a stuffed crow on it. She turned and saw the crow's beady eyes staring blankly at her, and felt a shiver run through her body. Mayor Hercules chuckled.

"I apologize for the birds," Mayor Hercules said. "But I've always been fascinated with them."

Kristin smiled weakly as Mayor Hercules sat across from her. The ceiling fan above them twirled slowly, circulating the hot air in the room. The furniture was dusty and made the room smelled old, like burnt incense and stale air.

"Would you like some tea?" he asked.

Kristin shook her head no. From the state of his living quarters, she could only imagine how clean his dishes were.

Mayor Hercules shrugged and removed his jacket. Although he was not sweating, he fanned himself with a newspaper that had been lying nearby.

"I apologize for the heat. I don't have a working air conditioner. Would you like to remove your scarf?" he asked, noticing that she was sweating profusely.

"No, no, I'm fine," she said, touching her scarf nervously. He watched her open her backpack and pull out his book. "I finally read it."

She handed it to him, *The Handbook of Hell and Its Demons*, and he put it on a table next to a crow, a being that was an omen of death or suffering, according to the book. It frightened her that he filled his home with them, especially since he knew what they represented.

"What made you finally decide to read it?" he asked.

"I want to prepare for what's in store for me," she said flatly.

Mayor Hercules raised his eyebrows, surprised by her bluntness. She had already gone to trial for Ronnie's death, and the jury found her innocent. The court of public opinion, however, believed she was guilty. With that mark branded on her, she figured she could do whatever she wanted because she had nothing to lose.

Mayor Hercules gazed at her with sympathy. He understood her inner turmoil more than he wanted to admit.

"I know that you did not kill that boy," he said. "That the demons in Hell snatched him to play. I also know that you were at the church on Halloween night. I know your lawyer said otherwise, but that's another story in itself, isn't it?"

There was something very gentle about the old man sitting across from her, and it made her want to tell him all about that night. About how Ashley manipulated them. About how the hands snatched Ronnie into the church. About how the aftermath tore the group of friends apart. About the nightmares she still experienced.

Yet, she kept quiet because deep down, she knew she was just as much to blame as Ashley.

"Have They come for you?" he asked.

She nodded, not even questioning how he knew.

"And have you accepted their invitation?" he asked.

She nodded again.

"Then you've come for advice," he said.

Kristin adjusted the scarf covering her sweaty neck. "How can I beat the Game?" she asked.

Mayor Hercules rose from his seat and walked to the window. He stared at the barren trees in his backyard, remembering how they were once lush and covered with pink flowers.

"Mayor Hercules?" Kristin asked.

Mayor Hercules remembered how his children used to play in the yard. They loved it especially in the fall, when the leaves piled up underneath the trees. He would watch them as they jumped into those piles, without a care in the world.

Kristin chewed on her bottom lip, nervous that she had upset him.

"I think you should come with me," he said.

**

Kristin ran, harder than she had ever run before. Her face flushed red. Her hair and the towel around her neck soaked with sweat and dirt. As the air began to escape her brain, she worried she was going to die.

Mayor Hercules stood in the sidelines of the track, still wearing his suit. He shook his head.

"You're too slow, Kristin," he said as she rounded the corner. She slowed to a stop, heaving, out of breath. She hunched over on the clay-colored track of the high school field, fighting to keep from vomiting.

"I didn't realize you were this unfit," he added.

"I'll get better," she said in between breaths.

"The Game requires you not only be at peak mental capacity, but also peak physical shape."

Kristin glared at him. He had forced her to run five miles in the hot Kansas heat, and now he was lecturing her as if she wasn't aware of how important it was for her to win.

"I said I'll get better."

She collapsed into the grass and closed her eyes.

"Who else has been invited?" he asked.

"I don't know. I don't talk to the others…"

"You must find out! If you are the only one, then you have less of a chance surviving than if you are with a team."

"Jake's still in juvie, Ashley just moved to New York, and Ashton…"

A lump in her throat formed anytime she thought about Ashton.

"Stop your excuses," he said as he gazed down at her. She crawled to her backpack and pulled out a bottle of water. "They only exist because you have too much pride, and pride is one of the seven deadly sins. It is pride that will cause you to stay in Hell. Remember the knowledge you read in my books. Remember that there is a Higher Power than yourself. Remember that it is okay to lean on others in your time of need. Go home and prepare your body, mind, and soul to be as strong as it can be before The Game begins, and tell the others to do the same. That is the only real advice I can give you, but that advice is what will help you conquer."

She eyed him, letting his message process in her brain. Should she swallow her pride and call Ashley? How was she going to contact Jake? She looked at Mayor Hercules, who continued to bore into her with his sad gray eyes.

"Can you train us?" she asked.

"I'm an old man, Kristin. You'll have to train yourself."

She glared at him. Why had he reached out to her if he could do nothing? He started to walk away.

"Is that it?" she called as she jumped to her feet. Her anger brought her a sudden burst of energy.

He stopped and turned. "You can come by anytime you want to gather more books. My purpose here is only to educate you. Nothing more."

She rushed over to him, ready to give him a piece of her mind. "I don't need books," she said, grabbing his sleeve. "I need someone to train me!"

He looked at her in a way that said he was done for the day. She backed away, suddenly afraid. She wasn't sure if he was going to speak or perish on the spot.

Finally, he took a deep breath and replied in a tired voice. "There is sin everywhere, Kristin. If you read the books, if you have faith that you're doing the right thing, then you'll be able to recognize evil when you see it, and you'll be able to do it on your own. That is one of the greatest tools you can bring to the Game and to your life on Earth if you return to it."

"Is that all you have to say?" Kristin asked.

He nodded. "Good luck," he whispered before he walked away.

**

Steve and Rosie Victor led Jake to his room, and although they were happy to have him home, a strange tension existed between the parents and their child. Since they had brought Jake home from the detention facility, he had been distant, as if his body was there but his soul had died. He had hugged his father and his mother when they had come to get him, but it was almost as if they were being hugged by the wind, a presence that could be felt, but was not human.

"We didn't change a thing, honey," Rosie said as Steve opened the door. Jake entered his bedroom and looked around as his parents waited patiently in the doorway. He saw his football gear in the corner of the room, next to the shelf full of his athletic awards and newspaper clippings. He saw the athletic posters on the walls, pictures of men he had wanted to be. He saw his made bed with its faded blue bedding, his desk covered with old papers, and his dresser decorated with empty frames that once held pictures of him and Ashley.

"Did you want to go out to dinner tonight?" Steve asked. "We weren't sure if you wanted to rest or go out. It's up to you."

Jake thought about the question before he looked at his father, who had gray hair and more wrinkles around his eyes than he had remembered him having. If he went out, surely people would whisper about how Jake Victor was out of juvie. They would probably stare and he would stare back, making them uncomfortable. Or, he could take the second option and hide. Be invisible in a town that had condemned him.

"Let's go out," Jake said.

**

Deer Creek didn't offer many dining options. There were the usual fast food restaurants along the strip, along with a few upscale restaurants downtown that the Victors couldn't afford. That left only one sit-down restaurant for them, which was McCue's, a diner on the edge of town that was popular and had the best meat loaf in town. Despite the affordability and quality of food, Jake's parents were hesitant to eat there. "Are you sure, honey?" Rosie asked. Jake felt their trepidation, but he didn't want them to have to walk on eggshells around town because of him. Any type of conflict that came their way, they would have to face and fight.

The diner was packed that evening, and the smell of steak, eggs, and coffee permeated the tiny dining room. Though the diner was small and sat only fifty people, it was manned by one tired waitress with strawberry blonde hair, Monica Smalls, Ronnie's mother. When Steve, Rosie, and Jake entered, the dining room grew silent. Some patrons glared at Jake and his parents. Others looked at them with sympathy.

Monica, who was clearing off a table, stopped bussing to stare at the entrance. When she saw Jake, her jaw dropped.

"Maybe this wasn't a good idea," Rosie whispered as she reached for her husband's hand.

"We can't leave now," Steve said.

Monica approached, and everyone in the restaurant watched as if this were the most riveting television show they had ever seen.

"Three tonight?" Monica asked.

"Yes," Steve replied.

When Monica did not appear to be upset, the tension in the room dissolved and the conversations resumed. As the Victor family sat in a booth at the back, some people continued to sneak glances at them.

"How are you, Monica?" Rosie asked. The two women had once been good friends, but after Ronnie's death, they had avoided each other awkwardly until the Smalls had moved to the trailer park across town.

"Surviving," Monica replied with no edge in her voice. She handed the Victors their menus, and as she handed Jake his, she examined him closely. He looked older, harder. With his cropped haircut, his weathered face, and his overly exercised body, it was clear that the two years in the facility had not been easy on him. "I know you weren't the only one with Ronnie that night," Monica said to everyone's surprise. Steve and Rosie didn't know what to say, and Jake swallowed hard. "I want you to know that I don't hate you, and I don't blame you."

Jake's eyes welled with tears as he nodded his head.

"I'll be back to take your order," Monica said.

Once she was out of sight, Jake noticed a pair of familiar eyes staring at him. It took him a second to recognize who they belonged to at first because she looked so different. Her once girlishly long locks were now cut short into a boyish pixie cut, and her makeup was harsh and angry-looking. She wore a scarf around her neck.

Jake didn't know whether to say hello or not, and he and Kristin continued to stare at one another until she broke the spell.

"Meet me outside," Kristin mouthed as she motioned toward the entrance with her head. She was sitting beside her mother, who wore a scarf to cover up most of her face, like the women in old movies did. Across from the table, Kristin's father Bryan sat, his shoulders hunched. He ate in a perfunctory manner as if unhappy to be there.

During his time in the facility, Jake had prepared speeches to all the people he had unresolved business with in town. Ashley and Ashton. Ronnie's parents. His own parents. For some reason, he had forgotten about Kristin, but it didn't matter. So far, the other speeches he had prepared weren't happening the way he had wanted, so he figured it was best to see what happened organically.

"I need some air," Kristin said to her parents. She looked to Jake as she removed herself from her mother and father's table, and Jake quickly did the same.

Standing before Kristin next to McCue's Diner, Jake was confused to see her so filled with fear. Why was she so terrified? After all, she hadn't been found guilty in a court of law. She hadn't gone to jail with teenage criminals. What was she so damn upset about?

"You got out," Kristin said.

Jake fought to not say a rude comeback. "I was released today," he said. "It's my birthday, you know."

"Happy birthday."

"I guess."

As they awkwardly avoided looking at each other, both tried to find more pleasantries to say. A middle-aged couple walked up to the entrance of McCue's. When they saw Kristin and Jake, their lips curled.

"God bless you," the woman said, and her husband shushed her as they went inside.

"You too!" Kristin snapped.

Jake was amazed at her attitude. She was just as bad as Ashley had been.

"Why are you looking at me like that?" she asked.

"How was graduation?" he asked, ignoring her question.

"I dropped out."

This surprised Jake. Although Kristin was never more than an above-average student, she seemed to like learning. He studied her and her makeover, wondering what had happened while he was away, but too afraid to ask.

While he pondered what to say next, Kristin took the lead. "I'm sorry about what happened to you," she said.

There were a million different things Jake could have said to her at that moment such as "Well, you shouldn't have helped put me there," or, "Looks like your life ended up sucking, too." But he kept his mouth shut.

It pained her to feel the tension between them, but she had to continue. "You must hate me…" she said.

Jake looked at her, pondering her statement, and as he stared into her beautiful brown eyes, he found the opposite to be true.

"Don't say that," Jake said. He stepped away from her, more confused than anything by what was happening at this very moment.

"Why not?" she asked. "It's true, isn't it?"

"How's Ashley?" Jake asked, changing the subject. While he was away, he thought a lot about his former friends. He thought about Ashley's manipulative nature, about Ashton going along with everything his sister wanted instead of being his own person, about Kristin being afraid to have her own voice. During those two years of being detained, when he had nothing but time and his thoughts, he had wanted to blame Ashley, to hate her for what had happened, but he couldn't, not fully at least. By no means had he found peace with the others or with what had happened, by no means had the anger completely washed away, but mostly he found that he hated himself for not doing what was right.

Kristin shifted uncomfortably at the sound of Ashley's name. "I don't know," she said. "We don't talk."

"You guys seemed to talk during the trial," he said matter-of-factly. "There was a lot of collusion going on."

She didn't understand the term, but from his tone, she could tell it was something negative. "What's collusion?"

He stared at her, noticing that she no longer had the baby fat that had once made her so cute. Her face was now chiseled, her body lean. It appeared to him as if she had been heavily exercising.

"It's a word I learned at the facility," he said, realizing he was taking too long to answer. Kristin nervously fidgeted with the scarf around her neck. "It describes when a group of people conspire for illegal purposes."

Kristin didn't like the sound of that. "I'm sorry," she said, avoiding his eyes.

"How's Ashton?" Jake asked.

Kristin looked at him again, her brown eyes boring into him. "No one told you?" she asked.

"Told me what?"

She paused, unsure of how to say it. She decided the direct approach was the best.

"Ashton committed suicide after the trial," Kristin said. Jake stepped back. "How did he die?"

"He shot himself in his father's office at church."

A visual of Ashton dead with blood running along the office's wooden floor rushed immediately into Jake's mind. He shook his head, trying to make the image go away, but it stuck there and wouldn't go away.

"I need to ask you something," Kristin said, noticing he was distracted. The pleasantries were over between them; it was now time for business.

"What do you want?" he asked, taken aback that she would ask him for a favor. His tone caused her to bristle even more than before. He hadn't meant to be so harsh, but that was how she interpreted it.

She looked into his eyes. "I want to ask if you got a letter," she said.

"A letter?"

"Were you invited to play the Game?"

"The game? What game? What the hell are you talking about?"

She shook her head, realizing she sounded crazy. Of course, he hadn't. After all, she was the only one who had the strange vision of the hands. She was the only one who saw Ashton's gunshot wound before he died. She was the only one with the psychic abilities. She looked at Jake, whose neck was bare, and Kristin cursed herself for being so foolish. She should've just looked there in the first place.

"Never mind. I guess it's only my problem then. I didn't mean to scare you," she said as she headed inside.

Jake was annoyed now. What was she babbling about, and why was she looking at him so strangely?

"What are you talking about, Kristin?" he said. "Why would I be scared?"

"Never mind!" she said, and the door slammed behind her.

CHAPTER SIX

For the rest of Jake's life, he would never forget the headline: "Trial awaits four accused of murdering teen." Underneath the giant bolded letters were class photographs, one each of Jake, Ashley, Ashton, and Kristin. The four of them were smiling and attractive, the picture of innocence and lucky youth. Underneath their pictures was a larger picture of a gruesomely slaughtered Ronnie, still wearing his letterman jacket from that night. It was a shocking addition, but the editor of the paper hated the Geminis and wanted the town to hate them too.

The article had mentioned nothing about Halloween, and the language in the piece suggested that he was slain after the holiday, during the first week of November. It was careful to avoid accusations of devil-worship or ritual slaughter, but the picture of Ronnie was gruesome and suggested it anyway.

CHAPTER SEVEN

Ashley's fist flew into the masked man's face. His head jerked to the side, his helmet flying off onto the ground. She saw his exposed face and took the opportunity to strike from below, up into his nose. She hit him so hard that his nose cracked, and then she jammed her knee into his groin. She grunted with pleasure at the sound of his pain, but before she could strike again, she heard a police whistle.

"That's enough," her trainer said. They stood in the New York Martial Arts Studio on the Upper West Side of Manhattan. It was the middle of the week in August, and despite the fans blowing in the room, it was muggy and hot.

Ashley stepped back and smiled as her assailant clutched at his bloody, broken nose.

"Son of a bitch," he mumbled before leaving the studio to go on break.

"She's a natural," the trainer said to Ashley's mother Heather who sat in the bleachers against the wall. "That skilled after only two lessons? It's impressive."

Wearing her tight workout clothes, Ashley laughed, happy with her results. Heather tried her best to appear proud of her daughter, but inside she was horrified. She had come up to help Ashley move into her dorm at Columbia University, Benedict's Alma Mater, and Ashley suggested that she enroll in a self-defense class. Heather liked the idea of Ashley being able to take care of herself in such a dangerous city, but to her surprise, her daughter had proven to be more violent than any criminal she could imagine. It wasn't that she was good at kicking or punching that bothered Heather; it was the happy smile on her face as she inflicted pain.

"How do you feel, Ashley?" the trainer asked.

She wiped the sweat off of her face with a towel. "Good," she replied as if nothing had just happened.

The trainer looked again to Heather. "Your daughter's tough. I don't think anyone stands a chance against her."

Heather gazed at her beautiful daughter, who had just broken someone's nose and had no remorse about it.

"That's my girl," Heather said, but she really wanted to say, "Yes, that's my monster."

**

"I heard Jake was let out of prison yesterday," Heather said. After the defense class, she and Ashley decided to spend the rest of the day shopping. They stood in the outerwear section of Bloomingdales looking at designer coats.

"Oh," Ashley said. She knew that her mother was only trying to make conversation, but Jake's name still filled her with dread. Ever since the trial, she had banned all items that had reminded her of him, all places, all conversations. This was the first time someone had directly mentioned him to her in a long time, and of course that person was her clueless mother.

"I heard they let him out on good behavior. I knew they would never keep him locked up for too long."

"That's nice," Ashley replied in a tone that seemed to say she didn't care. She was afraid to say more because she didn't want her voice to shake. She hated losing control in front of other people, especially in front of her parents.

She eyed a selection of Calvin Klein trench coats, but then she thought against it. She preferred to get something warmer.

"Are you going to call him?" Heather asked.

"What would I say?" Ashley replied, focusing more on the outerwear in front of her than the conversation.

"I don't know. Tell him you want to make sure he's okay."

"I don't think he'd care to hear from me, Mother."

"It never hurts to say hello. I'm sure he'd love to hear from a friend."

Ashley glared at her beautiful, dense mother. Was she really so delusional to think that she and Jake were still friends? After what the Geminis had done to him? That Ashley could just call him up and that they'd have a friendly chat? What would they talk about? "Hi, Ashley. Thanks for pinning Ronnie's death on me and ruining my future. How are you?" "I'm doing great, Jake. My Dad pulled some strings at Columbia, and I'm starting school in a week. Isn't that amazing? I'm going to an Ivy League school and starting a new life in New York City. How was juvie?"

"So are you going to call him?" Heather asked. She hated that whenever she asked Ashley questions, her daughter's mind would float off into space. When Ashley was younger, the two of them were very close, but when Ashley was nine, she began to pull away. Heather almost suspected that something had happened to Ashley, but she didn't know what.

"Um…sure," Ashley said. "Let me think about it."

Heather sighed. "Fine. Do what you want. I just want you to do the right thing."

Ashley stared back at Heather, annoyed by how much her mother cared about etiquette and what other people thought. Even when the town had turned against the Geminis after Jake was sent to juvie, Heather still wanted people to like her. After the trial, attendance at the church lowered, and whenever Heather Gemini went out, she heard the whispers that she and her supposed God-fearing husband had used their money to buy their children's freedom and condemn the town Golden Boy.

"It's not fair," Heather had whined to her husband after the trial. "All we wanted was to protect our children, and the town treats us like we're pariahs."

"The storm will blow over. God will protect us, and the truth will come out with time," Pastor Benedict Gemini had replied.

Heather grew quiet. She wanted to ask him something, but she was afraid to say it aloud.

"What's on your mind?" he asked.

"You don't think…"

"Think what?"

"You don't think we were wrong? You don't think the twins were part of the murder?"

Benedict shook his head. "Our children are good. We raised them right. If they were in any way responsible for that boy's death, then a jury would not have found our daughter and son innocent. Jake Victor had the same legal process that Ashton and Ashley had, and the law saw that he was guilty."

Heather's eyes lowered. Although she was happy that her children were set free, deep down, she never understood why the jury made the decision that they did. She almost wondered if it would have been better if all four of them had been found guilty, then there would have been no resentment, there would have been fair justice.

Benedict picked up on her hesitation, her worry, her fear. He stepped towards her, and she cowered as if he was about to hit her.

"Heather, honey, stop your thinking. The reason all of this happened was because of Jake, and he got what he deserved. *He* was Ronnie's friend. *He* invited that boy out that night, and *he* drove everyone to the cemetery. If Jake had never orchestrated the whole prank, then Ronnie never would have left the house that night. Ashton and Ashley didn't know him. Only Jake did. That's why he was found guilty and that's why he's serving time."

For weeks, she had listened to her husband's argument and buried her own intellect, which told her he was wrong. However, things changed when she had found Ashton in Benedict's office with a hole in his head and a gun lying on the floor beside him. Ashton had left a brief letter, which Benedict had destroyed before the police had arrived. Even though the letter was gone, she still remembered its haunting words:

"Dear Mom and Dad: I'm sorry. We did it. May God have mercy on our souls."

Now, as Heather browsed the denim department with her daughter, she gazed at Ashley and found herself wondering how someone so beautiful could be so cold and inhuman. It troubled her to think that her daughter had no soul, but perhaps it was true. After all, in the past two years, she was with a boy the night he was murdered, she had watched her ex-boyfriend be sentenced to jail for a crime she was possibly involved in, and she had survived her twin brother's suicide; and yet, here she was. Buying designer clothing as if this were any other afternoon.

Ashley noticed that her mother was eyeing her strangely. "What are you thinking about?"

Heather caught herself and returned to acting as if everything was fine.

"Oh, nothing. Just how much I'm going to miss you when I leave."

"Oh, shut up, Mother. You know I'm coming home for Thanksgiving."

"Oh, right."

Heather awkwardly smiled, and Ashley smiled back before she picked up another expensive item of clothing. She was busy gazing at the wool of the fabric, excited by the style, when she felt a pair of eyes upon her. She looked over to her left and she gasped. Eric Whitehorse, the handsome cop who had discovered the body of Ronnie Smalls, was staring judgmentally at her, the way he had in the courtroom when he testified against her.

"Ashley?" Heather asked.

Ashley glanced at her mother, and then back at Eric, but he was no longer there. He had only been a figment of her imagination, the face of her guilt for what had happened to Ronnie and Jake. Ashley shook her head, trying to forget her memory, trying to deny what she had done.

"Ashley?" Heather repeated, and her daughter smiled as she held up the coat she had been eyeing.

"I'd like this one," Ashley said, and Heather nodded that she would purchase it for her.

∗∗

Ashley's mother had left for the evening to retire at her hotel room at the Four Seasons, and Ashley had opted to stay at her dorm. Her roommate had not moved in yet, and most of the floor was also empty. Ashley started hanging up her new clothes in her closet, disappointed that the space was so small. When she had finished that task, she neatly folded her Bloomingdales, Saks, and Nordstrom bags and placed them underneath her bed, which was already covered with her expensive white and pink bedding. As she sat on the edge of the bed, she looked at her roommate's empty space. She wondered what kind of girl she'd be living with for the next year. Would she be a goth? A pretentious intellectual? An annoying sorority girl? Ashley prayed that she would not be given the sorority princess. After all, although *she* was like that, she despised other girls who came from that mold.

In actuality, Ashley hoped that she would get a roommate like Kristin—or someone who was like Kristin before Halloween two years ago. Someone who was sweet and non-confrontational. Someone who didn't mind doing what other people told her to do, but was so nice that most people didn't take advantage. After that night, Kristin had cut Ashton and Ashley out of her life. The twins had hoped with time that Kristin would forgive them, but forgiveness had never come.

There was a loud sliding noise from the doorway, and Ashley jerked her head. To her surprise, near the door was a plain white envelope on the floor with her name neatly typed on the front. Ashley got off the bed and retrieved the envelope, noticing it was sealed with a horse stamped into white wax.

"What the hell is this?" she muttered.

She tore into the envelope and pulled out a single sheet of white paper, a sparse invitation written in formal language. Below the writing was a stencil of a horse.

Dear Ashley Gemini,

We, the Gamemakers, cordially invite you to play a game on Halloween Night of this year in Deer Creek, Kansas, at the Deer Creek Cemetery. Your presence is greatly appreciated and the prize of this game will be the freedom of Ronnie Smalls' soul from our domain. If you choose to not play, then we will take that as an RSVP to Hell upon your death on Earth. We look forward to hearing your immediate reply.

Best,
The Gamemakers.

Ashley's hands shook. Color drained from her face.

"What the hell?" she screamed as she tore up the paper. "Who the hell sent this?"

The pieces dropped to the floor and scattered near her feet. She heaved loudly, trying to catch her breath. Someone was playing a trick on her, and that someone had followed her from Deer Creek to New York City. If that person had intended to scare her, fine, but he was going to be sorry he messed with Ashley Gemini.

**

Jake held a trash bag in one hand as he carefully removed his awards from his bookshelf. The Student of the Month award from sophomore year. The state champion ring from his freshman year. The ribbons of high achievement from his childhood sports teams. They all found a new home in Jake's trash bag. He didn't feel like a winner anymore, and the shrine of his prior achievements was only a sad reminder of what he once was. What he now could never be.

"You're throwing everything away?" Rosie asked. Jake turned to see his mother standing in the doorway with a small stack of mail wrapped inside of a rubber band.

"I don't want to look at it anymore," Jake replied.

"I can store them in the attic if you'd like. Maybe you'll change your mind."

"No," he said. "I won't."

Rosie gazed at him with sympathy, but she decided it was best to not press the issue further. Jake looked at the stack of mail in her hand.

"Is that for me?" he asked.

"It's mostly magazines and a few letters of support from people in town."

Jake took the stack from her. He glanced down and immediately noticed a handwritten card from one of his former teachers. The card made him think of an invitation, which made him remember the strange conversation he had with Kristin in front of McCue's Diner.

"Is something wrong?" Rosie asked.

Jake removed the rubber band, dropping the magazines to the floor and flipping through the stack. His mother stared at him strangely as he tore through each envelope, scanning it quickly before discarding it haphazardly.

"Did I receive an invitation of any sort?" Jake asked.

His question confused Rosie. Jake had only been out of the detention facility for two days. Why would he expect to receive invitations so soon, and where did he want to be invited to? She figured that he must have felt left out and hoped that being imprisoned hadn't made him delusional.

He finished searching through the stack, but the way he looked at Rosie concerned her. Why was there so much fear in his eyes?

"This is it?" he asked.

"This is all that came. You haven't received any invitations. I'm sorry, Jake."

She stared at him, trying to figure out what was wrong with her son. His paranoia reminded her of her own father, when he had come back from war.

"Let me know if you need anything, honey," Rosie said.

"Thanks, Mom," Jake said, feeling embarrassed. He was thankful when she left the room, and quickly resumed throwing his awards away. This time he didn't bother to look at what was going in the trash bag. Everything just disappeared.

When he was finished, he gazed at the magazines and opened letters on the floor, shaking his head at his idiocy. He had let Kristin's irrational fear spread to him, but why? Kristin was no longer the girl he had thought she was. If she was, then she never would've helped put him away, and really, Jake didn't know what she had been up to in the last two years. Why had she quit school? Was she into drugs? Had she fallen into a bad crowd, and that's why she looked the way she did? Why did she make up that nonsense about the invitation?

Jake bent to pick up the opened letters and stuffed them into the trash bag. As he came close to finishing, he noticed he had missed one envelope with no return address, only his name typed on the front.

He couldn't believe that he hadn't seen the card earlier. "What's this?" he asked as he tore into the envelope. He removed a single sheet of paper and saw a stencil of a white horse. As he read, his eyes widened.

Dear Jake Victor,

We, the Gamemakers, cordially invite you to play a game on Halloween…

**

It was dark when Jake pushed the doorbell of the Grace's home. He couldn't tell if the bell was working or not, so he pushed again. Then again. Then again for the fourth time. When a response didn't come fast enough, he banged on the front door with his fist. When it flew open, he jumped back, alarmed that he had almost punched Kristin in the face.

"What's wrong with you?" she said. "I heard the bell the first time. I was just upstairs with my Mom."

"I need to talk," Jake said, holding up the invitation. Kristin immediately recognized the paper with the white horse stencil. She stepped onto the porch and shut the door behind her. She was dressed in a t-shirt and her ugly black scarf. Jake watched as she rubbed her folded arms to keep warm.

"You got an invitation," she said. He handed it to her. She read the message and shook her head. "You know, when I first got this, I thought it was a joke."

"How do you know it's not?" Jake asked. He had thought about the invitation on the drive over. What if someone was playing with them?

Kristin stared into his eyes. Even with all of her heavy makeup, he was spellbound by how beautiful they were. At that moment, he wanted to kiss her, but she stepped away.

"This isn't *I Know What You Did Last Summer*. This is real," she said.

"Okay, but how do you know for sure?" he asked. "Just because it's written all spooky doesn't mean that some sick asshole didn't pen this…"

"Did you RSVP yet?" she asked, cutting him off and avoiding his question.

"How am I supposed to RSVP? It doesn't have any contact information. I don't know who the Gamemakers are. I don't understand what this is all about!"

"You need to RSVP, Jake. Just make a decision and say it aloud."

"I don't get it. How could playing a game bring Ronnie back?"

"We're not playing to bring him back. We're playing to set him free. To set ourselves free from what we've done."

Jake shook his head. "I still don't get it. What kind of game would we be playing anyway? Are we playing a sport like football or some board game like Monopoly?"

"Is this a joke to you?!" she screamed. Jake was taken aback. In the past two years, meek Kristin had become as crazy and hard as Ashley.

"How do I know to take this seriously?"

Kristin slowly unraveled her scarf. "You'll take it seriously when this happens to you." She exposed her bare neck.

Jake stared at her, unsure of what he was looking at. "I don't understand," he said.

They locked eyes before she turned around, revealing *666* tattooed on the back of her neck.

Jake stepped back in alarm.

"That's not funny, Kristin."

"You think I did this to myself?" she screeched.

He stared at her, wishing she had.

"Two days after I got my letter, this mark burned itself onto my neck. I don't know how it happened, but one morning, I woke up and it was there. I've got the Sign of the Beast on me, and you're next."

Jake stared at the letter in her hand. It looked so inconspicuous, yet its content was so evil. It almost made sense to him that the Gamemakers, the demons behind the invite, would toy with them in this way.

"You haven't been marked yet?" Kristin asked.

Jake shook his head. "I just found this tonight."

"You'll be marked," she said.

"So what are we supposed to?" he asked.

She took a step towards him. Knowing that he was doomed to play like she was made her feel closer to him. They were in this together.

"We have to do what we have to do," she said. "We've got to play."

CHAPTER EIGHT

Mayor Hercules sat on a bench in his backyard. He stared up at the barren trees, his mind wandering to the past, back when the leaves and flowers had once bloomed on their branches. He closed his eyes and saw his children, ten-year-old Brytani and seven-year-old Michael, running through the yard.

"Daddy! Mommy! Watch me!" Brytani called as she jumped into a pile of red leaves.

Mayor Hercules smiled.

**

It was a cool day in 1968. Next to Mayor Hercules, his redheaded wife Myra sat on the bench with him, smiling as she wrapped her arm around her husband's waist. The couple was very much in love, and they had a happy family.

"Mayor Hercules. Myra," a singsong voice said.

They turned to see their neighbor, Lily Breystrus, appear with a tray of cupcakes. She wore a beautiful polka dot dress that complemented her pale skin, her cherry lips, and her dark curled hair. She was the embodiment of a perfect housewife.

"Good afternoon, Lily," Mayor Hercules said with a joyous smile.

"You didn't have to bring us cupcakes!" Myra said, eyeing the beautiful treats. Lily always baked treats for the neighbors, and her goods were as enticing as any from a professional bakery. "You're already doing so much for us."

"Oh, stop," Lily said, her voice sultry and sweet. "Taking the kids out on Halloween is no trouble at all."

"Let us pay you for your troubles," Mayor Hercules said.

Lily put up her hand to say no. "I refuse your payment," she said. "I feel as if taking the children out on Halloween will be a gift to me just as much to you."

She smiled at Mayor Hercules and Myra before her attention turned to Brytani and Michael splashing each other with the leaves.

"They love to laugh. Don't they?" Lily asked.

"They have so much life in them," Myra said.

"I'm counting on that," Lily replied with a smile.

Mayor Hercules and Myra held hands and looked away from their neighbor, which was a shame. After all, had they been paying attention, they would have noticed how cold her dark eyes were. How wicked her grin was. There were evil thoughts churning in her mind, and if only they had paid attention, maybe they wouldn't have let their children go with her on Halloween night.

**

"This place gives me the creeps," Jake said. Kristin rolled her eyes. They walked through the basement of the Deer Creek Library, which had rows and rows of empty shelves along its dusty tables and creaky chairs.

"Maybe because you hate reading," Kristin said.

"For your information, I read a lot in juvie."

"Oh, yeah? Like what? *The Hardy Boys?*"

Jake laughed as they found an empty table near the back. He plopped his backpack onto the table and pulled out several heavy, old books.

"I read a bit of everything," he said.

Kristin sat next to him and opened up a black book with gold trim.

"What was your favorite book?" she asked.

"*Heart of Darkness*" Jake said. "It's about a British guy who takes an assignment as a river boat captain in Africa. While he's there, we see the evils of British colonization, and the book examines the evil that humans can inflict on other humans, the darkness within every person to create evil…"

Kristin stared at him and then at the pages opened before her. There was a detailed drawing of a demon with horns whispering into a woman's ear. The woman smiled with glee as she drowned her baby in a tub of water. The graphic violence made Kristin want to be sick.

She looked at Jake, who now stared at the drawing, too.

"Humans are capable of such monstrous things," he said.

She tugged at the scarf around her neck and wiped the sweat off of her brow. "I hate how stuffy this place is," she said.

"You chose the location," he replied.

"It's the only place I know we can go where we can study without any disturbances."

Jake gazed around the room, which was dimly lit with blue light and in serious need of cleaning.

Suddenly a cold droplet landed on his head. He looked up and saw a damp area in the ceiling.

"That's weird," he said.

"What is?" Kristin asked.

"The ceiling's leaking."

She scooted over, pulling the books. "Make sure the books don't get wet."

"Thanks for worrying about me," he said with a smile.

Kristin gazed at him and his perfect white teeth. Was he flirting with her? They looked at each other, an attraction building, but before anything could happen, she turned away, avoiding his eyes. Jake looked at the heavy books on the table. "So he gave you three books?" he asked.

"He said these would help us prepare for what would be in store for us."

"And what would be in store for us?"

"He said to expect the unexpected."

Jake's eyebrows raised with skepticism. "Mayor Hercules sure is helpful."

"Don't be sarcastic," Kristin said as she flipped through the black book's pages. "He had a good point. The Devil is full of tricks, and if we are always aware of that, then we have won half of the battle."

Jake read the first chapter of the second book, thick and blue with yellowed pages. The chapter focused on the Seven Deadly Sins that plagued man.

Gluttony.

Wrath.

Envy.

Sloth.

Lust.

Greed.

Pride.

The Seven Deadly Sins came in different forms, and they were the origin of other sins, other vices. Those sins could be as trivial as stealing a pack of gum or as grave as murdering one's parents. Jake scanned page after page of images of the different forms the seven sins could take.

"This is some heavy stuff," he said. He gazed at Kristin's delicate jaw line, the way her eyes sparkled, even in the dingy light. He swallowed before shifting in his hard chair. "Maybe we could study somewhere else. Somewhere not so intense and dingy."

Another droplet hit the table.

"Where do you want to go?" Kristin asked.

"Why don't we go back to my place? My parents aren't home."

Kristin cocked an eyebrow. "Are you serious?"

He made a show of looking indignant. "Whoa, whoa, whoa. What are you thinking I'm thinking?"

She stared at him, suddenly embarrassed. Maybe he wasn't trying to flirt with her, but now he was making her feel stupid for thinking otherwise.

A droplet fell on her head.

"Eww," she said.

Jake felt embarrassed. "I'm not that gross, Kristin," he said.

"No, it's not that," she said. She touched the top of her head and another droplet landed. She looked up, her mouth hanging open as another droplet fell. She jumped back in alarm and she gagged out what she had swallowed.

"What happened?" Jake said.

"It's blood," she said.

To his horror, Jake looked up and saw that blood was dropping down from the ceiling. The damaged ceiling was starting to tear further, creating an even greater spillage of blood.

"Grab the books," Kristin said. "We've got to get out of here!" The blood had already formed a thick, red puddle on the floor.

She and Jake scrambled to grab the books, as the hole in the ceiling widened. The liquid above was so heavy that the hole burst like a split seam and gallons and gallons of blood rushed to the floor, filling the room.

Jake rushed away from the table, but Kristin slipped on the blood and banged her head against the table.

"Ow," she cried. Jake bent to help pick her up. She grabbed his arm, and he pulled her to her feet. They sloshed through the blood, its ooze sticking to the bottom of her shoe. Soaked with the red liquid, Jake and Kristin made it to the staircase. They watched in disbelief as the room began to fill.

"Let's go," Jake said. He extended his hand, and Kristin grabbed it. The moment their hands touched, the sound of the blood falling stopped. They turned to look at the basement, and to their surprise, it was as empty as when they had first arrived.

"You saw it, didn't you?" Kristin asked.

"Yeah," Jake said.

Kristin's eyes watered with frustration. "They're not going to leave us alone until we play."

He nodded as he continued to hold her hand. "That's why we've gotta win."

"Hey! Who's down here?"

Jake and Kristin looked up the stairs to see policeman Eric shining his flashlight on them. When Eric spotted them, his eyes flashed with recognition, and Jake felt chills as he remembered how Eric had testified at the trial, had appeared at his hearing. It seemed as if Eric only appeared during the most horrible moments in Jake's life.

"What are you two doing?" Eric said. "I got a call that there was a disturbance down here. This area is closed, you know."

"We were just leaving," Jake said.

Eric eyed the two of them as they walked past him on the stairs. Jake felt his eyes on their backs as they left, but he exhaled with relief, happy that Eric had not arrested them. They didn't need any more trouble in their lives.

**

Mayor Hercules breathed slowly as he made his way up the stairs. The crows along the staircase and on the chandelier stared down at him. Although they were dead and stuffed, they appeared to be waiting for the old man to fall to his knees and perish.

"Don't worry," he said to the birds. "My moment will come."

Even though he had nowhere to go today or anyone to see, he wore a nice black suit, a handkerchief hanging out of his coat pocket. He tried to remain composed as he took each step, but this afternoon, he felt dizzy and wheezed noisily. He made his way onto the landing and slowly walked to his library, a grand room with floor-to-ceiling shelves full of books of the occult. He sat in front of the secretary, removing a pen and parchment. He paused as he recounted the memory that had been haunting him for years.

**

Lily Breystrus wore a maroon hooded robe on Halloween Night of 1968. When she pressed the doorbell to Mayor Hercules' home, she stood before a group neighborhood children, all wearing costumes and holding large sacks, eager to collect their candy.

The door flew open, and she smiled at Mayor Hercules, Myra, and their children, Brytani and Michael, dressed as a witch and a pirate, respectively. Lily gazed at Brytani's outfit in approval.

"I see we have a little witch!" Lily said, and Brytani's parents both laughed.

"Would you like to come in for some dessert?" Myra asked. "I just made a fresh pumpkin pie."

"I thought that was cinnamon I smelled," Lily replied, "but we must be off. I can't keep the children out too late."

"What time will you have Brytani and Michael home?" Myra asked.

Mayor Hercules gently nudged his wife. "Oh, Myra. Let Lily have fun with the kids." He looked to Lily, who smiled as if her face was made of plastic. "Take care of our babies."

"Oh, I will," she said. Brytani and Michael joined the gaggle of other kids behind her as Mayor Hercules and his wife smiled and waved goodbye, unaware that this would be the last time they ever saw their children alive.

**

The witch brought the children to the Deer Creek Cemetery Church at 10:30 pm.

"Why are we here, Lily?" a six-year-old dressed as a cat asked.

"I want to show you something," she replied.

The children milled about the inside of the church, which was a simple room with wooden pews and a wooden pulpit. Brytani and Michael gazed around the space, confused as to why they were there.

"I want you all to gather in a circle," Lily instructed. "And hold hands."

"What are we doing?" Brytani asked.

"We're having a party," Lily answered, and the children liked the sound of that. As they gathered into a circle and held hands, Lily counted each head, making sure every child from the neighborhood was there. When she was satisfied, she pulled out an ancient book that had been hidden behind the pulpit, then turned to the page about The Gateway to Hell and the instructions on how to open it.

"I have to go to the bathroom," the ten-year-old boy next to Brytani said. He was dressed like a skeleton, in a costume of black sweatpants with white bones painted onto it. Brytani had a slight crush on him, and to her disappointment, he let go of her hand and snuck out of the church while Lily was busy reading.

**

That boy was the only witness to the disappearance. He had returned to the church only to find its eyes glowing with fire. He heard his friends screaming inside, before the doors flew open and the screaming stopped. Filled with bravery, he ran up to the church and saw that no one was in there. It was like a horrific magic show, and he didn't know what to do.

He ran home, crying and scared, and told his parents what had happened. In their pajamas, his parents burst out of their house and banged on the doors of everyone else who had lost their children. They created a mob, which included Mayor Hercules and Myra, and drove to the church to see what had happened.

"What if the boy's lying?" someone asked.

"What if he's not?"

The mob arrived at the cemetery, and the church appeared to be nothing more than an old building. Creepy, but harmless.

Crying and hysterical, Myra ran to the boy and she shook him hard. "Where are Brytani and Michael? Where did she take them?"

The boy's mother rushed to push Myra out of the way.

"She took them here. I promise!" the boy said. "That church came alive like it was owned by The Devil!"

Mayor Hercules stood next to a group of men, who looked to him for guidance on what to do. Ever since he was a young boy, he had read the occult books that were handed down to him by father and his grandfather. They had told him the stories of the Gateway to Hell, how it was one of seven openings on Earth to the Underworld. Now he knew that those stories were true.

"Burn it," Mayor Hercules said.

"Are you sure?" a man asked.

"Burn it."

One of the men found a lighter in his pocket, while the others gathered brush from around the cemetery. They lit the base of the church on fire, and everyone watched as the church went up in flames.

"It's not coming down," Myra said, and it was true.

The wood disintegrated and the furniture inside perished, but the metal entrance, the pagan cross on the roof, and the heavy stones of the outside walls remained.

A group of men rushed over with sledgehammers, ready to break down the walls. The second their hammers touched the stones, however, the fire leaped towards them, catching their clothes. They screamed in pain as the others in the crowd gasped.

"This place really is evil," Mayor Hercules whispered. He looked over at his wife, whose heart was breaking. There was no denying anymore that what the boy witness had claimed was true.

**

Mayor Hercules rubbed at his temples. He had just finished composing his letter to Kristin, documenting to her how the children had disappeared, how his own children had disappeared, and how his wife had died years later of a broken heart. He wrote to Kristin about how sorry he was that the curfew had failed her and her friends, and he wrote to her that he prayed that she would beat Hell's Game. And then, finally, he asked that if she were to come across his children in Hell that he would tell them how sorry he was that he had let them go out on that night.

Mayor Hercules turned off the lamp next to a framed picture of Mayor Hercules and his wife and children. He left the library of his Victorian, taking slow steps to his master bedroom, which was decorated with dark green wallpaper and black furniture. He gingerly removed his jacket and pants, then slipped them over his high-backed chair. He climbed into his four-poster bed in his underwear and socks, and he pulled the thick covers over his body. After his head hit the satin pillows, he closed his eyes, prepared to have the nightmare that came to him every night, but the nightmare did not come. Instead, the Grim Reaper took him that evening, and that was the best thing that had happened to him in decades.

CHAPTER NINE

Rebecca put her bucket of toiletries on the tiled floor. The dormitory bathroom had three stalls, and the middle one was occupied. She stepped into the first stall and disrobed. She thought about how hard her first day of class at Columbia University was and all she wanted to do was de-stress under a hot stream of water. As she turned the faucet knobs, she waited for the water to pour, but nothing would come out.

"What the..." she asked.

She put on her robe and stepped out of the shower. She grabbed her bucket of toiletries and walked to the third stall. She attempted to turn on the water, but that shower was broken as well.

"Are you almost finished?" Rebecca asked the girl in the middle stall. Rebecca had been in the bathroom for at least five minutes and figured that the girl had to be close to finishing by now.

The girl in the shower ignored her and continued soaking her blonde hair.

"Hello?" Rebecca asked. Her tone emerged ruder than she had wanted, but she couldn't believe that she was being ignored.

"I heard you the first time, *bitch*," Ashley replied coolly.

Rebecca loudly *tsked* her tongue. "What the hell?" she muttered.

"I just got into the shower. Use the other stalls."

"They're broken!"

Ashley rolled her eyes. That was not her problem.

"Then wait like a normal person."

"I'm going to report you!" Rebecca said.

"Go ahead," Ashley snapped back.

Rebecca glared at the stall door before she stormed out of the bathroom. She imagined the punishment the mean girl would receive from the floor's resident advisor as she slammed the door behind her, causing an echo that reverberated throughout the heavily tiled room.

Ashley smiled with satisfaction, having won the battle. How dare that the girl think she could just step in on Ashley's time? After all, Ashley had to wait over an hour for her turn, and she was not about to let some spoiled co-ed cut into her time.

"*I'm going to report you!*" Ashley mimicked in Rebecca's voice. She found it ridiculous that the girl thought that anyone was going to do anything to reprimand her.

She rolled her eyes as she squeezed out her expensive shampoo into her hand. She massaged it into her scalp as she closed her eyes, enjoying the sensation, and she began to hum the song that she had heard when she was a little girl.

"*I'll take care of you, until the end of the time. I'll always love you, but I can't make you mine...*"

Ashley hadn't sung that tune for years, and she wasn't sure why it had popped into her head at the moment but it was there, dying to escape.

"*I'm sorry we can't be together, pretty girl, but I promise through the darkness that I will guide you to the light...*"

As Ashley got further into the song, the lights of the bathroom flickered. Her eyes flew open, and she gasped as the warm water suddenly became ice cold. She glanced down and saw the water knobs slowly turn on their own.

"Aaaasssssssssssshhhhhllllleeeyyy..." a soft voice whispered from above.

Ashley grabbed her towel and jumped out of the stall without turning off the water. As she raced out of the bathroom, her foot slipped onto a puddle of water. She crashed down, hands first, her face hitting the hard-tiled floor. She groaned in pain.

Behind her, the knobs of all three showers turned slowly to scalding hot. Water poured out, even from the two broken faucets. The steam from the water filled the room and covered the giant, singular mirror over the sinks.

The lights flicked back on, and Ashley slowly lifted her head to see letters appear on the steam of the glass.

"P. L. A..." Ashley read aloud as the letters appeared, slowly becoming words. Ashley stood up and approached the mirror. She gasped as the phrase fully formed.

Play the game, it said.

The water in the showers turned off, and the lights turned off again.

Breaking her spell of curiosity, Ashley raced for the door. One hand held onto her towel and the other reached for the knob, but before she could exit, she cried out in pain. Her free hand jerked back to touch her neck where it felt as if someone was slicing her with a scalpel.

She continued to hold her neck as the pain intensified, but it became so unbearable that she fell to her knees. The cutting sensation continued, and she closed her eyes wishing that it would stop.

"Please, God," she begged as tears emitted from her eyes.

After seconds that felt like hours, the slicing ended, and she was left with a strange burning feeling on the back of her neck. Ashley removed her hand, checking to see if there was blood, but her hand was clean.

"Aaaassssssssssshhhhlllleeeyyy..." the voice said again. Ashley looked upwards, worried what other pain was in store for her.

"Please," she said, crying. "Please, no more."

As if the voice had heard her, the lights came back on. Ashley blinked, trying to adjust her vision. She groggily rose to her knees, and as she stood, she caught the reflection of her backside in the mirror.

"What the…" she said as she touched her neck again, making sure that what she saw was real. As her fingers caressed her skin, outlining the numbers *666* branded into her flesh, she further realized with horror that the game was real, and that if she didn't play, The Devil was coming for her soul.

CHAPTER TEN

Ashley sat against the concrete wall of her dorm room, holding her knees against her chest. She stared at a speck in the tile of the floor in such a way that her roommate, Liz, a brunette artsy girl, grew alarmed.

"Are you okay?" Liz asked.

Ashley rubbed at the back of her neck. She wasn't close to her roommate and besides, would she believe her if she told her that a spirit had carved *666* on the back of her neck while she was in the bathroom?

"I'm fine," Ashley lied.

Liz continued to stare, and Ashley knew she had to get out of her dorm. She climbed out of bed and put on her pea coat. She grabbed her purse and cell phone, and without saying goodbye to her concerned roommate, she hurried out the door.

With long strides, Ashley walked the streets of Manhattan. All around her, people rushed past, not paying any attention to one another, too concerned with where they needed to be. Ashley closed her eyes and thought about Jake and the trial from two years ago. Recounting what had happened, she knew what she and her parents' lawyers had concocted was wrong. Yet that didn't stop her from taking out her cell phone and dialing Jake, right there in the middle of the busy Manhattan sidewalk.

"What do you want?" Jake asked.

"Is that how you greet all of your exes?" Ashley asked.

Jake rolled his eyes.

"You got your invite?" he asked.

"Did you get yours?" she asked.

"Kristin and I both did."

"Did you get the mark?"

"Not yet."

Ashley nearly ran into an elderly woman in a fur coat. The woman looked Ashley up and down and glared at her. "Watch where you're going, you harlot!" the woman yelled, and Jake heard it through the line.

"I see you're making friends in every city," Jake said.

"Enough with the pleasantries," Ashley said. "What are we supposed to do?"

As she walked through the crowded street, she thought she saw the Deer Creek cop, Eric, staring at her from a distance. When she blinked, he was gone.

"We're going to play the game," Jake said, "And we hope you're going to join us."

Ashley rounded a corner and stepped close to the wall of the building, where she stood masked in the shadows.

"I don't know if I can do that..." Ashley said.

Jake closed the book and sat up with alarm. "You have to play, Ashley. Kristin got advice from Mayor Hercules. He said we need to band together if we're going to survive. He seemed to know a lot about this stuff."

Ashley stared at the beautiful stores across the street, at the wealthy New Yorkers walking by. She hated the idea of giving up New York City to return to Deer Creek, only to play a game for her soul in Hell.

"The letter said we don't have to play if we don't want to," she said.

"It also said if you don't play, then they'll take that as your RSVP to Hell when you die."

"Well, I'd rather deal with it fifty years from now than in a few weeks."

Jake couldn't believe how selfish she was being. "What about Ronnie?" he asked.

The image of Pencil Dick Smalls flashed in her brain, and she winced. She didn't want to think about him. She only wanted to think about herself.

Jake waited for her to respond, to change her mind, but the line remained quiet.

"Ashley?" he asked. He knew she was there. "Ashley, if you're not coming home then why did you call?"

She took a deep breath, trying to find the right words. Across the street, Eric Whitehorse stared at her, shaking his head. She tried to hide her face from him even though she knew she was being stupid. He wasn't there at all.

"I wanted to hear your voice, Jake," she said.

It was this time that *he* kept quiet.

"Jake?" she asked. "Are you there?"

He couldn't tell if she was trying to manipulate him or not, and he found his face flushing with anger.

"Jake?"

His jaw tightened.

"Jake?"

"Ashley, I think that…"

He dropped his phone before he could finish his thought. He felt a searing pain on the back of his neck, a type of sensation that he had never experienced before in his life.

"Jake?" Ashley asked in alarm as she heard him scream. "Jake?"

The line went dead. Ashley tried to call back, but even though there was no answer, she knew exactly what was happening.

**

"Kristin?" Bryan Grace said as he knocked on her bedroom door. Kristin, who had been doing sit-ups on her floor, looked at the door in alarm as it opened. The sight of her father surprised her. Bryan Grace wa a medium-sized man with a tubby belly, and he seemed nervous as he walked into her room.

"Are you okay?" Kristin asked. Something was wrong, but she didn't know what it was.

"You should sit down," Bryan said.

Kristin realized at that moment that she wasn't wearing her scarf. Bryan noticed the *666* carved into her neck, and he frowned but said nothing about it.

She eased onto the edge of her bed as he pulled up a chair beside her.

"What's up?" Kristin said.

Bryan took a deep breath. "I'm just going to say it," he said, and Kristin braced herself, unsure of what he was going to tell her. "Your mother and I are getting a divorce."

Kristin felt her heart break. Even though her father had been absent a lot since her mother's disfigurement, she still hoped that there was still love between them.

"Is this because of me?" Kristin asked.

"No, honey," Bryan replied. "It's not anyone's fault. Your mother and I just don't love each other anymore."

Kristin knew that was a lie. Her mother loved her father. Every time he went away, she stayed at home, waiting for him while he did whatever he wanted. She also knew that her father had a hard time looking at Susie ever since she had become scarred. It was sad to see that every time Bryan pulled away, Susie only needed him more.

"What's going to happen now?" Kristin asked.

"Your mother wants to move in with Aunt Leslie."

"But Aunt Leslie doesn't want to stay in Deer Creek anymore, now that Lenora moved."

"There's nothing I can do about that. That's what she wants."

Kristin crossed her arms and looked to the side, avoiding her father's eyes. "I hate you!" she screamed.

He believed she hated herself more.

"Why did you get a tattoo?" he asked.

He stood to approach and examine it, but Kristin sprang away. She searched the room for her jacket, grabbed it and then hurried towards the door.

"Where are you going, Kristin?"

"It's none of your business!" she said as she wiped at her eyes. She slammed the bedroom door so hard that the paint cracked. As she dashed down the stairs, she had hoped to hear her father coming after her, trying to plead with her not to go, trying to make her understand why he had stopped loving her mother.

Kristin exited through the house's front door and heard only silence coming from inside.

"Bye, Dad," Kristin whispered to the air as the door shut behind her.

CHAPTER ELEVEN

Even though it was nighttime, Kristin rode her bike to the cemetery. As the moonlight reflected off of her *666* tattoo and the sweat on her forehead, she pedaled furiously, the anger of her parents' divorce fueling her. She knew that her father had been using business as an excuse to be away from his wife, who he could no longer bear to look at. She knew that her mother didn't blame her for her disfigurement, and that made her feel worse all the same. Kristin knew that the divorce ultimately was the result of what she had done as a child.

Once Kristin arrived at her destination, she hopped off of her bike and left it in the dirt. She took long strides through the rows of tombstones until she found the marble marker that had the name Ashton Gemini carved into it.

The moment she saw it, she fell into the grass on her knees. As she stared at the marker, she thought about how much Ashton had loved her before he died.

"What if I hadn't broken up with you when you came to see me that afternoon?" Kristin asked, remembering the way the sunflowers had fallen to the ground. Was it egotistical for her to think that if she had remained his girlfriend, that he wouldn't have shot himself? After they broke up, he began to write her love letters. In a normal circumstance, maybe the letters would have worked, but there was something scary about his hurried proclamations of "I'll love you forever, no matter where we end up…"

"Kristin?" she heard Ashton ask.

Kristin jumped, startled. She turned around, expecting to see Ashton standing behind her, pale as a ghost.

"Ashton?" Kristin said. She gazed around and saw that he wasn't there. She realized then that she was close to losing her mind, and remembered Mayor Hercules advice to be as strong in mind as she was in body and soul. If she were to head into Hell's Game now, there was no way she would be able to win.

**

Jake stepped out of the shower, the steam filling the tiny bathroom of his home. He wrapped a towel around his waist after patting dry the rest of his body, which was chiseled, every muscle pronounced and throbbing. He wiped the perspiration off of the mirror, and then turned, trying to get a good look at the *666* branded onto his neck. When the branding occurred, he felt a sharp sting on his flesh, and fear seized him, the feeling he was going to die. After the pain had subsided, he wondered, "If this is what the invite feels like, what will the game entail?"

"Jake?" his mother Rosie asked from the other side of the door.

"Yeah, Mom?"

"Kristin's here to see you," she said.

"I'll be out in a minute."

With only a few weeks left until Halloween, he and Kristin were still preparing themselves for the game. They had finished studying the three books from Mayor Hercules, and planned to go back to his house that morning to get more.

Jake got dressed in a blue hooded sweatshirt and jeans before walking into the living room to find Kristin sitting with his mother. She wore a white sweater, black and white scarf, and jeans, and he noticed that today she had put on a little bit of makeup and left the gel out of her hair.

Jake found himself staring. He had never met a punk girl so pretty.

"Where are you two off to today?" Rosie asked.

Jake stared at the rash on his mother's face. Her eyes looked tired, and she sat on the couch, bundled up in a blanket. It pained him to see his mother when she was sick, and he was thankful that Kristin was comfortable in her presence.

"We're going to study," Jake replied.

"You've been doing that quite a bit lately," Rosie said with pride. "Are you two thinking of going to college?"

"I'm not sure," Kristin said to be polite. After Halloween, she wasn't even sure if she'd be alive, let alone become a studious co-ed.

She stood and joined Jake.

"See you, Mom," Jake said.

"Bye, guys. See you later," Rosie said as she closed her eyes.

**

While Jake drove his Mustang, Kristin sat in the passenger seat, thinking about how this had once been Ashley's place. She looked at her reflection in the side mirror, amazed at how different she looked from two years ago.

Jake stared ahead at the road, and Kristin glanced his way. She stared at his hardened jaw, his dark brown eyes, and his straight nose. He really was handsome.

"What are you thinking about?" Kristin asked.

"My Mom," Jake replied.

Kristin had noticed that Rosie looked sicker than she had in the past. She knew that she suffered from lupus, but never once had she and Jake discussed his mother.

Jake continued, relieved to have someone to talk to. "She's been getting worse. She was sick before I went away, but I think the stress of it all has really taken a toll on her."

"I'm sorry," Kristin said, unsure of what to say.

"I've been thinking a lot about what would happen to her, well, to both my parents if I don't make it out of the game…"

Kristin reached over and touched his hand on the wheel. She gazed into his eyes, letting him know that she was in it with him.

"We're going to win," Kristin said. "We're smart, we're strong, and we've got Mayor Hercules as a guide. We're going to be okay."

"What if that's not enough?" Jake asked.

Kristin stared ahead, thinking of what life had become since Ronnie's disappearance.

"My parents are getting a divorce," she said. "If I die in the game, my mother's going to be alone."

"What about your father?" Jake asked.

Kristin took a deep breath, stunned that she was spilling everything. It wasn't like her to delve deep into her feelings, but because of what was happening with the game, she felt incredibly close to him.

"I don't know if I can say I really know much about my father," she added. "It's funny; I had spent my whole childhood adoring him and hating her, but I never really knew him."

"I'm sorry," Jake said.

Kristin appreciated his sympathy, but she didn't want to talk about her parents anymore.

Jake pulled in front of Mayor Hercules' spooky Victorian and turned off the Mustang's engine. He and Kristin got out of the car, with Jake holding the backpack full of Mayor Hercules' books.

When they stepped onto the porch, he pressed the doorbell. They heard the chimes ring inside, and after a few seconds of waiting, he pressed again. No answer.

"He knows we're coming, right?" Jake asked.

"He said we can come anytime, day or night," Kristin said.

Jake pressed the button, and again, no answer.

"Maybe he's not home…" Jake said.

Kristin shook her head. "Where else would he be? He never leaves his house, except for church."

"Well, what do you suggest we do?" Jake asked.

Kristin lifted up the floor mat, but Jake couldn't believe that someone like Mayor Hercules would leave his house key underneath it.

"I really doubt he'd hide his key there," Jake said.

"You hide your key on your porch," Kristin replied. She moved on to the porch bench, where she ran her hand along the bottom. The key wasn't there. "Check the railing," Kristin instructed Jake. He looked, but no key was there, either.

"Let's just come back another time," Jake said.

Kristin sighed. "Let's ring him one more time," she said. She pressed the doorbell and waited. "I think I hear something in there." She turned the doorknob and to her amazement, the door popped open.

"He doesn't lock up?" Jake asked, and Kristin shrugged as they stepped inside.

Immediately, they were hit with a foul, rotten stench. They looked to the stairs and saw a raccoon scurrying upwards.

"There's your noise," Jake said as he plugged up his nose.

"Mayor Hercules?" Kristin called. "Hello?"

Jake walked around the first floor. He returned to Kristin in the entryway. "I don't think he's here…"

"There's something wrong. He wouldn't just leave his house smelling rank and letting vermin walk in and out."

Jake looked to the crows and then to the stairs. "I guess we can check upstairs," he said.

He and Kristin walked up to the second level, where the smell was so bad that they wanted to retch.

"Mayor Hercules?" Kristin called. She knew that he wouldn't answer, but she figured she would give it one last shot.

Jake pushed his bedroom door opened, and the smell that escaped was a hundred times worse than anything they had ever experienced. He and Kristin entered the room, horrified to see the mayor dead in his bed.

"He must've died sleeping," Jake said.

Kristin covered her mouth, her eyes watering. Even though he was old, she had still hoped that this day wouldn't come.

"We should call the police." As Jake searched for a phone, he noticed the letter addressed to Kristin. "He left this for you…"

Kristin tore into the envelope, and her eyes darted from left to right, reading the paragraphs about his family and how he lost his children decades ago, how he wished she would win the game, and how he wanted her to find his children in Hell.

"What's it say?" Jake asked.

Kristin folded the letter and put it into her pocket. She looked at Mayor Hercules, who had died with his eyes closed, the covers over his body.

"He's resting peacefully," Kristin said. "That's all that matters."

**

Before moving to New York City, Ashley avoided stepping into any church to pray, despite the fact that she attended her father's service every Sunday. Every time he had stepped up to the podium in his slick suit, flashing his phony smile, Ashley had shut out his words, instead dreaming of what it would be like to be free of her parents and of Deer Creek.

As Ashley wandered the streets of Manhattan on a chilly October afternoon, she thought about her options. She had only a few weeks to decide whether or not she would return to the Deer Creek Cemetery for Halloween, but she was scared. She had originally intended to find a church near her dorm in Morningside so that she could ask God for help, but at every building, she hesitated, finding different excuses.

This church seemed uninviting.

This one seemed like no one was inside.

That church catered to non-English-speaking parishioners.

However, after several hours and several city blocks later, Ashley realized that she was lying to herself, something she had done for the majority of her life. All of the churches scared her, but that was a problem within her, not their buildings.

Near dinnertime, she stood in front of a massive Catholic cathedral close to New York University, alarmed that she had walked this far south. The church was massive, five stories high with giant stained-glassed windows and a gold-colored rooftop. Its front door opened as a woman in an ugly brown dress stepped out. She avoided Ashley's gaze, but something about her presence assured Ashley that it was okay to go inside.

Ashley entered a room full of tea light candles in small red holders. Half of the candles were lit, and she passed by a man who was in the process of lighting one. He whispered something to himself in Spanish, but she couldn't understand him. Feeling uncomfortable for invading his private moment, she hurried past, her black boots pressing quickly into the red carpet that led to the velvet-covered pews. Relieved to find this giant room empty, she removed her pea coat and white scarf. She then looked up at the high ceiling and was amazed to see a beautiful mural as detailed as Michelangelo's.

In one of the middle pews, Ashley sat forward and clasped her hands together. She stared ahead at the large gold cross at the front of the church, and her lip curled with disgust. Its ostentatious appearance reminded her of her father, which she didn't like, but she didn't feel uncomfortable chills the way she did in his church either. After a few seconds, she relaxed and bowed her head, the way she had been taught to pray when she was a child.

"Dear Lord," she said aloud in a hushed voice. "I know it looks bad that I'm coming to you now, and I'm sorry for the timing, but I don't know what else to do." She opened her eyes and looked at the cross again. She felt like a huge phony, and she was sure God knew she was one, too. She unclasped her hands and sat back. She paused for a moment, contemplating whether or not to proceed. She ran her fingers through her blonde hair before they reached the back of her neck, where the *666* still existed, burned in her flesh. She decided to proceed.

She sat forward, clasping her hands, trying again. This time, the fear of what would happen to her soul outweighed her fear of looking stupid in front of God.

"Look," she said in the bitchy tone she had once reserved for her peers at Deer Creek High. "I'm going to be straight up with you. After what you let happen to me and Ashton, you owe me a free pass because that was bullshit. We were kids. We didn't know any better, and you watched us, and you let it happen, and people wonder why I'm not a nicer person, but how could I be when I have to carry around that baggage, knowing that shitty people can get away with shitty things and nice people get taken advantage of by shitty people?" Her voice cracked with anger. "I know what I did to Ronnie was wrong, but you shouldn't have taken Ashton away. Two wrongs don't make a right, and besides—you did way more wrong to us than we ever intended to do to Ronnie. I'm sorry, and I was wrong, but I never thought that the Gateway was real. You know that. If you're out there, you can read my thoughts, and you know that I didn't really believe it was real. After what you let happen to me, I didn't believe that *you* existed, let alone the Devil..."

She was crying now. Her tears warmed her cheeks.

"I'm sorry, God. This doesn't sound like much of a plea for help, but I don't know what do. I'm not good with words, but I need an answer. I need help."

She wiped away her tears and sat back again. "There," she thought. "I did it." Now she wondered how long it would take for God to send her an answer or if He would send one at all. After all, where was he when she was a child, screaming for help? Where was he when Ashton pulled the trigger over a year ago? Where was he two years ago when Ronnie was pulled into the Gateway to Hell?

Ashley crossed her arms over her chest as her bitter, angry memories rushed through her. What was she doing here? This was a big waste of time, and she was only kidding herself for believing that God would ever help her.

"Thanks for the sign, asshole," Ashley muttered as she made a grab for her jacket and scarf next to her.

"Miss?" she heard someone say.

Ashley looked up to see a young priest hovering over her.

"Yes?" Ashley snapped.

"You should go."

Ashley stared at him, and although she had heard what he said, she wasn't positive he had said it.

"What?" she asked.

"You need to go."

She stared at him blankly. Had God really sent her a sign? Was he really using this priest to tell her to play the game?

"It's important that you go," the priest said. "We're holding a wedding here in an hour, and we need to set up. I'm sorry."

"Oh," Ashley said, hurrying out of her seat. "Sorry."

As he watched, she quickly put on her jacket and left the church. She couldn't believe that God had given her an answer.

PART THREE: HELL'S GAME

Even though I walk through the valley of the shadow of death, I will fear no evil, for you are with me; your rod and your staff, they comfort me.

-Psalm 23:4

CHAPTER TWELVE

The night felt cold, just as it had two years ago. Ashley stood in the middle of the Deer Creek Cemetery, shivering underneath her pea coat and scarf. She gazed up at the church, which still looked like a sad face, and she wished that she wasn't the only one standing there. Had Jake and Kristin backed out? She knew that they were invited, and from the *666* on the back of her neck, she knew the invitation was real, but they could have still changed their minds. After all, fear of the present was just as powerful as fear of the inevitable.

It was eerily silent. No creatures stirring. No crickets chirping. No fireflies dancing in the sky. Ashley remembered how quiet it was that Halloween night, but hadn't realized back then that it was because all the animals in the forest were hiding.

"Hey," Jake said as he approached Ashley from behind. His deep voice sent excitement throughout her body. She hadn't seen him in so long, and she missed him. When she turned, however, her face fell.

Jake stood next to Kristin, and both of them had hardened over time. Jake looked weathered and older than eighteen, and his once lustrous brown locks were buzzed short. Kristin looked older, too. She had short hair and wore too much eye-makeup, which made her almond-shaped orbs look gigantic and alien-like. Her once meek demeanor was replaced by an angry shell, and Ashley recognized that shell of anger because she wore it herself.

"Hey," Ashley replied. She waited for Kristin to say something, but she didn't. Ashley was bothered by the idea that Kristin still hated her, and bothered that she and Jake had shown up together, in solidarity, while she had come alone. "What are we supposed to do now?" Ashley said.

"I guess wait," Kristin replied.

Ashley nodded awkwardly and continued to watch Jake and Kristin standing close to one another. The sexual energy between them was palpable. In the time that she was in New York, had the two of them connected?

Kristin stared hard at Ashley, who still looked like a magazine model, even more so with her fancy New York attire. Even though she knew it was petty, Kristin resented that Ashley had not suffered the same physical toll as Jake and she had.

Eleven o'clock was only four minutes away, but to Ashley, it felt like four hours were going by. The three of them stood tensely, facing one another, shivering from the cold in front of a haunted church, the silence only amplifying the anticipation for whatever evil things were about to happen.

Ashley wished that The Gamemakers would have given them more hints as to what was to come. Would they be playing a game filled with physical torture, or would it mostly be mental? Would they see actual demons or would they have to confront their own?

"So…" Ashley said.

"So," Jake said.

"You look good," Ashley lied to Kristin.

Kristin glared back at her. This was no time to be patronizing. "I heard you go to Columbia now," she said.

"I do," Ashley replied.

"I don't remember your grades being very good."

Ashley bristled. Jake shot Kristin a warning look before he looked at his watch again. What were they waiting for?

Suddenly, the tolls of a clock chimed eleven times. Kristin and Ashley jerked their heads.

"Where'd that come from?" Ashley said.

"There's no clock in town," Kristin said.

Jake stared at the face of the church. He half-expected its eyes to light up again, or to hear the evil laughter, or to see the gnarled hands jump out of the church doors.

Yet, the church remained still. Eerily still.

"What now?" Kristin asked.

"Should we go up to the church?" Ashley asked.

Kristin and Jake stared at her as though she had just said something extremely offensive. Ashley found their reaction puzzling since going into the church seemed like the only logical thing to do.

"Is this part of the game?" Kristin asked.

"Not telling us what to do or where to go doesn't seem very fair," Jake said.

"They branded us with *666*. I doubt these fuckers care about fairness," Ashley griped.

"Nice vocabulary, as usual," Kristin sniped.

"Maybe that's part of the game," Jake said. "We have to figure out how to get *into* the game first."

Kristin heard a strange buzzing in her ears and looked around curiously. "Do you hear that?" she asked. Ashley and Jake perked up, also hearing the sound.

"What's that noise?" Ashley asked, surprised that the silence was finally broken.

Kristin, Jake, and Ashley looked up to the sky. Everything appeared normal, except for a square patch of dark gray in the middle of the clear, starry sky. The more they stared at the patch, the bigger it became.

As the buzz grew louder and the patch came closer, Jake, Kristin, and Ashley realized that they were staring at a swarm of wasps closing in on them.

"Run," Jake said.

The three of them scattered, covering their faces with their hands. Ashley ran towards the woods, Jake took off towards the parking lot, and Kristin ran towards the tombstones.

The wasps broke up into groups of three before shooting down at Ashley, Jake, and Kristin. Ashley fell to the grass, never making it to the woods. The wasps' stingers felt like a thousand needles piercing her body simultaneously; the pain was just as intense as when the sixes were cut into her neck. The athletic Jake ran towards the parking lot, only yards away. The wasps came for him, but he swerved, avoiding them. He took out his car keys, zigzagging closer to his car when he heard Kristin screaming in pain.

"Help! Help!"

Jake ran towards her, the wasps still coming for him. From a distance, he could see Kristin amidst dusty graves, writhing on the grass. There were boils all over her face and body, but luckily, her group of wasps had left her.

Jake looked behind him and saw the wasps zeroing in. He swerved before they could sting him, quickly making his way to Kristin.

"Kristin!" Jake cried.

"Jake," she whispered in pain, unable to open her swollen eyes. "Get away from me. Save yourself…"

"I'm not going to leave you," he said. He glanced behind him and saw that he had seconds before the wasps would catch up to him. He calculated that there was just enough time to scoop up Kristin and take her to safety.

Towards the woods, Ashley lay paralyzed in the grass. Though her eyes could barely stay open, she watched as Jake bent to lift Kristin, who had collapsed near the tombstones.

"Jake…" Ashley whispered, wishing he had come to save her instead.

Jake struggled to lift Kristin. Although he could pick her up, he had miscalculated would be light as a feather, and lifting her took him longer than he had planned, all while the buzzing intensified behind him.

"No…" Kristin whispered in horror as the wasps darted down with their stingers. Jake winced as the first sting occurred, closing his eyes as his flesh was pierced with dozens and dozens more. He dropped Kristin to the ground, where she landed with a hard thud. He closed his eyes as the stingers entered one by one, then dozens and dozens at a time, and he felt each prick until a red fog misted inside of his brain and he fell asleep.

CHAPTER THIRTEEN

"Ugh…" Jake moaned as he opened his eyes, which were flooded with extremely bright light. He felt as if he had just come out of being anesthetized. His head felt groggy, his body moving slowly as it readjusted to consciousness. As he tried to shield his eyes, he heard a familiar female voice.

"Jesus Christ," Ashley muttered as she touched her head. She looked around and saw Jake and Kristin lying beside her, swathed in light as though they were all in a giant white room with a million spotlights blasting on them from different directions.

"What happened?" Kristin asked, highly confused. She recalled going to the cemetery and the swarm of wasps, but from there, she didn't know how she ended up in the room of white. She figured that the Gamemakers had transported them to this site, but the bright lights confused her. Would they really take the trio to Heaven?

"What's this?" Ashley asked, seeing an old gold timepiece on a chain in her hand. She opened its cover and saw that it was broken.

"Where'd you get that?" Kristin asked. She reached into her pockets, wondering if she had received a gift, but she only discovered that her pockets were empty. The cell phone, keys, and wallet she had taken with her to the cemetery were gone.

"I don't know," Ashley said. "I just woke up and found it in my hand. It doesn't even work…"

Jake checked his wrist, only to see that his watch was missing. He also noticed that the boils and the stings from the wasps had disappeared. His skin was restored to what it was, and the clothes he had worn to the cemetery were clean.

"Welcome to Hell's Game," a voice said, and it echoed throughout the space. Jake, Ashley and Kristin gazed around, trying to find out where the voice was coming from. "I hope that your journey here wasn't too off-putting."

"No way," Ashley shot back, putting the timepiece in her pocket. "Stinging us to death wasn't off-putting at all."

Jake gazed around. "I recognize that voice," he muttered, and suddenly the lights dimmed to a normal brightness, revealing that the trio was in the foyer of a majestic castle. The room had high ceilings, and its walls were made of heavy stone. The floor-to-ceiling windows were covered with beautiful purple tapestries, making the room look fit for a king.

"Is this where we'll play the game?" Kristin asked.

"One level of it," the voice said. Kristin, Jake, and Ashley jerked their heads to a hallway entry, where a handsome prince dressed in regal white apparel appeared. The trio glared when they saw him.

"Eric Whitehorse," Jake said.

Eric smiled. "I'm glad that I don't need a formal introduction." He paused, letting them react to the realization that the same cop from Deer Creek was part of the game. "Welcome to Hell, and thank you for playing our game. I am your host for this evening."

Ashley scowled at him.

"Why the long face?" Eric asked Ashley. "Are you not excited to be here? After all, The Gamemakers have set up the game so that you'll be nothing but entertained."

"I'll bet," she mumbled. She thought about his testimony at their trial. How serious he had appeared. How aw-shucks and wholesome. He had seemed like nothing more than a small town cop who cared about justice, but now she realized that he was a part of a bigger picture. He was a demon who had played with them for years before bringing them to the scariest chapter of their lives.

"So," he said, walking around the foyer, enjoying the beauty of the environment. They stared back at him, still in shock that he was introducing them to Hell's Game. "You're probably wondering what the rules are."

"No shit," Ashley said.

"Ashley!" Kristin reprimanded. This entire ordeal was overwhelming and scary enough as it was. They didn't need to add more trouble for themselves by angering their host.

"Are you ready to learn the rules, or do you want to continue wasting your time being petulant children? After all, you're only allotted a small window on each level, and you're only making things harder for yourselves…"

"I'm not making things harder for us," Ashley griped.

Eric *tsked* as he shook his head. "So ungrateful. Even after I gave you an advantage that many other players would kill to have."

Jake raised his eyebrow. "What advantage?"

"The time piece," Eric said, pointing at Ashley's pocket. "We normally do not give players the advantage of knowing the time, but for you three, I made an exception."

"Tell us the rules," Jake said before quickly shooting Ashley a silencing glance. He didn't want her to do anything more to irritate their host.

Eric smiled, pleased.

"I'm sure you all have been wondering what kind of game you would be playing tonight, and you'll be happy to know that the Gamemakers have made the careful decision to put you three on a Scavenger Hunt."

"A scavenger hunt?" Kristin asked.

"Give me a break," Ashley muttered.

Jake and Kristin glared at her, hoping she would shut up.

"There are seven levels of the game, and you will have one hour to complete each one," Eric said. "At each level—except for the final one—you will hunt for one of these." Eric removed from his pocket a shiny white horse made of stone. The token was no bigger than a quarter, but it shined like a diamond in the light.

"How are we supposed to find them?" Jake asked.

"You will either be given clues as to where the horse is located or expected to find your own clues. Once you are in possession, a door will appear. If you do not exit by the time that hour is up, you will be stuck in that level, in Hell, for all of eternity."

Jake, Kristin and Ashley were speechless, too scared to argue. Eric went on.

"You are all aware of the stakes of the game. If you complete each level, you will earn the chance to free Ronnie's soul from Hell, and in turn free yourselves from the Mark of the Beast."

Kristin gazed at the *666* burned onto Jake's neck. She felt her own scar, and though she couldn't feel or see it, she knew it was there. She looked at Ashley, whose blond hair covered her neck, but she was positive her mark was there as well.

"Do you have any questions?" Eric asked.

Not knowing what to expect, the three of them didn't want to waste any time. They shook their heads, ready.

"Good," Eric said. "If you ever need me, just call out my name. For every one of you, you will be given one opportunity to ask for my help. Use it wisely." He paused for dramatic effect as the information sunk in. "Good luck with the game. I'll be watching."

Before they could speak, he turned to walk away.

"What do we do now?" Ashley asked, confused about what would happen next.

Eric didn't even look back as he answered. "In a marble hall white as milk/ Lined with skin as soft as silk/ Within a fountain crystal-clear/ A golden apple doth appear / No doors there are to this stronghold/ Yet thieves break in to steal its gold."

"What does that mean?" Kristin asked.

But Eric had already disappeared down the hall.

**

Kristin, Jake, and Ashley stared at one another, unsure of what to do. Ashley glanced at the time piece in her hand and realized that its hand moved at a rapid pace, as if keeping time for only one hour, not twelve.

"Our time's started," Ashley said.

"Shit," Jake said. "What are we supposed to do?"

Kristin looked down the hallway where Eric had disappeared. "I guess we should start exploring," she said.

The three walked down the wide, long hallway, with its gigantic floor-to-ceiling windows covered with luxurious tapestries. Even though the décor was vastly different from the Kansas State Juvenile Detention Facility, the hallway reminded Jake of the one that he had walked down numerous times.

"Watch for clues," Jake said.

"I don't see anything that could be a clue," Kristin said.

"I think there's a room up ahead," Ashley said, noticing a large entry-way. She noted that it looked incomplete without its doors.

"There aren't any doors," Jake said, saying aloud what Ashley had been thinking.

"That makes sense," Kristin said. "It means the only door we will see will be our escape."

The trio walked past the entry and were immediately hit with the exquisite smell of roasted meats, mashed potatoes, thick sauces, and desserts. Kristin, Jake, and Ashley stood in a grand banquet hall before a table set up in a way that reminded them of a Thanksgiving feast on a more elaborate scale. They closed their eyes, savoring the foods' aromas.

The room was cavernous. The high ceiling was made of glass, and seemed three stories high. There were three moons out in the sky, along with dozens of shooting stars. The floors were shiny and made of a dark marble, covered with giant Oriental rugs. The furniture was heavy and intricate, as if the makers had carved each piece from a tree.

"I didn't think Hell would be beautiful," Kristin said as they gazed around.

"How else is Evil going to entice the innocent?" Ashley asked. Her ears perked at the sound of wet noshing, similar to the sound of the ocean hitting sand. "What's that noise?" she asked.

Jake listened, while Kristin grimaced. The sound reminded her of someone chewing with his mouth open, and it made her want to vomit.

"Who dares to perturb my scrumptious feast on the nightfall of my merriment?"

The three all turned toward the loud, theatrical voice as it boomed through the room.

"What the hell did he say?" Ashley asked.

"It sounded like a woman," Kristin said.

"It's a dude, Kristin! A dude that sounded like Carol Channing, but still."

Kristin glared at Ashley.

"Whatever it is, it wants to know who's intruding on its dinner," Jake translated.

"When did you become so book smart?" Ashley asked.

"I had a lot of time to read in juvie," Jake replied, and Ashley looked away, guilty. Kristin noticed and shot Ashley a disdainful glance.

"How come you didn't know what she said?" she asked. "Aren't you the one studying at an Ivy League school?"

"Whatever. It's just being a blowhard. Why can't it talk like a normal person?" Ashley said.

"This isn't the time for fighting," Jake whispered.

"Interlopers! I am aware of your trespass. Approach my table and gorge with me," the voice said.

The three of them exchanged looks. "Should we do it?" Kristin asked.

"What other choice do we have?" Jake said.

Ashley looked to her timepiece. They only had fifty minutes to find the first horse token.

"We don't have much time," she said.

"Yeah, but what if we're supposed to hang out with that thing as part of the game?" Jake asked.

"Can you see him?" Kristin asked. Her view was obscured by the pillars and hanging tapestries throughout the room.

"No, but I don't know what else to do," Ashley said. "I thought Eric would be giving us clues."

"We could use a lifeline," Kristin said.

"I'm not wasting a lifeline on the first level," Jake griped.

"You wouldn't use a lifeline ever," Ashley said.

"What's that supposed to mean?" Jake shot back.

Ashley rolled her eyes. Jake had way too much pride to ever accept assistance. He would rather give up and perish than get help from someone like Eric.

"All of this food is making me hungry," Kristin said.

"Me too," Ashley said.

Kristin suddenly remembered a chapter she read in one of Mayor Hercules's books. She remembered the Greek story of Hades, Ruler of the Underworld, and his reluctant bride, Persephone. To keep her trapped in Hell, he tricked her into eating six seeds from a pomegranate, and each seed kept her condemned for one month in Hell. When Persephone informed her mother Ceres that she had eaten the food from Hades' world, her mother wept. "Didn't you know that the food from the Underworld is cursed? No one can stay on Earth once ingesting that poison." Kristin shuddered to think that there was truth to that legend.

"We can't eat anything, though," Kristin said.

"Why not?" Ashley asked.

"Because…"

Jake knew there wasn't enough time to explain to Ashley anything that they had read. "Ignore the food," he said. "We need to figure out where the horse is."

Before Ashley could tell Jake to go screw himself for his bossy tone, an angry voice yelled out, "It is improper to intrude on one's meal and then refute their invitation to join the table." The angry voice was so powerful that it sent shockwaves throughout the hall. The waves blew the tapestries and the trio's hair back, and their lips curled in disgust at the foul smell of the speaker's breath. The stench was worse than that of the rotting corpse of Mayor Hercules.

Kristin's eyebrows raised. "I didn't know demons in hell were passive aggressive," she said.

Jake and Kristin exchanged nervous glances, and without a word, they walked towards the voice, unsure of what they would find. With each step, the wet slurping sound intensified.

Kristin, Jake, and Ashley approached a grand table that easily could fit a hundred guests. Amidst beautiful ice sculpture centerpieces lay a buffet of every scrumptious thing ever created: roasted poultry, ham, curries, pies, cakes, casseroles, breads, and more. The trio's stomachs grumbled with hunger as their eyes feasted on the various dishes, but when their eyes moved from the food to the head of the table, their jaws dropped.

Sitting regally in front of a mysterious glowing light, a twelve-foot-tall troll sat on the floor, her gigantic, bulbous body too large to fit into a chair. Her tiny legs appeared sprouted underneath her rolls of flesh, and her torso resembled the shape of a blueberry. Her arms were long and proportionate to her large body because if they weren't, they would never be able to shovel the food into her mouth. The light backlit her face, which was human-like but androgynous. She had tiny brown eyes, a pig-shaped nose, and thin lips. Her hair was short, brown and curly and looked like little worms on her head. Her tiny teeth were brown like coffee, and when she breathed, she released a loud huff of air that smelled like a baby's dirty diaper.

"I told you it was a woman," Kristin whispered.

Before Ashley could retort, the being exclaimed, "Could you humble guests not find my table?" As she spoke, bits of turkey dripped out of her mouth and hit one of her chins. She spoke with sugary-sweet concern that stank of condescension and sulfur.

"Eww… gross," Ashley whispered, as Jake and Kristin held their breath.

The troll smacked its lips as it threw the giant turkey leg's bone onto the floor behind her. She motioned for them to sit beside her, and the trio grimaced. "I invited you to gorge, so please sit. Join me, for no one enjoys eating alone."

Kristin, Jake, and Ashley inched closer to the chairs at the end of the table as the troll stared at them, appalled by their rudeness.

"Do not sit at a far distance from your esteemed host. Please, dine next to me as my privileged friends."

Eyeing each other, they got out of their hard-backed chairs and slowly walked closer to the head of the table. She smiled at them, revealing a mouth filled with bits of food. She then motioned again for them to sit. Awkwardly, the three took seats next to each other on the troll's left side.

"Welcome! Allow me to introduce myself. My name is Zuzan! Please, inform me of your namesakes."

Zuzan reached for a raw egg inside of a golden bowl. She cracked it on the table and then grabbed the yolk and smashed it into her mouth.

Kristin covered her mouth, wanting to vomit again. Ashley's face twisted in disgust. Jake, on the other hand, tried to be hospitable and cleared his throat.

"I'm Jake," he said. It was hard to speak, let alone breathe because of Zuzan's terrible stench.

"I'm Ashley."

"Kristin."

"Wonderful!" Zuzan said, clapping.

Kristin noticed that she had tiny baby hands connected to her giant arms and fought the urge to cring.

"Now eat!" Zuzan commanded.

The trio stared at the food, their stomachs grumbling. The dishes not touched by Zuzan looked appetizing. "Don't eat anything," Kristin advised. She looked at Zuzan and the bits of bread dribbling down her face, sticking in the crevices of her body. Kristin and the others soon lost their appetites.

"Consume!" Zuzan said. She grabbed a plate of mini hamburgers and shoved them into Jake's face.

He winced and closed his mouth, making sure to breath from his nostrils.

Zuzan glared at him and his reluctance to eat, and then as though she could read Kristin's mind, she growled. "This is not like Hades' Hell where he tricked his dear wife Persephone to devour the pomegranate, imprisoning her to months in his bedchamber! This is my realm, where my guests may feast and enjoy themselves for all of eternity, tasting morsels until their taste buds can no longer savor the flavors. So enjoy. Gorge, gorge. That is all I want from you."

Ashley stared at the blueberry muffins that were in arm's reach and beside the bowl of eggs. The muffins looked delicious and smelled wonderful. She was stretching out her hand to grab one when Kristin suddenly slapped it away.

"Ow!" Ashley cried.

"What are you doing?" Kristin asked.

"I'm hungry…"

"I told you not to eat anything."

"What's the problem? It said it was okay…"

"Don't eat anything, Ashley! The monsters in Hell always lie."

Overhearing, an angry Zuzan smacked a plate of tarts off of the table and onto the floor. As she spoke, bits of strawberries and pastry flew out of her mouth, along with a shiny, black, baby eel. The pastry bits landed onto Jake, Kristin and Ashley's faces, and Ashley and Kristin immediately wiped them away. Jake, however, was fixated on the black eel which slithered down the table, disappearing from sight.

"How dare you question my hospitality? I am not asking you to bite the apple, Eve. I am only offering you sumptuous pies and cakes, yet you rebuff me. I never knew such spoiled children existed until I laid my eyes on you three."

"What a pretentious blow hard," Ashley muttered.

"Shut up, Ashley," Jake said.

"What, Jake? I'm sure it can't hear me. It's too busy using big words and talking out of its ass. I didn't know that being in Hell meant dealing with annoying, stupid people."

"Shut up, Ashley," Kristin whispered.

Ashley gazed around at the items on the table. "Where is that stupid white horse? If I'm going to be trapped in Hell for all of eternity, I'm not going to be trapped eating myself to death and listening to a condescending freak show who loves to hear itself talk."

"Silence!" Zuzan screamed out in a deep, demonic voice that did not match the one that had come out of her mouth earlier. "I attempted to invite you to dine with me in the most jovial of manners, but I see now that my kindness was not reciprocated."

Ashley ignored the troll and looked at her timepiece. Only fifteen minutes remained in this realm, and they were nowhere close to finding the token. Panicked, she continued to scan the table, trying to find the key to her escape.

"Now, I am not a verbose creature that enjoys repeating herself, so I will only speak this once," Zuzan said in her original voice. "Join me in my gluttony, or *I will make you regret denying me.*" The demonic voice returned.

Kristin and Jake stared back at Zuzan with fear, but they were equally afraid to eat her food. They glanced at the tasty-looking items, but they were in Hell, after all. What if the food was poisoned, or what if they took a bite and nasty creatures like cockroaches crawled out and into their mouths? After all, they just watched a baby eel escape Zuzan's mouth.

Ashley focused on the bits of meat and sauces stuck on Zuzan's flesh, and like Kristin, the sight made her want to vomit. If Zuzan hoped to make them gluttons, then she had failed miserably. After this night, Ashley never wanted to eat again.

"Time is running out," Ashley whispered.

"I thought Eric said there would be clues," Kristin said.

"He didn't give us any clues," Jake said.

"I'm sure he did," Ashley said. "We're just not looking hard enough."

"I don't see a clue anywhere!" Jake yelled in frustration.

"Enough chatter!" Zuzan screamed. "You have been nothing but ungracious attendees!"

Ashley rolled her eyes, glancing at the time once again. Six minutes.

Without thinking, she said, "Oh, blow me, fat ass."

Zuzan's eyes grew wide as she held her breath with anger. Kristin and Jake stared at Ashley in shock , unsure of what was to happen next.

"Did you just call me fat?" Zuzan asked.

Ashley remained still, like a child who had just been caught with her hand in the cookie jar.

"No," Ashley lied, but Zuzan was not foolish enough to believe her.

"Hmph," Zuzan said. She held her breath until her peach flesh-tone changed into a putrid pea green. Her eyes enlarged so wide that they appeared as if she was about to pop as steam literally smoldered out of the top of her head. Her green face began to contort with pain, as if her stomach hurt—just as the trio heard a loud squeak of flatulence.

"Oh, God, the smell," Kristin whispered as she plugged her nose.

Zuzan shot her a dirty look as she continued to emit gas.

Ashley and Jake, meanwhile, were immobile, uncertain of what to do.

"Should we run?" Ashley whispered through clenched teeth.

"I'd say so," Jake said.

They bolted from the tables, pushing their chairs haphazardly to the floor. Kristin continued to plug her nose, and Ashley coughed, the smell catching up to her. Zuzan's face twisted further, a volcano about to erupt.

"She's going to barf," Kristin said with realization. They hiked up their speed, but it was too late.

Zuzan's mouth opened into a giant O, but instead of vomiting up the many meals she had previously consumed, she shot out thousands of slimy, black, eel-like creatures with no appendages, just gray beads for eyes and a small holes for mouths. Ashley and Kristin squealed as the creatures shot at their backs, leaving cold goo on their bodies. While Jake ran to help his friends, he was knocked out by a bombardment of eels as well. The creatures leached onto his back, and he shouted out in pain.

Behind them, Zuzan continued to spew the creatures, which squeaked in delight. As they flew out, Zuzan's body deflated like a punctured balloon, as if all this time, Zuzan's form was only a giant canteen holding the true monsters inside. The banquet hall slowly began to fill with the creatures, like water flooding a room. They slithered amongst the food, crawled up into the trio's clothes, caressing the trio's bodies. The outside body of Zuzan lay on the floor, where it finally resembled a real human being—a five-foot-tall woman, obese but not monstrous. The woman softly breathed, happy to be free of the eels.

"We didn't find a door!" Ashley said. The tried to swim upwards through the sea of eels, afraid that if she plunged underneath them, they would crawl into her mouth. They slithered inside of her clothes, prying their way close to her underwear. Their slimy bodies were gross enough against her flesh, but she hated the sound of their squeaking as they slid around.

"That bastard didn't give us any clues!" Jake said.

"We can call for help!" Kristin said.

"He's not going to help us," Jake said.

"You don't know that, Jake!" Kristin said.

The creatures began to move the trio closer to the table, like a tidal wave moving a lost surfer away from shore. They set Kristin, Ashley, and Jake at the table, placing Jake in Zuzan's spot. The eels then banded together to form giant black hands.

"Don't eat any…" Jake said, right before an eel-formed hand shoved apple pie into his mouth. Though it tasted warm and gooey and well-seasoned with nutmeg and cinnamon, he spit it out.

The hands shoveled food towards Kristin, who closed her eyes and tried to look away. To avoid choking, Ashley swallowed a spoonful of chocolate pudding. As she complied, the creatures fed her with less force.

"If you eat, they'll ease up on you!" Ashley said, but Jake and Kristin wouldn't listen. They knew that if they ate, they would share Zuzan's fate.

"We have to…" Jake said in between spitting out his dessert, "Find…The horse…Or…we'll be…stuck here…forever!"

Ashley watched as the eel creatures hugged Kristin and Jake tighter, making it harder for them to breathe. "Kristin, just eat something!" Ashley screamed.

Kristin felt the hold around her body. Her eyes started to glaze over and her mouth parted open. The dark hand brought a spoonful of couscous to her mouth, and she realized that if she didn't eat, the creatures would squeeze her to death.

"Kristin, don't fight it!" Ashley said as Kristin swallowed the couscous. With just one swallow, they loosened their grip, and Kristin fell forward in her chair, happy to breathe. The eels brought Ashley a spoonful of puree. She grimaced as the spoon came near her, but closed her eyes and opened her mouth, the agony clear on her face.

The freed Kristin watched Ashley and Jake get tortured by the food. She clutched at the table and she screamed out, "Eric Whitehorse! Eric Whitehorse, I want to use a lifeline!"

There was a crack of lightning above her, and through the glass ceiling, she could see dark storm clouds obscure the three moons. Kristin realized at that moment that time had stopped. The eels had stopped squirming, Jake and Ashley were frozen, and Zuzan stopped breathing on the floor.

"Using a lifeline after only one level?" Eric asked. He wore a dashing white suit, more suitable for a Hollywood mogul than a host at an eel-filled dinner party. "I was sure that you, in particular, would want to use it on the next round, but no matter." He stood on the table, amidst the eel creatures and the tainted food.

"How are we supposed to get out of here?" Kristin asked. She looked at her friends, who were as still as photographs— Ashley, who looked horrified as the eels brought a strawberry puree up her mouth, and Jake, who spit out beef chunks as the eels squeezed him so tightly that the veins on his head popped.

"I told you the rules," Eric said. "You will be given clues to find the white horse, and once you find it, a door will appear. You have one hour to complete each level or you will be stuck in Hell forever." Eric smirked as he eyed Ashley. "Such a skinny girl. She never liked food much, did she?"

"We didn't get a clue!" Kristin said.

His eyes darkened as he returned his attention to Kristin. He wasn't as fond of her as he was with Ashley.

Eric clapped his hands and a giant hourglass appeared in the sky, just above the glass of the ceiling.

"You called me just in time. You only had one minute left on this level. If it weren't for me, you all would've been as fat and gluttonous as Zuzan." Eric casually walked along the table as if they were part of a runway, kicking the slimy eels away as if they were nothing more than dust underneath his shoe. "Do you remember the Mother Goose poem I recited to you?"

"What? No. What Mother Goose poem?"

"As I was leaving? You don't remember me saying this: 'In a marble hall white as milk/ Lined with skin as soft as silk/ Within a fountain crystal-clear/ A golden apple doth appear / No doors there are to this stronghold/ Yet thieves break in to steal its gold.'"

"We didn't know what you were talking about," Kristin said.

Eric shook his head. He bent down towards the plate of ostrich eggs in a golden bowl, the bowl Zuzan had eaten from earlier. "If you three want to survive Hell, you're going to have to try harder. Nothing worthwhile is ever just given to people. You have to fight to win." He picked up the largest egg and cracked it on the table. Kristin watched the yolk and the egg white emerge from the shattered shell, and out of the debris, Eric picked up a shiny white horse.

Kristin gasped, amazed that the level had been so simple.

"'In a marble hall white as milk/ Lined with skin as soft as silk/ Within a fountain crystal-clear/ A golden apple doth appear...'"

"An egg..." Kristin said.

Eric nodded. "An egg. How simple was it to find an egg?"

He jumped off the table and walked towards Kristin, over the eels as if they were solid matter. He grabbed Kristin's hand and placed the horse into it. Behind Jake, a white door appeared.

"Thank you," Kristin said, so happy to be free of the eels.

Eric studied her. although he shouldn't have, he felt sorry for her. He stepped closer and Kristin tensed, worried that he was about to kiss her. Instead, he leaned and whispered in her ear.

"You shouldn't thank me," he said, his warm breath sending shivers down her spine. "There's much worse in store for you. All I can say is the best is yet to come."

CHAPTER FOURTEEN

Kristin stared at Eric, fully aware that he was threatening her. "What do you mean?" she asked, hoping that if she asked directly, he would tell her more clues.

He stared back at her, a smile in his eyes.

"Your lifeline is over," Eric said, and then there was a crack of lightning, just like when he had arrived.

Kristin blinked from the bright light, and when she opened her eyes, he was gone. The scene reanimated as if nothing had ever happened.

Ashley squealed as strawberry puree fell from her mouth, while Jake struggled to break free from the eels' grasp. Kristin jumped from her seat and yelled as hard as she could, "There's the door!"

Ashley and Jake jerked their heads in the direction Kristin was pointing. Kristin ran towards Ashley and grabbed a serving spoon. She beat at the stack of eels holding Ashley until they loosened up, enough so that Ashley wrangled herself free.

Ashley and Kristin then hurried towards Jake. The eels around them began to regroup, a few leaping towards Kristin and Ashley's backs and sucking on them like leaches.

"Oww!" Kristin screamed, but that didn't stop her from running towards Jake. As she beat the eels with her serving spoon, Ashley scanned the table for a weapon. Her eyes found a long carving knife and she grabbed it, ready to fight.

All around them, the eels squeaked, creating a grotesquely loud squishing sound.

"We have less than a minute!" Ashley screamed, her eyes trained on the door.

"Leave without me!" Jake yelled as Kristin struggled to set him free.

"We're not going without you," Kristin said as she looked deeply into Jake's eyes. He nodded as he watched her beat at the eels surrounding him.

Ashley glanced at the door, which seemed to be fading. "*Leave them…*" a voice in the back of her head whispered. The *666* on the back of her neck glowed as she thought about the door and what it would be like to race through it without her friends.

"*Leave them…*" the voice whispered again.

Ashley continued to stare at the door when she heard Kristin scream in frustration. Ashley turned and watched her friends struggling, and she knew that she couldn't leave them. The *666* on her neck returned to neutral as she hurried behind Jake, sliding the knife in between the wrapped eels and the chair. She closed her eyes as she pulled the knife towards her, slicing the eels as if they were nothing but an old rope. Jake limped forward as he became free from the monsters, while Kristin quickly put his arm around her shoulder. "Come on," she said, as Ashley quickly moved to help with his other arm.

The door blinked as if it were about to disappear, but Ashley, Jake, and Kristin glided faster through the slush of eel bodies that rested amidst their feet.

"Hurry!" Kristin said, grabbing the door handle. The three of them raced through to the other side. Once the door shut behind them, it disintegrated into a million grains of sand. The remaining eels around the banquet table stopped to stare at the door, unsure of what had just happened. For a moment, the cavernous hall was silent.

"*Squeeeeee…..*" an eel shouted.

The squeaking intensified as the eels returned to their mission of consumption. They devoured the remaining food on the table, the furniture in the room, and the newly formed sand on the flood. Once everything was eaten away and the skinny eels had grown fat and lumpy, they formed a long line and slithered towards Zuzan's body, ready to fill her once again.

**

There was a burst of white light as Jake, Kristin, and Ashley crossed over to Level Two of The Game, and a stream of images flooded into each of their heads.

For Jake, the images were of the day he fended off the bullies who picked on Ronnie. The first football game he had ever won. Seeing his mother in the hospital when he was a little boy.

For Kristin, she saw her mother picking her up from school when she was a child. Kristin didn't see her when she had pulled over to the curb, so her mother had yelled for her in a screeching voice. Kristin remembered how her cheeks reddened at the sound of her mother's accent. She remembered when a group of boys behind her called her "Ching-chong" and started to mimic her mother's harsh tones.

For Ashley, she remembered hiding underneath her father's giant desk in the church when she was a child, waiting for Ashton to find her when they played hide and seek. She remembered as a teenager how he would hold her after she had a bad day at school, just as she remembered bawling her eyes out when she found his body in their father's office at church, a gaping wound in his head and a gun on the floor.

The light, their transportation device into Level Two, then disappeared, leaving the trio in a small room covered with mirrors. Their three reflections reflected multiple times, creating hundreds of Jakes, Kristins, and Ashleys. Each one of their reflections looked tired, defeated. They were not cleaned up or as healthy as they were when they first arrived following the wasp attack. As the game progressed, they would have to muster up as much energy as they could sustain to fight.

"This is the second level of Hell?" Ashley asked. "It looks like a funhouse."

"Don't speak too soon," Jake said. "Remember how beautiful the castle appeared in Level One?"

"Don't remind me," Ashley said, as she gazed at her reflection. Her face appeared worn, and her beautiful designer clothes were dirty and torn. She touched her hair, which was greasy and flat, then slowly pulled her hair up to reveal the tattoo of *666* on the back of her neck. She grimaced. For some reason, she had hoped that it would've disappeared.

"I recognize where we are," Kristin said, dread filling her voice. "This is the carnival where my Mom was attacked."

Jake and Ashley stared at her in shock. Then shock gave way to anger for Ashley, and she stepped away from the mirror, shaking her head.

"That wasn't a part of the deal," Ashley yelled to The Gamemakers, even though she had no idea whether they were listening, watching her from above, or behind the mirrors, like policemen behind their double-sided glass. "We shouldn't have to relive our pasts! That shouldn't be what the game is about!"

Jake stared at Ashley. This was Kristin's nightmare—why was Ashley going berserk?

"You said this was a scavenger hunt!" Ashley screamed as she kicked at her reflection, her pointy boot cracking the glass. She jumped back in pain as blood flowed from her toe. She removed her shoe, and Jake and Kristin ran over to inspect it.

"You're bleeding…" Jake said.

"No shit," Ashley said.

"That means we can get hurt here," Kristin said.

"That is correct!" a jolly voice called out, causing the trio jumped in alarm. Eric Whitehorse appeared a thousand times as a reflection in the mirror, but he was nowhere in the room.

Now dressed in a white blazer over a white t-shirt and white pants, he smiled at them with his perfect white teeth.

"Why so angry?" Eric asked, staring at Ashley.

"You know why I'm angry," Ashley growled. "Making us relive our memories shouldn't be a part of the game!"

Eric gazed at her foot in its blood-soaked sock, and he feigned sympathy.

"You, Miss Ashley, should control your temper. You know as well as I do that you have no authority to tell us what we *should* or *shouldn't* do. Your little manipulative mind games don't work beyond your classmates and the adults in your pathetic town. And really, you three are in Hell. What constitutes Hell more than reliving the worst moments of your life in vivid detail?"

"Where's the horse?" Jake asked. He was tired of Eric's mind games. He just wanted to get through the game as quickly as possible.

Eric glanced briefly at Jake before focusing his attention on Kristin.

"I gave you such an easy clue last time, and you three just squandered it. One lifeline gone. Two remain…"

Jake rolled his eyes. "We'll do better next time. What's the clue?"

Eric smiled at him, his eyes flashing with mischief. Jake recognized it as the same look that Ashley had when she came up with the idea to play a prank on Ronnie.

"Ask that one," he said, pointing to Kristin. "This is her memory. Where would the white horse be hiding?"

Ashley stared at Kristin, hoping that she would be able to get them out of Level Two as quickly and easy as possible. "Where's the horse, Kristin?" Ashley asked, her gaze boring into Kristin.

But Kristin's eyes were completely blank. She was too busy thinking about her and her mother, ten years earlier.

**

Kristin remembered how excited her mother was to take her to the carnival in Lucky, Kansas, a town that resided twenty miles west of Deer Creek. Eight-year-old Kristin had never been to a carnival before, and Susie was sure that the two of them would have a lot of fun. To her surprise, though, Kristin didn't want to attend.

"Are you ashame of your mother?" Susie had asked.

Kristin glared back. Of course she was ashamed. She hated her mother's black hair. Her slanted eyes. Her round face. She didn't want to be seen in public with Susie. She only wanted to be seen with her handsome father, who people looked at with respect.

"If you no want to go, fine," Susie said quietly, and Kristin smiled with satisfaction.

However, when her father Bryan had heard the news, he was furious. "You're going with your mother, young lady," he said. "I don't want to hear anything else about the matter. You understand me?"

Kristin looked up at him in shock. She had never seen him so angry.

"No, no," Susie had said. "It okay. Kristin no have to go."

Bryan squatted so that he and Kristin were at eye level, staring deeply into her eyes, daring her to disobey. "She's going," Bryan said, "And she's going to be happy you're taking her. Aren't you, Kristin?"

But Kristin only stared back, too afraid to answer.

On the day of the carnival, Susie wore a yellow shirt with a Mandarin collar and tan linen pants. Kristin remembered glaring at the outfit, thinking it looked too different from what she had seen other mothers in town wearing. Susie had purchased the clothing in China, and the style was Chinese, not American. Kristin folded her arms in annoyance, irritated that she had to be seen with such a freak. However, she remembered her father's reprimand and said nothing.

Susie had driven Kristin the twenty miles to reach Lucky, and the entire way, they rode in silence, with Kristin's arms crossed and her brows furrowed. When they arrived, Susie smiled at her daughter, who continued to pout in the passenger seat. Susie tried her best not to cry. She couldn't understand why her daughter hated her so much.

"Are you ready to go?" Susie asked, trying not to let her voice crack. "I can buy you cotton candy or an ice cream cone…"

Kristin glared at her mother. "Whatever," she said.

The two of them got out of the car and walked towards the carnival located on Lucky's fairground, behind an old brown fence. Kristin remembered staring up at the Ferris Wheel in wonderment at its twinkling yellow lights, but when Susie asked her if she would like to ride it with her, she snapped, "No! You're not the boss of me!"

Susie winced as if Kristin had thrown fire on her, but she hid her pain with a smile.

"Let's go inside," Susie said. She offered her hand, unsure if Kristin would take it, and when she felt her daughter's tiny hand in hers, she smiled.

Once they stepped on the grounds, they were immediately met with sensory overload. The carnival was packed with people, none of whom looked or dressed like Susie. Kristin hid behind her mother, embarrassed by her and yet wanting her protection at the same time.

"Do you want a hot dog?" Susie asked, and Kristin shook her head no.

A group of men with bald heads walked past, giving Kristin and Susie dirty looks. Kristin flushed at the negative attention, but Susie seemed to not notice or mind. "Are you sure you don't want to ride the Ferris Wheel? I can wait on the ground as you ride."

Kristin heard the hurt in her mother's voice, but she ignored it. She was just happy to get away from her mother, even if it were only for a few minutes.

Kristin remembered how free she had felt when she had boarded the Ferris Wheel all by herself. The carnie manning the ride stared at her quizzically. "You aren't with your parents?" he asked, and Kristin glared at him defiantly.

"I'm here alone," she replied.

He shrugged and took her ticket. She remembered how the ride had slowly taken her to the top, where she had a view of the entire carnival.

"I'm like a bird," she thought. She stared down at Susie, who gazed up at her, and for a moment, Kristin felt cruel. "What if I ran away?" she thought. She imagined how frightened her mother would be if she were to take off. She imagined what Bryan would say later when Susie told her that their only daughter had abandoned them.

"I should never have made her go to the carnival with you!" Bryan would scream. "Kristin doesn't love you. She hates you!"

Eight-year-old Kristin smiled at the thought of it. As the wheel took another spin around, she decided then and there what she was going to do when she returned to the ground.

"Okay, miss," the carnie said as he unlocked her bucket. Kristin saw her mother waiting on the grass, behind the long line that had formed. Without hesitation, she sprang in the opposite direction, away from the other riders who were exiting, while Susie watched with horror as her daughter ran away.

"Kristin!" Susie screamed. Kristin remembered cringing at the sound of her accent. "Kristin! Kristin, come back!"

Kristin continued to run, fueled by her shame, fueled by her hatred. She'd show Susie what it was like to suffer. She'd show Susie and afterwards, she would forever treasure the joy she'd feel because of her suffering.

**

"Kristin? Kristin?" Ashley repeated. She shook Kristin, trying to break her from her daze, but the harder she shook, the more Kristin's head bobbed back and forth.

"Careful," Eric said. "You die in this game, you die on earth."

Ashley gazed at her bloody foot, regretting her tantrum. Then she glanced at Kristin, who had seemed to awaken from her memory.

Eric smiled, savoring the line he was about to deliver. "And then you'll join your brother and Ronnie in Hell forever."

The glib mention of her brother sent boiling rage throughout Ashley's body.

"Don't talk about Ashton like that," Ashley said.

"Why not? It's true. Would you like to see him?" Eric disappeared from the mirror and flames appeared behind the glass. Ashley, Kristin, and Jake watched as Ashton's burnt face appeared in the hellfire, his voice screaming in agony.

Tears streamed down Ashley's face. "Turn it off," she commanded, as if instructing someone to turn off the television.

"You didn't believe me," Eric's voice said from above. Ashton continued to scream, and Ashley looked away as her twin's burnt flesh fell from his bone.

"Turn it off!" Ashley screamed, her command now a plea.

"You didn't believe..."

"Turn it off!" Ashley screamed again. She pulled off her shoe and beat the mirror with the shoe until its cracks shattered and the pieces fell to the floor. "Turn it off!"

Some mirror bits flew back and scratched at Ashley's skin. Jake ran forward, grabbing her hand and holding her back.

"Ashley, stop it!" Jake said.

"Turn it off!" she said as her body convulsed.

Ashley had tears rolling down her eyes. She attempted to wrangle out of Jake's arms, but he was too strong. "Don't talk about Ashton like that, you fuckers!"

From the unbroken mirrors, Eric stared at her as if she were a science experiment and he the cold data collector.

"Ashley, stop it. You're giving them what they want..." Jake said. As he held her tight, Kristin stared, envious. Ashley sobbed and Jake held her tighter, and Kristin forced herself to look away.

"Ashton's not in Hell…" Ashley said.

"Don't let him get to you."

"Eric's lying…"

"We all miss Ashton, but you're going to be okay."

Kristin stared at the floor. She couldn't watch Jake hold Ashley. It hurt her too much.

Eric, also, had seen enough. The flames dissolved, and he reappeared, clearing his throat.

"Your hour starts now," he said. Kristin, Ashley, and Jake heard a loud *crack* and the room went black. When the lights returned, the trio was amazed to find the mirrors restored and Ashley's foot wound-free.

"Son of a…" Ashley said.

"Why does he always help us?" Kristin asked.

"Does it matter?" Ashley asked.

"Only if it's because he wants us to reach the end," Kristin said. "What if he wants us there, healthy, so he can really mess with us then?"

"There's only one way to find out," Jake said. He gazed around the room full of mirrors, at the walls that appeared solid. How were they to get out? "Eric said Kristin knew where to find the horse," Jake said.

"Yeah, but Kristin goes catatonic if you ask her to think about this place," Ashley griped.

"Well, let's start small then," he said, turning to Kristin. "You said you recognized this place. How do we get out of here?"

Kristin gazed around at the mirrors, remembering how she stood in the same room ten years ago.

"There was a panel that looked like a mirror, but it was actually an opening," Kristin said. She felt along the walls, which were cool to the touch. She continued to glide her fingers along the glass until one panel fell forward. "There," she said, stepping through what looked like the wall. Instead it was the opening to the exit.

"That was too easy," Ashley muttered.

Easy was a bad omen in Hell.

The three followed a light to the exit, which was a doorway with no door. They stepped out into the open air, where carnival music played and twinkling yellow lights illuminated the grounds. It smelled like peanuts, cotton candy, and funnel cakes, and although the rides were moving and the buzz of conversation traveled throughout the air, no one was present at the carnival.

"Why isn't there anyone here?" Ashley asked.

"I don't know," Jake said.

Kristin, on the other hand, looked around in terror. She saw a group of teenagers rush past, ice cream cones in their hands. A couple holding hands as they walked towards the Ferris Wheel. Carnies tearing tickets from the people in line. She heard the chatter of people waiting in line for rides, the vendors shouting out to come to their tables, the laughter of children running to and fro. The scene was exactly the same as it had been ten years earlier.

"So, this was the carnival?" Jake asked her.

Kristin was too afraid to answer.

"If The Gamemakers want you to experience that nightmare, then why take away the people? Wouldn't it be scarier to recreate the night exactly as it was?" Ashley asked.

"It *is* exactly like it was…" Kristin said.

Jake and Ashley stared at her with confusion. How could it be the same scene if no one was there?

"I don't understand…" Ashley said.

"They want me to face my memory alone," Kristin said.

Ashley felt sympathy for Kristin, but her own dread was much more powerful. She knew exactly what memory she herself was most afraid of facing, and the thought of reliving that nightmare terrified her.

Jake, on the other hand, remained levelheaded. "We can get out of here as soon as we find the white horse," he said.

"It was in an egg last time," Ashley added.

"I doubt they'd put it in an egg again."

"Maybe we should look for a riddle."

"Where are we going to find one? Eric just gave it to us last time."

"I don't know," Ashley said, looking at her timepiece. "But our hour has already started."

"Then let's start looking," Jake said, and he motioned for them to begin walking. Ashley followed his lead, but Kristin remained in place, frozen. She saw the various carnival patrons stare at her as if she were a freak show, the hatred in their eyes palpable. She swallowed hard, wishing she was invisible.

"Kristin, come on," Ashley said. She pushed at her gently, and in a daze, Kristin followed them.

Jake led them past the spinning Ferris Wheel, down towards the games. Jake and Ashley saw darts being thrown at targets, balls being thrown at milk jugs, and wheels being spun, but only Kristin saw the people playing.

"Maybe this is a clue?" Jake said. "After all, we're playing a big game. Maybe we're supposed to be playing more games within the game."

"That makes sense," Ashley said. "We had to solve a riddle to find the horse in Level One."

Jake looked around for the first game to catch his eye. He saw a booth with various empty fishbowls set up, and ping pong balls flew around, trying to land into them. "Let's try that one," Jake said.

Ashley followed him up to the booth, and Kristin watched as they shoved people out of the way, earning dirty looks. How did Ashley and Jake not see them?

A carnie noticed Jake and Ashley and brought them three balls each. Jake and Ashley only saw balls fly towards them, and Jake took this as a good sign.

"This has to be the clue," Jake said.

Ashley looked at her timepiece. "We've got forty-five minutes."

"Why are you wasting your time, Kristin?" a fifty-year-old woman whispered. Kristin jerked her head to see a fortuneteller standing in front of a small tent. The woman had long red hair, a tired face, and cold black eyes. She wore a long black skirt and a maroon shawl. Her many bracelets clanked together as she beckoned for Kristin to walk closer. "Come inside, and I will give you your clue to show you the way."

Kristin looked to Ashley and Jake, who were seriously into the game, trying hard to make their ball fall into the bowl.

"Guys, do you see her?" Kristin asked. She tugged at Jake's shirt, but his focus was unwavering. "Ashley?" Kristin asked, but she was just as obsessed with playing as Jake was.

The woman continued to beckon for Kristin to join her. "Only you can see me, sweetheart," the woman said. "You know that."

Kristin hesitated. She didn't want to go alone with the woman, but at the same time, she wanted the clue.

"Hurry, Kristin," the fortuneteller said as she bore into Kristin's eyes. You don't have much time to leave this level, and I would hate to have you relive this night for the rest of your afterlife."

**

Kristin entered the fortuneteller's purple tent, a small, dark space lit by a circle of white candles. In the middle of the room, a green table was set up with a crystal ball, two chairs, a plush, high-backed chair covered with velvet and a small stool.

"Sit across from me," the fortuneteller said, directing Kristin to the stool. As Kristin obliged, the fortuneteller gazed at the *666* on the back of her neck. "How are you liking The Game so far, child?" she asked.

Kristin stared at her, thinking her question was the stupidest thing she had ever heard. "It's Hell," Kristin replied.

The fortuneteller nodded at her, understanding. There was something about her, a quiet sadness that caught Kristin off guard. Was this woman not a demon? Was she a lost soul imprisoned in Hell like Ronnie and Ashton?

"You're looking for the white horse," the fortuneteller said as she stroked the crystal ball. Inside, dark clouds began to circle and lightning cracked. Kristin was reminded of when Eric had arrived in Level One to give her a lifeline.

"Where is it?" Kristin asked. She didn't have the timepiece, but she knew there wasn't much time before the hour would be up.

"There's a reason why this level is a manifestation of your worst nightmare."

"This isn't my worst nightmare," Kristin said defensively. She knew she was being stupid trying to trick the fortuneteller, but for a split second she hoped that she could convince Hell that other things were scarier to her. Maybe in the process, she could also convince herself.

"Oh?" the fortuneteller said. She sat back and crossed her arms.

"I'm very afraid of spiders," Kristin said matter-of-factly.

The woman stared at Kristin for several moments, studying her, until finally she smiled with a condescending smirk. Kristin shifted uncomfortably.

"You only think about the superficial," the woman finally said. "But to truly win this game, you must dig deep. You must confront not only the evil of your surroundings, you must fight the evil within yourself."

The clouds within the crystal ball darkened.

"There's a lot of hatred within you," the fortuneteller continued. "Self-loathing of who you are. Hatred of where you come from. You have to stop lying to yourself that you are happy when you know you truly are not."

Kristin glared at her, not pleased with what she was hearing.

"You are ashamed of your mother."

Kristin's eyes watered. She was so frustrated and upset with what she was hearing that she just wanted to run out of the room and bawl her eyes out. She pictured her mother's round face and dark, almond shaped eyes. She could see her smiling mother with her hideous scars, and felt her face flush with anger. She wasn't ashamed of her the way this woman was suggesting. Sometimes her mother embarrassed her, but that was normal for any teen. It was unfair of this stranger to imply that Kristin's case was extraordinary.

"That's not true..." Kristin whispered.

"Then why do you make her wear scarves when you go out? Why did you run away from her when she took you to the carnival? You were the reason she was in the alley on this night. You were the reason her face is scarred, why she was attacked."

Kristin shook her head, tears falling. "That's not true..." She wanted to find other words to say, but that was the only thing that could fall from her mouth.

"You don't look like your father," the woman said. "You look like your mother. You shouldn't be ashamed of that. She was a beautiful woman. She *is* a beautiful woman still, even if you can't see that."

Suddenly the crystal ball became a mirror, showing Kristin her reflection. She had delicate features. Pretty brown eyes. A round face. The mirror gave way to an image of a younger Susie, and Kristin gasped. She and her mother easily could have been mistaken for twins.

"I don't deserve this," Kristin said as she looked up and bore into the fortuneteller's eyes.

The fortuneteller felt no sympathy for her and waved her hand in dismissal. "Honor thy mother and father," she said. "Isn't that how the saying goes?"

Kristin's throat choked up, and she wiped at her eyes. "Who are you?" she asked, thinking the woman really was a demon.

The fortuneteller sat forward, rubbing the crystal ball as it turned completely black, matching the color of her eyes.

"Before I came here, I had a husband and two children. We lived in a small town and we were simple people, but we were happy," she answered.

Kristin was taken aback. "How'd you end up here?"

The sadness that Kristin had picked up on earlier returned the woman's face. She looked away as she thought about her life on Earth. "The damned end up in different parts of Hell, and some have their memories wiped clean but are tortured for all of eternity; others retain their memories and are tortured with those reminders. I'm part of the latter."

"What did you do?"

The woman gazed at the ball as though her memories were hidden inside. Her dark eyes misted as she cradled the ball into her hands. "My children were stolen from me, and so I ended my life. My husband thought I had a heart attack, but I induced my death myself."

Hearing the story, Kristin thought about Mayor Hercules' final letter to her.

"Myra Hercules?" Kristin asked.

The fortuneteller shook her head, not wanting to discuss her past any longer.

"You need to find the horse, child," she said, giving Kristin a cue to leave. "You've wasted too much time here with me."

"You didn't give me a clue..." Kristin said.

"I told you the answer to solving this level involves your worst fear. That's as much as I can say."

The woman waved her away, her bangles clinking together. Kristin stood up, realizing that there was nothing more to be said. As Kristin walked to the tent's exit, she took one last gaze at the woman, watching her stare sadly at her crystal ball of memories.

**

"Come on, come on…" Jake said as he threw another ball. It soared through the air in a perfect arch, but when it was about to land in the fishbowl, it suddenly veered left and bounced off of the rim. "Son of a…" he muttered as the invisible Carnie gave him another set of balls.

Next to him, Ashley tossed her ball, but the other balls flying around knocked hers away. "Damn it!" Ashley said. She gazed at the small stuffed bear on the counter in front of her. She had won it on her first try, but to her confusion, she couldn't seem to win now. She stared at the gigantic stuffed bears hanging from the booth's ceiling. If only she could win three more bears, she would be able to trade it in for the gigantic one.

Jake tossed more balls. He and Ashley hadn't realized that Kristin wasn't with them, nor did they realize that they had been playing this toss game for thirty minutes.

Kristin emerged from the fortuneteller's tent and saw Jake and Ashley intensely playing the fishbowl ball toss. She was amazed to see that they hadn't stopped or moved on to another booth. When she approached them, they continued to toss balls, missing the bowls. They didn't even notice her arrive.

"Guys, we need to go," Kristin said.

Jake and Ashley ignored her.

"Seriously. We need to move on from this…"

Jake and Ashley were handed more balls. Kristin rolled her eyes and searched for the time piece, seeing that it hung around Ashley's neck. Kristin touched it without Ashley even noticing, and she saw that they were running out of time.

"Stop playing this," Kristin pleaded. "We've got to find the horse!" She tugged at Ashley's shirt.

Ashley turned to glare at her. "What's wrong with you?" Ashley said angrily. "It's not your turn!"

"What's wrong with you? If you keep playing this, you're going to be stuck in Hell forever!"

Ashley stared at Kristin blankly, and there was something about her gaze that reminded her of a drug addict looking for a fix. Shocked, Kristin stepped back.

"You have to stop playing this," Kristin said. She thought about Mayor Hercules' books, how they had warned her of demon trickery.

"Why? It's fun," Ashley said. She turned her back to Kristin and grabbed more balls.

Kristin watched the balls fly around the booth with alarm. The Carnie smiled at Kristin, baring jagged teeth as his eyes burned with fire.

"This game's worse than Zuzan's food," Kristin said, but her friends wouldn't listen. "You guys have to stop!"

"Would you like to try a game?" The Carnie asked. "You play once, you play forever."

"No!" Kristin said. She slapped the balls out of Ashley and Jake's hands. "We have to go, guys!"

They stared at her as if she wasn't speaking English. Her eyes quickly moved to the timepiece. Only twenty minutes left. She had wasted too much time trying to convince them, and not enough time searching for the horse. That moment, she made a decision.

"Ow!" Ashley said as Kristin snatched the timepiece off of her neck. Kristin ran off, and Ashley picked up another ping pong ball, ready to play.

Kristin ran away from the games and saw an angry young girl with a black bob and bangs scurry past, towards the house of mirrors. Her fists were balled, and she moved with a speed atypical for a little girl.

"Kristin!" Kristin yelled, trying to stop herself from hiding in the house of mirrors.

Eight-year-old Kristin ignored her. Her parents and teachers at school had told her to never talk to strangers, so she kept walking.

"Kristin, go back to your Mom!"

Young Kristin whirled around. Who was this stranger talking to? Who did this stranger think she was?

"You can't tell me what to do!" young Kristin screamed.

Teen Kristin stared at her in shock. She remembered that being her favorite phrase as a child, how she thought the phrase was so powerful. Now, hearing the childishness and anger from an outsider's point of view, it made her wince.

"Your mother's looking for you," Kristin said. "She's alone and she's scared."

"I don't care about her! I don't care about you! She's ugly! You're ugly!"

Kristin was awestruck. Was she really this difficult? This angry? She realized suddenly how much of a handful she must have been, and felt guilty for the way young Kristin talked about her mother.

"Was Susie behind you?" Teen Kristin asked. She prayed that her mother hadn't lost track of her.

Young Kristin crossed her arms and pouted. She would be a pretty girl if she smiled.

"I'm not telling you!" young Kristin said, before darting away towards the funhouse. Teen Kristin wondered if she should follow her and convince her to tell her where her mother was, but Kristin—knowing Kristin—realized it was a better decision to look for Susie herself.

Kristin gazed at the timepiece. Only twenty minutes left.

She ran away from the house of mirrors funhouse and raced down the row of carnival rides and back to the Ferris Wheel where it had all started. As her feet pounded on the ground, her mind cleared, and she suddenly thought of the fortuneteller's words. *The alley where your mother was attacked…*

"An alley," Kristin said.

Her mind raced. Where would an alley be? She had already checked out the majority of the fairgrounds, and saw no hidden place for an attack to occur. She scanned her mind, wondering where an alley existed where her mother could be alone, where strangers could hurt her.

"The parking lot is too open," Kristin said. "The woods behind the carnival aren't an alley. The only place that would be considered an alley is…"

The space between the fence and the house of mirrors.

Kristin turned and ran as fast as she could, channeling the energy she had as a child. She ran until her heart hurt, until her breath escaped into gasps, and as she approached the alley, she heard men shouting slurs.

"Look at the gook, thinking she can hang in our neighborhood," one of the men said. He was a tall man with a shaved head and two earrings dangling from his elephant lobes.

Kristin's face reddened when she saw her mother being held by two other men. Susie was crying. Her yellow blouse was ripped and blood was on her knees. Kristin gasped when she realized the men were the bald ones who had sneered at her and her mother when they had first entered the carnival grounds.

There were five men total. Their ages ranged from 35 to 50, but they all had shaved heads and scowls on their faces. The man who had first spoken held a bat, one he had won earlier at a game booth. Kristin watched in horror as he swung at Susie, the wood smacking her stomach with a loud *crack*. Blood emitted from Susie's mouth and nose. Kristin stood paralyzed as she watched a second man remove the cap from a red gasoline container. She closed her eyes, realizing that this was the moment that the men were about to set her mother on fire.

"Get off of her!" Kristin screamed. She looked around for a weapon of her own, seeing nothing but a security golf cart against the fence. The men stopped their assault to glare at Kristin, examining her from head to toe.

"Look what we have here," the first man, clearly the leader of the group, said.

The man who held the gasoline licked his lips. "A young gook wants to join our party," he said.

"If you want me," Kristin said. "Come and get me."

They smiled at the challenge and released Susie. She fell to the ground, wheezing, but left alone, for now.

Kristin ran away from the alley, back towards the carnival. She rushed towards the Ferris Wheel, where the carnival patrons stared at her strangely as she raced past.

"There she is!" Kristin heard one of the men say.

She didn't look behind her, but she could tell that they were closing in. She thought about what Eric had said earlier in the house of mirrors: any injury inflicted in Hell would affect one's vessel on Earth. There was no way that she was going to let the men who hurt her mother hurt her, too.

"Where are you going, girly?" another man said.

Kristin's eyes did a quick scan of the rides: the Teacups, the Spider, the Spinning Swings. Even if she cut everyone in line, the carnie would still need to activate the ride, leaving Kristin vulnerable to abduction. She ran away from that area and towards the games. She rushed past Jake and Ashley who were still mesmerized by the ping pong balls flying into the fishbowls. She wanted to stop and ask them for help, but she knew it would be a lost cause. She was on her own.

Kristin glanced quickly at the timepiece. There were only fifteen minutes left.

In the game section, she saw kids launch darts at paper stars, and wondered what would happen if she threw a few at the men.

They would be annoyed at best.

She saw a man throw a lasso at a wooden horse, and when he missed, he cursed at the carnie to give him another chance. Kristin realized that this section of the park was fraught with possible weapon choices, but she had to choose quickly.

She was about to grab a lasso, but noticed a better weapon in the booth next door.

"Excuse me!" Kristin said to a little boy who was about to aim his BB gun at the sitting ducks in front of him. She snatched the gun from him, and he yelled at her as she sprinted away. "Sorry!" Kristin called back, but he didn't accept her apology.

She ran away from the games area, clutching the gun to her chest. When she looked behind her, she saw the men huffing. She, herself, felt sick, using all of her energy to sprint. She would never be able to hit them if she shot at them while running, nor would she be able to fight them off by herself either. The only way she could hurt the men would be to surprise them, but how?

"Think, Kristin," she said to herself. Where could she hide in such an open space?

A security guard in a golf cart whizzed past without noticing her. The guard was an overweight, short man who seemed to need the golf cart to do his rounds. Kristin remembered that he was the one who had found her mother that night and called the police. Kristin remembered how helpful and kind he was, but he was not of a physical stature that could fight off the men.

Kristin watched as the cart sped towards the house of mirrors.

"Of course," Kristin said with realization.

She raced behind the cart. The men behind her were catching up to her, but they stopped running to play it cool at the sight of the guard in the distance. Kristin shot a glance behind her, and the leader with his large earlobes pointed at her and mouthed, "I'm coming for you." Only one of his cronies had a weapon, the bat, while the other three were weaponless but physically strong.

Kristin's eyes widened when she saw a thin chain hanging from the leader's neck. On that chain, the white horse token dangled.

"*The leader is who I want*," Kristin thought. She kept this mantra in her mind as she ran into the funhouse. She entered the long hallway, remembering the lack of doors.

"Where are you, girly?" she heard a voice call out. Kristin ran down another mirrored hallway. No time to stare at the hundreds of Kristins that ran beside her. "Come out, come out, wherever you are!"

Kristin raced down the hallway until she reached a dead end. She heard the leader scream out, "Split up! We're bound to find her somewhere."

Kristin panicked as she stared at her direct reflection, the bright fluorescent lights above her glowing. She touched the glass, her hand touching her own, and that was when she remembered that entryways were optical illusions. They existed, but looked like walls.

She quickly backtracked and felt along the walls. She found an opening and when she raced through it, she heard the footsteps of one of the men.

"Where are you, girly?" the voice from earlier repeated. Kristin pushed herself against the wall of the room and closed her eyes, trying to catch her breath. She held the BB gun close to her, waiting for the man to reach the end of the hallway.

"What the hell?" the man said as he reached the dead end. He was gawking stupidly around him and at all of his reflections when Kristin darted out. She aimed her gun and shot, hoping to hit him in the chest, but the BB bullet slammed into the glass behind him, shattering it into pieces.

"Bitch!" the man screamed.

Kristin realized that aiming for the man was foolish, especially with only so many BBs available.

Ignoring the man's name-calling, she aimed her gun upwards, shooting at the lights. The hallway instantly went pitch black, and Kristin darted back into her room, where she shot out more lights. In the darkness of the hallway, the man futilely searched, terrified and confused. He stumbled around, trying to get out of the hallway. Once he entered the room where Kristin had been hiding, she took the opportunity to jet, leaving him to figure his way out.

"Help!" the man screamed as Kristin ran towards the light. "Help me!"

Kristin rounded a corner, the other Kristins running beside her in the mirrors, their guns pointed and ready. She kept running until she heard voices. She stopped, trying to figure out where the noise was originating.

Carefully scanned the walls, Kristin looked for something slightly off, hoping to find the opening from the hallway to the room. She moved swiftly, still holding her gun, and when she heard someone coughing, her ears perked up.

Kristin saw the opening and stepped through it. Before the two men in the other room realized that Kristin had appeared, she shot upwards, blasting out the lights. When it was dark, she fired rounds of BBs at the direction of the men, and this time, she was lucky enough to hit them in their chest and arms.

"Oww!" they screamed as she took off, blasting the lights in the hallway behind her.

Now she had a system. She knew where she had been, based on the light versus the dark. She had dealt with three men, and there were only two left—one of whom was the leader with her ticket out of Level Two.

Her body filled with adrenaline, she ran, her armpits perspiring, her hands shaking. She held the gun, which seemed to be getting heavier, but she knew she had to keep going. She had to find the leader with the white horse.

"What are you doing?" a voice asked from the side.

Kristin jumped, aiming her gun at the speaker, but the girl at the gun's receiving end stared at her with wide eyes.

"Kristin, get out of here!" Teen Kristin said.

"I'm having fun. You can't tell me what to do," child Kristin replied, and Teen Kristin couldn't believe her attitude.

"You're not safe here!"

"You're ugly!" child Kristin screamed before darting out of the room and down the hallway. Kristin followed after her, wondering what would happen if the bald men got a hold of her younger self. If they harmed her, would Kristin also feel the pain?

Child Kristin reached a T in the hallway and turned right. Teen Kristin hurried after her until she heard a voice that sent chills throughout her body.

"Come out, come out, wherever you are!"

Kristin darted around, afraid that the leader was about to ambush her the way her younger self had. When she looked around her, he was nowhere in sight.

"There's no point in hiding, girly. We're going to get you!"

Kristin listened for the origin of his voice. He was somewhere to her left; she just had to find the opening.

It was her dumb luck that he stood in the room where the trio had begun this level. As he stared at his own reflection, admiring his bald head and his overly exercised body in its tight t-shirt, Kristin realized that to get the white horse she would have to take him down. There could be no black-out, no escape. She had to aim, and she had to make it hurt.

She raised her gun and took a deep breath. Steadying her arm and focusing her aim, she silently prayed to God to give her the ability to shoot. Miraculously, the leader turned around just then, and Kristin's gun was pointed right between his eyes. Before he could move, she pulled the trigger, just as the bat came crashing down on her back and she slumped onto the floor.

CHAPTER FIFTEEN

Kristin's head throbbed as she gazed up at the white horse dangling before her face.

The leader of the bald men sneered down at her, the fluorescent lights backlighting his face.

"Got you," he said.

Kristin glared at him, her eyes darting to his hands and seeing the BB gun. Behind him, the man with the bat stood. He patted it against his hand, as if reminding Kristin that it was he who had knocked her out.

After he had struck her, she had fallen to the floor, her BB missing her original mark of the leader. Its bullet sped to the mirror behind him, shattering it to the floor, and the shards laid behind Kristin. She sat up on the floor and faced the leader as if he were her executioner. Her nose bled and her back ached from the blow.

"See what happens when you don't mind your business, girly?" the leader asked.

Kristin shouted a million obscenities in her head, but she knew better than to voice them aloud. She looked to the second man with the bat before turning to the cruel face of the leader, pockmarked and ugly. She searched for signs of humanity, but there were none. After all, how could a human being order a group of men to brutally beat and burn a woman because of the color of her skin?

"Cat got your tongue?" the leader said.

Kristin howled in pain as a BB punctured the skin of her arm. The leader smiled as he stepped closer, wielding his gun. Kristin slid backwards, closer to the jagged mirror pieces as he shot at her again. The BB hit her stomach, and she doubled over in pain. The wounds were not enough to hit any organs, but they were painful welts that tore at her flesh.

"You wanna talk now, girly?" the leader said.

The gun went *pow*, another bullet hitting her skin. Kristin screamed in pain, but she didn't want to give him the satisfaction of responding to his cruelty. He shot at her again until she bore into his eyes and shouted out.

"Screw you!" Kristin said.

He laughed cruelly and looked to the man behind him with the bat. "This one's more fun than the old lady. She didn't say shit even as you whacked at her."

The man with the bat chuckled awkwardly. The anger that boiled inside of Kristin caused her to shake, but she knew that she couldn't take them both.

And then, Kristin saved herself.

"What's that?" the leader said as he caught the reflection of young Kristin running past.

"What's what?" the other man asked.

"A kid's in the funhouse. Go get her, make sure she didn't see anything."

The man with the bat stared at him, uncomfortable with the request. Kristin used this moment of conflict between them to quickly glance behind her. She saw a large shard of glass and wrapped her fingers around it, pulling it behind her.

"I'm not going to hurt a kid, Adam," the man with the bat said.

The leader, Adam, lowered his eyes. "Do it," he said.

"Adam, I don't…"

"I said do it!" Adam growled, and the man with the bat obliged.

At that moment, Kristin thought about herself and Ashley. How often she had gone through with Ashley's schemes, even when she didn't agree with them, even when they hurt people. She remembered Ashley's plan to play with Ronnie on Halloween, and she remembered how cruel it had sounded. Then she thought about her own cruelty—how she had run away from her mother, just to hurt her, when all Susie ever wanted was to love her daughter and be loved in return.

As Kristin watched the man with the bat leave to find young Kristin, she realized that she was the same as him and no better.

"What're you looking at, girly?" Adam said.

The anger inside her began to subside, evolving into a calm power that she harnessed within.

"A nobody," Kristin said.

Her response took Adam aback. "What did you say?" he asked, aiming his gun at her face.

"You're a nobody. A prick. An asshole who abuses women and children because you're too chicken to pick on someone your own size."

"I'll teach you!" Adam snarled, pulling the trigger.

Kristin winced, moving her face out of the way, but to her amazement and his shock, the gun was out of BBs.

"What the?" Adam said as he looked at his gun. Kristin took this opportunity to attack. Fighting the pain in her body, she leapt upwards, bringing her mirror shard over her head and stabbing it down into his chest. His jaw dropped and he clutched at the shard. As he stepped back, Kristin grabbed the white horse dangling from the chain around his neck. Blood escaped from his mouth, and he fell to the floor, helpless.

Suddenly the room went black, and flames appeared in the mirror.

"Krrrriiiiiisssstttttiiiiinnn...." a demonic voice said. It was the same voice that Kristin heard the night Ronnie was abducted.

She saw a handsome young man in a black suit appear in the flames. He resembled Eric Whitehorse, but unlike Eric with his jokey game show host demeanor, this man was serious. There was something very heavy about the way he looked into Kristin's eyes.

"Who are you?" Kristin asked.

"Finish him," the man said. "Finish him, and end the game."

"What? No," Kristin said.

The man gazed down at Adam's still body, frozen the exact way the scene in Level One was frozen when Eric had arrived to give Kristin her lifeline.

"Kill the man who harmed you and your mother. Get your revenge."

"No. I won't. I can't…"

A large dagger suddenly appeared in Kristin's hand. The man looked at it and then at Kristin. He nodded, letting her know it was okay.

"Succumb to your anger. Punish him for what he did to you."

"No!" Kristin screamed. She threw the dagger onto the floor and kicked it away. As the lights came back on and the man and the flames disappeared, she dashed out of the room and out of the funhouse.

She needed to find the door to the next level.

**

Kristin hurried back to the games section of the carnival, looking at the timepiece. Only minutes left until the level would be over.

She pushed past families moseying around with cotton candy and candied apples, and made her way back to Jake and Ashley, still playing the fishbowl game as if it was the most important thing in the entire world. Next to the game, however, was a blessing—the door, a large wooden piece painted red, stood only a few yards away.

"How can I get them through it?" Kristin asked herself. She gazed around, seeing a teenager using the lasso. Nearby that booth, she saw the same kid from earlier shooting a BB gun.

She got an idea.

"Excuse me!" Kristin said.

As she approached the shooting kid, his face fell. "Not you again," he said.

Kristin snatched his gun from him and ran towards the teen using the lasso.

"Give me that," Kristin said, and the teenager defiantly stuck her hand on her hip and gave her a dirty look.

"You want to make me?" the teen asked.

Kristin pointed the gun in her face. "Give me the rope," Kristin commanded, and the teen quickly obliged.

"Hey! What are you doing?" an older male voice yelled.

Kristin turned to see the security guard pointing at her in the distance. The BB gun kid next to him.

"What a nark," Kristin muttered, but then she noticed the abandoned golf cart behind them.

"Come here," the guard said as he motioned for Kristin to walk over. Ignoring him, she ran past him to his cart, which thankfully still had the keys in them. "Hey!" the guard yelled as Kristin whizzed past him.

She raced the cart to the fishbowl game, stopping it in front of her friends. With speed, she ran out of the cart and pulled the lasso over Jake and Ashley, who didn't even notice as they tossed their ping-pong balls. Kristin squeezed the lasso tight around them before she tied the other end of the rope onto the back of the cart. She glanced back and saw the red-faced guard jogging towards her, but fortunately, he was too slow.

"Sorry, guys, but you'll thank me later," Kristin said as she hopped back into the golf cart. With only two minutes left, she gunned the gas, and the cart sped towards the closed door. Kristin closed her eyes as it broke through the wood of the door, and Jake and Ashley groaned in shock as their bodies were pulled through the doorway by the cart.

The white light engulfed them, and Kristin closed her eyes as they were transported to the next level. She felt nothing as the golf cart disappeared underneath her, nor when the skin on the back of her neck healed, erasing the Mark of the Beast.

CHAPTER SIXTEEN

"They should never have been given a timepiece."

"It's not the timepiece. It's the game that's too easy."

"It's not the game. It's Eric helping them. He's the reason."

The Council of the Gamemakers glared at Eric Whitehorse, dressed in his white button-down shirt and white slacks. He rubbed at his eyes, wanting to fall asleep. This council meeting was so boring.

"No man has ever removed *666* from his body."

"Well, this time wasn't a man either," Eric clarified. "It was a *woman*."

The council members glared again at him, but he only shrugged, unconcerned with the matter at hand.

In a brightly lit white space, the members of the council sat around a giant round table shaped like a ring and made of a material that reflected the bright light from above. Every other member wore either all black or all white, with table space before them made of onyx or marble, respectively.

"Is this a joke to you?" an older gentleman with black hair asked. He wore a sleek black suit with a gray and black striped tie. "The rules state that any human that reaches the end has the right to their prize and the saving of his or her soul, but if these kids win... they'll have the ability to alter their realities. Do you understand what they could do? No one has ever won the game!"

"Maybe their realities needed to be changed," Eric muttered under his breath.

"What did you say?" the suited man in black seethed. "We never should have elected you to be the host. You have too much invested in that girl."

Eric said nothing as he stared at the table.

"She'll never love you, Eric," a woman in a white dress said.

Eric shot her a dirty look.

"I'm sorry to say that," she continued, "but it's forbidden. It cannot be done."

I'll make it happen, Eric thought, but he remained silent.

"I say we cut our losses and end the game," a woman in black said. She had dark hair and bright red lips. "We agree to release Ronnie Smalls' soul to Heaven and exonerate Jake, Kristin, and Ashley from the crime. I would rather forfeit than give them a chance to win."

"That's generous of you," a woman in a white dress said.

The woman in black smiled. "Kristin and Jake will be good, but Ashley will end up here eventually, just like her brother." She shot Eric a smug grin, and though he glared at her, he refused to take the bait.

The Chair of the Gamemakers in Black banged his gavel. "Enough!" he said. "There will be no forfeit. I refuse to release four souls just because the players made it past two rounds. There are five more to go, after all."

"They didn't *just* pass two rounds," the woman with red lips said. "Kristin removed her Mark. What if they all remove their marks? What if they figure out how to free other souls from Hell?"

"I said enough!" the Chair said, glaring at her. She cowered in her seat, and those around her diverted their eyes, thankful it wasn't they who had spoken out of turn.

The Chair of the Gamemakers in White stood next to the Chair in Black. He was just as composed as the other Chair, but his face was softer, kinder. When he spoke, he spoke with the wisdom of a thousand years.

"Chair Black is right," he said, and everyone listened, even Eric. "Eric has twisted the rules. He has taken advantage of his role as the Host of this game, and we must address this issue." Chair White's gaze bore into Eric, who felt like a small child being berated by his father. "There is no question that the Game must continue, but there must be something taken for everything that was given."

Chair Black nodded in agreement. He commenced a discussion of what to do next in the game, while Chair White motioned for Eric to speak with him in the other room.

"What are you doing with that girl?" Chair White asked once they were out of earshot from the others.

"Don't believe the rumors. She's just a player in this game."

Chair White stared at him. "After this is over, you are never to see her again. Regardless of the outcome. Understand me?"

Eric didn't want to agree with that.

"If you disobey my order, you know what will happen to you. You've always been one of our best, Eric, but rules are rules."

Eric swallowed hard. He had to fight himself not to retort that in years of service, years of watching horrible things happen to his ward, he was now being questioned for not following the rules. "I understand," he said.

The Chair nodded, satisfied with that answer. With the discussion over, he walked back into the meeting, where the council was in the midst of a heated debate on what to do with the trio of Jake, Kristin, and Ashley.

**

"Holy shit. It's hot," Ashley whispered. Sweat beaded down her forehead and she wiped it away with the back of her hand. Next to her, Jake fanned out his t-shirt, already dripping with sweat, while a red-faced Kristin gazed at the ground that looked so dry that it cracked. They had only been on Level Three for a minute, but the door to entry had already disappeared.

"Are we in a desert?" Jake asked.

"We're on Level Three," Kristin said. "This can't be just any old desert."

Ashley looked at Kristin, at her bloody hands and torn clothing. She then glanced at herself and Jake and the rope burn marks around their waists.

"What happened?" Ashley asked.

"I'll tell you later," Kristin said, walking forward. They only had an hour to solve this level, and there was no time for explanations.

As Kristin walked ahead, Ashley stared at the back of her neck and gasped, grabbing Jake's hand.

"What?" Jake asked.

Ashley pointed at Kristin's neck, now smooth with the mark of the beast removed.

"She doesn't have her number," Ashley said.

Jake's eyes grew with surprise. He watched as Ashley marched up to Kristin as she stopped walking and stared at the ground again, entranced.

"Hey, you have to tell us what happened back there!"

But when Ashley saw what had caught Kristin's attention, she gasped again. The two girls stood on the edge of a dusty rock, and beneath them was a vast empire of flames. Amidst the fire, hands reached upwards as if trying to break free, an image reminiscent of when they were in Zuzan's castle, trying to swim through the eel monsters.

As Ashley gazed at the millions of anonymous souls burning in the fires of Hell, she thought of her brother and scanned the sea of faces, hoping not to find him.

"This is the Hell I've always imagined," Ashley said. "Ever since I was a little girl, I imagined it would look like this."

"This is where most of the souls end up in Hell," Eric said.

The three turned around to see him smiling at them, not a drop of sweat in sight.

"Why are you here?" Ashley snapped, and Eric's eyes flashed at her. She flinched, but quickly recovered as he smiled.

"Well, I'm here because I wanted to congratulate you all on making it to Level Three," Eric said. "Most people never make it this far."

"You came to congratulate us?" Ashley asked, suspicious.

Eric smiled at Kristin. "I'm sure you noticed that Kristin has successfully removed her Mark of the Beast. The Gamemakers were extremely impressed by her gusto. Well done."

Kristin reddened even more. She knew that everything in Hell came at a price, and for Eric to congratulate them part way through could only mean trouble.

"That's why I'm here! I wanted to let you know that The Gamemakers are offering a special prize!"

Eric spoke with game show host enthusiasm, but the trio only stared at him.

"What's the catch?" Jake asked.

"What is it?" Ashley asked.

Eric pointed at Kristin. "They're offering Kristin a chance to go home! Isn't that wonderful!"

Ashley's eyes widened with envy. "Her?"

Eric smiled. "She really impressed The Gamemakers. They think she's the best player and don't see a reason to challenge her anymore. After all, she conquered Level Two without you, and she saved you both from the Eels in Level One."

Eric circled around Jake, whose pride was hurt knowing that he hadn't done anything to help the girls. "We were really surprised, Jake. We had all bet that you would be the star, that you would be the hero. Who would've guessed that former weakling Kristin would be the only one of value in this equation?"

Jake looked at Kristin. She looked down as if apologetic. He then looked at Eric, who grinned at him condescendingly.

"So, Kristin, are you ready to go home?" Eric asked.

Kristin looked at Jake and then Ashley. Jake appeared proud, wanting her to leave so that he could be the man, while Ashley looked like she would claw Kristin's eyes out if that gave her the opportunity to win the Get Out of Hell card.

"I'm staying," Kristin said.

Eric feigned shock. "What? Why?"

"I'm staying. They need me."

"We don't need you," Jake said.

Hurt, Kristin looked at him. She remembered the strong connection that they had previously shared, but it seemed as though that bond had already splintered.

"Are you sure?" Kristin asked, looking into his eyes.

Ashley stood behind them, glaring. Eric focused his attention on her, wondering what she would do and say next.

"We should do a vote!" Ashley said. She stepped in between Jake and Kristin, stopping them before they could get close enough to kiss.

"What vote?" Jake asked.

"You heard Eric. Kristin's a superstar at this game. She doesn't need a free pass home—I do!"

Kristin stared at her with wide eyes, speechless.

"Can you hear yourself?" Jake asked.

"I don't care," Ashley said, unaware that the sixes on the back of her neck were aglow. "Why does she get a break? Her life has been nothing but easy. I deserve to go home! I don't deserve to be here!"

"You're being unreasonable, Ashley!" Kristin screamed back. "We're all in this together!"

Seeing her best friend's harsh reaction shocked Ashley, embarrassing her. "I'm sorry," Ashley said. "I'm just so scared."

Kristin hugged her. "I'm not going to leave you."

"I'm going to end up here no matter what happens," Ashley said.

"Don't say that."

Ashley closed her eyes. She could remain silent, but that didn't mean her words weren't true. Eric looked above, where he knew the Gamemakers were watching, wondering if they were satisfied with what they saw.

"Time's up, people," he said. "What's the decision?"

Kristin looked at Jake, who nodded, and then at Eric. "Take Ashley home," Kristin said.

"You don't want your free pass?" Eric asked.

She shook her head. "I don't want it. Give it to her."

Eric stared at them, touched. However, the trio didn't believe his moved expression, and when he began a slow clap of applause, they knew for sure that he was mocking them.

"Well done! Well done!" he said.

"You can stop making fun of us now," Jake said.

"That little expression of selflessness will serve you well here."

"If you're so impressed, then let us all go," Kristin said, but Eric shook his head.

"I can't. You may have removed your mark, but that girl to the left of you is still selfish and envious, and that boy to your right still has too much pride. You may have given up your pass to leave, but that doesn't mean the game is over. In fact, I want to tell you about surprise number three from The Gamemakers."

They stared at him, only more annoyed than they were surprised or scared.

"What now?" Ashley snapped.

"The Gamemakers are cutting your time to forty-five minutes!" Eric said.

Jake and Kristin's faces fell further. Ashley, on the other hand, became livid.

"You asshole!" she screamed as she attempted to slug him in the face. Kristin and Jake watched, appalled, but Eric remained expressionless as he caught her fist easily in his hand.

"You were always such a firecracker, even as a child."

"How would you know?" Ashley snapped, and for the first time, she noticed that Eric looked uncomfortable.

"I wouldn't," he said, but there was something about his reaction that caught Ashley off guard. He regained his composure and pointed upwards, where a giant hourglass appeared in the sky. "Remember to look for the white horse," he said. "In case you forgot—if your time runs out, then you're stuck in Hell forever." He looked to Kristin. "Even you. Don't you wish you had escaped when you had a chance?"

She refused to take the bait. "Are you going to give us a clue?" Kristin asked.

"I'm going to do something even better than that!" Eric said. He reached into his pocket and pulled out several white horse token. The trio's eyes stared at the token, mesmerized.

"You're just going to hand it to us?" Ashley asked.

"That's not how the game is played," Eric said. "You know that."

"No riddle?" Kristin asked. "No memory game?"

"Nope," Eric said as he made the token appear and reappear like a street magician demonstrating his sleight-of-hand. "We're going to play a game, but it's much more simple than any mind game."

"If you're holding the token, then what kind of game is that?" Ashley asked, unsure of where this was going.

"It's a game so simple that even dogs can play it," Eric said before hurling the token into the fiery abyss. The cliff they stood on bolted towards the sky, higher and higher until the four of them were a mile away from the fires. The tokens fell, disappearing into a soul's hand, its shine vanishing amongst the flames. Eric turned to stare at the trio, another smile on his face.

"Fetch," he said. He disappeared, and the particles of the hourglass above the trio slowly began to fall.

CHAPTER SEVENTEEN

His hand reached up for the particle that fell from the sky. He hoped that it was a teardrop from an angel, raining down to cool him from the fire, even if only for a few seconds. When his fingers wrapped around the cool metal token, he pulled it closer to him, pondering what it was. What was the meaning of a white horse?

From above, Ashley gazed down from her floating island, gasped when she saw the white horse disappear. She blinked again, unsure.

"Ashton!" she yelled.

Kristin and Jake turned to her in shock and saw the tears running down her face. With the flames reflecting in her blue eyes, she really looked like a mad woman.

"Ashley…" Kristin said, unable to think of Ashton in hell at all, let alone in the fire below.

Ashley whirled around. "Ashton has the horse!"

Kristin's eyes watered. She thought about that day when she was thirteen and Ashton had appeared on her doorstep with the sunflowers. She remembered how nervous he was, how he had stumbled on his words. She remembered how happy he was when she said yes, how he had kissed her after the dance. At first, she had believed that he only asked her out because of a bet or because Ashley put him up to it. However, when his lips hit hers for the first time, she felt his desire. He had held her in a way she thought could only happen in the movies.

Kristin turned and looked at Jake, who was staring at her, studying her reaction. *She loves him*, Jake thought, a feeling of sadness filling him.

Kristin noticed Jake staring at her, and quickly looked away, feeling guilty. "Ashton's not here," she said. "There's no way he'd be here."

"I saw him!" Ashley screamed back.

"You're hallucinating. It's too hot. We're melting here."

"Don't tell me what I didn't see. I saw my brother, and he's got a horse!"

Above them, the sand fell, too quickly for them to comfortably be standing around arguing. Jake rushed forward, stopping them.

"Girls!" Jake yelled. "We're running out of time."

"How are we supposed to get the horse?" Kristin asked.

"We know where it is," Jake said, glancing at the fire and the souls burning. Jake rubbed at his eyes. Did he just see Ronnie amidst the flames?

Kristin shook her head. "We can't go down there."

"We don't have a choice," Jake said.

"How are we supposed to get down there? There's no ladder. We're floating above the fire…There has to be another way; we've just got to think."

Ashley glared at her, a wild look in her eye. "You can try to stay rational about this whole thing, but your brother isn't down there burning. You may have a free pass to get out of here, but I don't and we're running out of time!"

"Ashley, this isn't what it's all about…"

"We need to jump!" Ashley interrupted.

"Are you serious?" Kristin asked. "We're going to burn to death. Remember, if we die here, we stay here!"

"We're not going to burn," Ashley said. "We're not damned like they are."

Jake looked at Ashley and Kristin, their clothes tattered, their faces scratched, their hair greasy. He knew Ashley still had The Mark of The Beast tattooed on the back of her neck, and shook his head. "I don't know," he said. "Kristin's right. When we're hurt here, we're hurt for real. I don't think it's a good idea to jump."

Ashley glanced up at the hourglass and then back at her friends.

"I'd rather try and fight to get out of here than just stand here until my time is up," Ashley snapped.

"You can't go down there!" Kristin said.

Ashley lowered her eyes. "Watch me," she replied before running towards the edge and leaping into the fiery abyss. Jake and Kristin ran to the edge of the rock and saw Ashley dive into the flames.

The lost souls of Mayor Hercules' children and their friends reached up for her as she descended, and when she was close enough, they wrapped their arms around her, pulling her into the flames. She screamed as the fire licked her skin. As Ashley felt her skin sear, she looked around for Ashton, but he was nowhere to be found. She realized just then what a huge mistake she had made, but it was too late.

"Oh, God," Kristin said.

She and Jake locked eyes, and he reached for her hand. Tears rolled down her cheeks. She wanted to give up so badly.

"What are we going to do?" she asked.

"Did you see anything in the other direction when you pulled us into this level?" Jake asked.

She shook her head. "It was just desert."

"And we saw Eric throw the token into the fire, so we know where it is."

Kristen was scared to take the leap, and at that moment, she wished that she had Ashley's recklessness, her courage. Kristin closed her eyes and prayed that she and her friends would be okay.

Jake gazed at her, wanting to make everything okay. He wanted to protect her, to lead her to the end.

"All we can do is jump," he said.

She knew he was right. She nodded at him, and he squeezed her hand tight.

"I trust you," she said.

They looked ahead, at the hellfire that awaited them. Sweat beaded down their bodies and faces.

"Are you ready?" Jake asked, and Kristin closed her eyes. She didn't want to see the fire or the souls when she fell, and her fear brought tears to her eyes.

Jake was just as afraid on the inside, but he chose to remain strong.

"Ready," Kristin lied, and then they leapt into the air.

CHAPTER EIGHTEEN

The hellfire licked at Jake and Kristin's bodies as the hands of the buried souls pulled them down into the flames. At first, they screamed, thinking the fire was burning their flesh. Instead, the sensation was only a foggy illusion.

As Jake and Kristin clutched each other, she noticed that the hands were pulling her through an open door. She closed her eyes, and everything went to black.

**

There was a flash before Jake and Kristin landed on the ground with a thud. They moaned as their bodies recovered from the fall.

"It's about time!" Ashley said. She had been waiting for minutes, wondering if her friends were brave enough to join her.

Kristin wiggled her fingers in the plush grass as Jake slowly lifted his head. He saw that they had arrived in a tropical location beside an ocean. Next to him, Kristin rose to her feet and gazed around. In front of them was a sparkling blue body of water, more magnificent than anything either of them had ever seen. The cerulean sky above them was clear and the sun shone brightly. Between the grass and the ocean was a long stretch of white sand, free of pollution. The location was more beautiful than anything on Earth.

"It's paradise," Kristin said, and she felt Jake's fingers reach for hers. He clutched her hand, grateful that they had made it to the next level in one piece.

Ashley stared at their hands, green with jealousy, but she stayed silent.

"I wonder what the catch is…" Jake said. He looked at Kristin, wanting to protect her.

"Have you two forgotten we have something to do?" Ashley said. "Get up already."

Jake and Kristin exchanged glances. There's their Ashley.

**

As Kristin, Jake, and Ashley walked towards the sand, they heard the waves crash along the shore.

"Do you still have the time piece?" Ashley asked.

Kristin revealed the watch hanging from a chain around her neck.

"How much time do we have?" Jake asked.

Kristin opened the cover and saw that the time piece was no longer for sixty minutes, but for forty-five. "We've already wasted five minutes," she said.

They walked along the beach, their shoes sloughing through the tiny grains of sand. Jake looked at Kristin, taking notice of the way the sun hit the angles of her cheeks. The light seemed to illuminate her skin, and even in her haggard state, she was incredibly beautiful.

"What are you looking at?" Kristin asked, feeling Jake's eyes on her.

"Nothing," he said, embarrassed that he had been caught.

Ashley gazed at the beautiful water, trying to ignore them. "I really could use a bath," she said.

"Do you think the water is safe?" Jake asked.

"I don't know," she replied.

Just as they stared at the waves, a dolphin jumped out of the water and flipped in the air. Their jaws dropped, utterly amazed at what was happening.

"There has to be a catch," Kristin said as she thought about Level One and how beautiful the castle was, only to see Zuzan and her eels. "What if the water is really scalding acid, or transforms us into something?"

"Like what, dolphins?"

"You joke, but what if it did?"

"I don't doubt that," Jake said, "but it's a Game. All we can do is play smart and take some chances."

Jake walked towards the water, stopping just before getting his feet wet. He turned to look at Kristin, who hesitated on the shore.

"Come on, the water will feel good," he said.

"I don't know," Kristin said, knowing that everything in Hell had come at a price.

"Come on, Kristin. Trust me…"

Annoyed, Ashley ran into the water first, leaving the wannabe lovebirds behind.

Suddenly, a massive wave rose from the sea and overtook Jake and Kristin, sweeping them away into the ocean.

"Jake!" Kristin yelled, paralyzed with fear.

Jake swam over to her. "The water's fine," he said.

She looked at him, and they locked eyes—the electricity between them palpable.

"This doesn't feel like Hell," Kristin said.

"If anything, Hell's only manageable because I'm here with you," he replied, making her blush.

At a short distance, Ashley closed her eyes as she let herself go underneath the surface. After everything else she had experienced in the Game, she was happy to get a break. And as her body dunked into the water, she contemplated what would happen if she didn't surface. Would Jake and Kristin even notice she was gone?

"Hello, there!" a woman yelled. Jake and Kristin sprung away from each other and turned their heads, afraid of what they would see. Ashley nearly choked on water from the surprise. They looked towards the shore and saw a beautiful man and woman, dressed brightly in red, turquoise, and gold. The couple smiled warmly.

"What do they want?" Kristin whispered.

"How can we run?" Jake asked. He looked around him in the vast ocean and knew there was no escape.

"We won't hurt you!" the tanned man said. He smiled, revealing extremely white, perfect teeth. He and the woman looked so happy and relaxed, it was hard for the trio to not trust them.

"We want to take care of you," the woman said. "Please, come to the shore!"

Ashley glanced at Jake and Kristin. "Should we listen to them?"

"It seems like we don't have a choice," Jake said.

"Hurry, Jake, Kristin, and Ashley!" the man said. "We want to properly greet you to your afterlife!"

Jake and Kristin stared at each other. Did they hear what they thought they heard?

Ashley felt a sense of panic. "Are we dead?" she asked.

"We couldn't have died…could we?" Jake said.

At that moment, a bottle floated towards them, jigsaw pieces inside. Ashley grabbed it. "It's a clue," she whispered.

The trio looked to the beautiful couple on the sand and then to the bottle in Ashley's hand.

They realized there was only one way out.

**

Dressed in jeweled robes, Jake, Kristin, and Ashley sat underneath a bright turquoise cabana while beautiful men and women who were heavily jeweled and provocatively dressed brought them fruit on silver platters.

Jake and Kristin awkwardly smiled at their hosts, Alexandria and Javier, the woman and man from the shore, sitting on chaises beside them.

"You look refreshed," Alexandria said in an exotic accent that none of them could place.

"The robes look wonderful on you," Javier added.

"Thank you," Ashley said, marveling at her elaborate clothing. The bottle with the jigsaw pieces remained hidden underneath her robe, pressed against her and reminding her to solve its puzzle.

"You really have been too kind..." Kristin said, feeling uncomfortable among such decadence.

Alexandria put up her hand playfully to shush her. "No, no. We want to take care of you. We want to pamper you. We want to show you how wonderful Heaven can be." She clapped her hands and more beautiful men and women appeared with pots of water and other tools for manicures, pedicures, and massages.

Jake stared at the beautiful people's gold jewelry, how it glistened in the sunlight, the way the white horse glistened. "We can't accept this," Jake said.

Javier laughed. "No need to be shy," he said as the beautiful men and woman began to work on pampering Kristin, Jake, and Ashley. They slid their feet into an herbal warm water soak, while the beautiful people massaged their shoulders and arms.

"Wow," Jake said. "I really feel like a king."

Alexandria and Javier laughed heartily at how new he was to this lifestyle.

"Heaven is a place for Kings and other high members of society," Alexandria explained. "The poor and meek have no place here because they do not understand the life of luxury. There is no reason to be shy."

"I can't wait to one day get to Heaven myself," Kristin replied, and Jake shot her a warning look.

Alexandria and Javier tried to hide their surprise before exchanging a look, as though unsure whether or not to speak. The beautiful people working on them exchanged nervous glances.

Kristin's face reddened. She shouldn't have said anything, especially if these demons could turn on them the way Zuzan did.

"Should we tell them?" Alexandria asked.

"I thought they knew what happened," Javier replied.

Kristin, Jake and Ashley stared at them, waiting for an explanation.

Alexandria reached over and gently touched Jake's hand, and he melted, sighing in ecstasy. Kristin and Ashley watched with jealousy as she gazed seductively into his eyes.

"I know it must be difficult for you all to realize this, but…" She paused, unsure of how to proceed. "You three died in the hellfire."

If Kristin didn't know better, she would have fully believed what she was about to say. She exchanged glances with Jake and Ashley. Was there any way that she was telling the truth?

Alexandria's beautiful, soft eyes seemed so sincere. "This must be a lot to process," she said with sympathy.

"Or you're just lying," Ashley shot back. "We're not dead, and we're not in Heaven."

"Could we have a minute?" Jake asked.

Alexandria looked to Javier. "Of course," she said. "But rest assured, what Javier and I are telling you is a fact. You can accept it now, or you can accept it later." She clapped her hands, and the beautiful men and women immediately stood up and followed her and Javier out of the cabana area.

Once they were at a distance, Kristin, Jake, and Ashley immediately scooted together and whispered.

"This is weird," Jake said.

"She's lying," Kristin added. "We're not dead."

"But where was Eric?" Ashley asked. "He always shows up at the beginning of the level…"

"But if we were to die, why would we go to Heaven? Eric said that if we die in the Game, we stay in Hell forever. That means if we really are dead, then…"

"We're still in Hell."

"Exactly."

Jake looked around at their paradise. What if this realm of Hell really was just a lazy life of luxury? It couldn't be that simple, could it?

"Do you remember Mayor Hercules' book?" he asked Kristin. "There was a chapter on the seven deadly sins…"

"Yeah, and we've seen gluttony," Kristin said, thinking of Zuzan. Then she considered Level Two at the carnival. "And wrath."

"What was the Hellfire?" Jake asked.

"A whole lot of bickering," Kristin said, shooting a look at Ashley.

"Maybe it was envy?" Jake said. "Eric tried to get us to turn against each other with jealousy…"

"He tried to get everyone to turn against *me*," she corrected.

Jake nodded. "So if we've already experienced gluttony, wrath, and envy, that leaves lust, greed, sloth, and pride."

"Maybe this is pride? Everyone here seems pretty full of themselves," Ashley said.

Jake glanced around, unsure. If this was pride, then he imagined there would be something more extreme. He thought about the peaceful setting, the luxury, the pampering, and realized that this level's intention was something else.

"They want us to be lazy," he said.

"Sloth," Kristin said, and Jake nodded in agreement.

"Let's see what's inside the bottle," Jake said.

Ashley pulled it out from underneath her robes and uncorked it, then shook out the thick jigsaw puzzle pieces. Jake looked behind him to see if Javier, Alexandria, and the others were returning, but they were nowhere in sight.

"We'd better hurry," he said as Ashley and Kristin began to organize the pieces together.

"I've never been good at puzzles," Kristin said.

Jake looked behind him again, making sure the coast was clear. He then looked into Kristin's pretty brown eyes. "We'll be fast if we work together," he said.

He joined them in putting the puzzle pieces together, and when they were halfway through, they heard Alexandria's lilting laughter as she approached. Jake and Kristin glanced over to see Javier and Alexandria lead their gorgeous army back to the cabana.

"She's coming," Kristin whispered, and Jake put the final piece in the puzzle. Once he snapped it in, the cracks of the puzzle disappeared and the jigsaw became one scroll. Kristin, Jake, and Ashley watched in amazement as lines appeared on the paper, drawing a detailed map of the island.

"This has to be a map to the white horse," Kristin said.

"Put it away," Jake said. "They're coming."

Ashley quickly hid the map beneath her robe just as Alexandria and Javier stepped onto the platform, glasses and a bottle of fine champagne in hand.

"We thought you'd like a drink!" Alexandria said before Javier popped the champagne. He poured as Alexandria held the glasses, and Kristin, Jake, and Ashley weakly smiled when she brought them the alcohol.

"We don't drink…" Jake said.

"Nonsense," Alexandria said, taking a seat on the chaise nearby. "Drink and be merry. Kristin, you look so tense. Danyela will attend to you. Marshall, attend to Jake. Ashley, have a sip."

The thought of drinking the champagne greatly appealed to Ashley, but she fought the urge to partake.

Meanwhile, Kristin stared at the champagne in her glass as a beautiful dark-skinned woman grabbed her feet and began to kneed fine oil into her cuticles. Next to her, a muscular man with brown hair and blue eyes massaged Jake's shoulders.

"Are you having fun?" Alexandria asked, and Kristin and Jake weakly smiled. Ashley kept her head down, afraid her suspicion would show on her face.

Pleased, Alexandria put on sunglasses and laid back on her pillow as a gorgeous set of twins rubbed lotion onto her calves. Javier sat on another chair nearby, enjoying a similar treatment.

"You're wasting your time, girl," Danyela whispered in a thick accent. "Don't get stuck here like we did."

"What?" Kristin asked.

Danyela lowered her eyes as she waited for Alexandria to look away. "Don't lose your time," she whispered. "Find the white horse."

Kristin's eyes widened, and Alexandria noticed. Her nostrils flared as she glared at Danyela, who dutifully soaked Kristin's feet.

"Is something wrong, Kristin?" Alexandria asked. "Is Danyela not making you happy? Perhaps we can find you someone else to do your nails?"

"No, no, she's doing a wonderful job," Kristin said quickly. "Thank you."

Danyela stared at Kristin's feet as she worked, avoiding Alexandria's cold, examining gaze. But when Kristin looked over at Alexandria, her hard face transformed back to her jovial, bubbly self, a quick change that sent chills down Kristin's spine.

Jake noticed it, too. "We really need to get going," he said as he sat upright.

Javier stood abruptly. He smiled, but his eyes showed that he was not pleased. "Why the rush? Perhaps we can go to the hot springs, and you three can take a nice dip in the waters? It will be wonderful."

Jake looked at Kristin, whose eyes told him it was time to go. He then turned to Ashley, signaling it was time to run.

Danyela continued to work as though nothing had happened.

Alexandria rose to her feet and joined Javier. She looked to her partner and wrapped her arm around his shoulders, smiling a wicked smile.

"The jig is up, Javier," Alexandria said. "Our guests may no longer appreciate the luxuries we give them, but no matter. They will soon be trapped with us forever…" Her eyes turned golden with a cat slit pupil, and a whip suddenly appeared in her hand. She smacked Danyela on the back, and Danyela writhed in pain. Alexandria smiled, enjoying the torture.

That is when it dawned on Kristin and Jake that the beautiful men and women serving them were not their hosts' friends but their hosts' slaves.

Javier nodded. He smiled, his teeth like fangs. "Soon our lazy guests will know what it is like to truly be a servant in Hell."

CHAPTER NINETEEN

Kristin, Jake, and Ashley stared at the beautiful men and women behind Javier and Alexandria, and at last noticed that the gold bands around their necks, ankles, and wrists were not jewelry but shackles.

Danyela cowered behind her master, gazing up at Kristin with fear. She wasn't sure what was to happen, to Kristin or to her and the other slaves for the matter, but knowing Alexandria, she knew it would be bad.

"So, friends," Alexandria said. "You have fifteen minutes left in our world before you're stuck here forever. What is your choice? Would you like to spend the rest of your time being pampered and lazy, or would you like a futile fight?"

"Where's the horse?" Jake asked.

Alexandria and Javier glanced at each other and smiled. "It seems, Alexandria, they prefer to stay here the hard way."

"What a pity," Alexandria said as she shook her head. "Most people who are resigned to stay with us were here because they were lazy and spoiled while alive on Earth. They felt entitled to luxury when in fact they were only sealing their fates in Hell for their sloth. You two may not deserve your fates, but you are about to share them with these heathens!"

Javier smiled. "I heard, Kristin, that you were quite fond of spiders," he said.

The trio watched as Alexandria grew to ten feet tall. Her body darkened to black and four limbs sprouted from her sides as her arms and legs lengthened.

"She's become a spider…" Ashley said.

Kristin thought about that day she had destroyed the web and smashed the spider at Mayor Hercules' house. "Karma," he had said, and karma was what was happening now.

Javier grinned, loving the fear he saw in their faces. Their slaves cowered and scattered in different directions, but invisible chains jerked them back. They screamed as Alexandria fully became a giant black widow.

Kristin, Jake, and Ashley ran towards the ocean, Javier calling out to them as Alexandria slinked towards them.

"You'll never find the white horse in the water!" he screamed.

"Do you think he's lying?" Ashley asked.

"They've lied about everything else," Jake said as they darted towards the ocean.

"Open the map!" Kristin said.

Ashley pulled out the map and unrolled it as she ran. She stared at its contents, trying to decipher what it all meant.

"I don't know where to go!" Ashley said.

"Give it to me!" Jake said. Annoyed, Ashley handed it to him as they continued to run. Jake looked behind him, seeing the spider closing in on them. On the map, he saw a giant red "X" located on a hill behind the forest.

"Where do we need to go?" Kristin asked.

"Stay away from the water. Follow me!"

He made a sharp turn towards the jungle. Kristin and Ashley huffed as they dashed after him. The jungle was only yards away, but the girls didn't have Jake's stamina or speed.

Alexandria hissed, her spider fangs opening and closing. Her eight legs glided over the sand, and she caught up to Kristin quickly, spitting a web around her. Kristin screamed.

"Jake!" Kristin cried out.

Jake stopped and pivoted, gasping at the sight of Kristin covered with slimy web that seemed to push her down into the sand. The giant black spider behind her slowed, savoring going in for the kill.

"Kristin!" Ashley screamed. She looked around the jungle for a weapon, stumbling upon a ragged branch.

Jake searched for a weapon, but all he could see were twigs and other debris blown on the sand from the jungle. He saw Alexandria open her fangs and slowly walk towards Kristin and knew he had to act fast. He grabbed the pointiest branch that he could find and ran towards Alexandria as if he were holding a javelin.

As Ashley smashed at the spider, Jake launched his twig at it.

"Suck on this!" Jake yelled. The twig plunged into Alexandria's belly. He smiled with victory as the giant spider convulsed and retched out webs.

Jake and Ashley ran to help Kristin pull herself out of the goo, and while she broke free, she cringed at the sticky, wet sensation on her flesh.

"We don't have much time," Ashley said as she helped Kristin to her feet.

Kristin nodded as she reached for Jake's extended hand, but before they could take off, they heard a loud *crack*.

"What's that?" Kristin asked.

They turned around and gaped in horror as the twig fell out of the spider's abdomen, which cracked open slowly like an egg breaking. The abdomen split in two, and Kristin, Jake and Ashley sprinted towards the forest, away from the millions of baby spiders that emerged from Alexandria's dead body.

Now in the lead, Ashly looked at the map and saw she was getting closer to the white horse.

As Jake and Kristin ran through the brush behind her, the leaves of giant exotic plants slapped across their faces.

Kristin glanced behind her and saw that the baby spiders were not as slow as their mother. Their thin legs danced towards them as they moved silently through the grass and dirt.

"They're gaining on us!" Kristin said.

"We're almost to the white horse!" Ashley said.

Kristin tried to push forward, but the baby spiders had already made it to her shoe, traveling up her pant legs and up to her torso. She grimaced as they caressed her body with their fragile legs, and she cried out in pain when a baby spider took its first bite on her back.

"Ow!" Kristin screamed as Jake pulled her along.

"We're almost there!"

"We're close to the horse!" Ashley said. They were only yards away from the clearing of the jungle.

But it didn't matter.

Kristin felt the bite blow up into an oily boil on her flesh, and she cried out again when another spider slid into her shoe and bit the ball of her foot.

"I can't make it, Jake!"

"Yes, you can!" Jake said, trying to get her to run beside him.

She winced, the pain on her body too strong. "Go without me!" she said.

"I can carry you," Jake said. "The spiders aren't trying to get me."

It was true. They seemed to only be attracted to Kristin, and Jake used that to his advantage. He stopped and attempted to hoist Kristin onto his back, but the spiders had formed a cocoon around her, pulling her in the opposite direction.

"Ashley, stop!" Jake screamed.

Ashley stopped, and turned. When she saw Kristin in her cocoon, her eyes filled with tears. "Oh, god," she whimpered.

Suddenly, the timepiece around Kristin's neck opened, and the hands of the clock showed that there were only minutes left.

"Leave me," Kristin said as the spiders began to cover her face. Some entered her ear canals while others traveled up her nose. She cried as they danced across her body, as they nibbled on her skin.

"I can't," Jake said with tears in his eyes.

"We're not going to leave you!" Ashley screamed.

"You have to save yourself," Kristin said. "Save Ronnie."

"It's not fair," Ashley cried. "You should've taken the deal. You could've been home." She looked around for another stick, but everything around them was too small and brittle.

Kristin's eyes watered as she attempted to remain strong. "You've got to go. I love you both."

Jake tried to break through the barrier of baby spiders so that he could grab Kristin, but they had formed an unbreakable bond. Jake watched in horror as they covered Kristin's entire face before dragging her to the ground, forcing her onto her knees. His eyes searched around for something to make fire with, for a weapon, for water, for anything, but there was nothing he could find to free her.

"We'll stay with you," Ashley said.

"Go! Beat Hell's Game," Kristin said before the rest of the spiders entered her mouth.

Jake and Ashley looked at one another. They only had moments to decide what they were going to do.

With tears in their eyes, Jake and Ashley broke free of their daze and raced out of the forest, towards the sunlight and the white horse token.

CHAPTER TWENTY

Since Ashton's suicide, Ashley had not entered her father's church, let alone his office. She found it eerie to walk through the space, to see her father's massive desk made of oak, to see his leather chair behind the desk.

She rubbed her arms.

The room was unbearably cold, unbearably quiet. She stood near the doorway without a door and gazed at the large space. The wood floors. The wood walls. The expensive leather furniture. She took a deep breath and gazed around the room, wondering where to find the white horse.

"We're in your father's office?" Jake asked, confused.

Both of them looked worn. Tired. Their eyes were still red from crying.

For a second, Ashley was able to hold herself together, but then she burst into sobs.

Jake hurried over to comfort her.

"Why are we here, Ashley?" Jake asked.

Before she could answer, the leather chair behind the desk creaked as it was pushed an inch away. Ashley's head darted to look in that direction. She walked over to the desk and bent down, having an inkling of what she would find. When she saw nine-year-old Ashton hiding behind the desk, her worst fear was confirmed.

"Hey, Ash," Ashley said to the young boy. He looked ahead, straight through her as if she weren't even there.

He said nothing.

"He can't see me," Ashley said, and when he didn't respond, she knew it was true.

"So what are we reliving?" Jake asked.

Ashley's sad eyes told him silently to wait and see.

The door creaked open, which surprised Ashley and Jake considering there were no physical doors present. They looked in the direction of the noise, and to her horror, Ashley saw herself as a little girl, wearing a pretty lace dress as she run into the room, giggling.

"Ashton!" young Ashley called out. "Ashton, where are you?"

Underneath the table, Ashton giggled. He loved playing hide-and-seek with his twin sister, and he especially loved to hide underneath this desk, his favorite spot. Ashley knew perfectly well where her brother was hiding, but it was fun to tease him a little.

"Ashton! Ashton! Come out!"

"Ashley, what are you doing here?"

The sound of the deep male voice brought chills down Teen Ashley's back. Her face paled, goose pimples forming all over her arms.

Young Ashley turned to see Tom Ryder, a friend of her father's who had come to Deer Creek for the weekend. He had been a friend of Benedict Gemini's since they were in college, and following graduation, Tom had taken over his family's oil empire. When Tom had come to visit the Gemini family, they were still living in the house next door to the Graces. They were modestly wealthy thanks to Heather's parents' money, but they were nothing compared to Tom, who wore tailored designer suits and came into town in a Ferrari.

Teen Ashley stared at Tom, who was handsome and charming with black hair and a square jaw, but he gazed at young Ashley in a way that no man should ever look at a child. Teen Ashley stepped back, covering her mouth with her hand.

"Not again," she whispered, as Tom locked the invisible door behind him.

"Can you keep a secret?" Tom Ryder asked nine-year-old Ashley as he hovered above her. Nine-year-old Ashley tensed, knowing something wasn't safe, but too innocent to know what was about to happen.

Jake could not believe what he was watching. He felt like he was going to vomit.

Behind them, teen Ashley watched, tears in her eyes. She had memorized this scene in her head, knowing everything that was about to be said, about to happen. She smelled his expensive, musky cologne. She heard the sound of him softly breathing. She felt the cold air on her skin.

"Tell him no, Ashley," teen Ashley said.

Jake looked at her, sorry that he had never known her dark secret, sorry that he could do nothing about it.

"I can keep a secret," child Ashley said, and Tom smiled.

He removed his expensive blazer and hung it over a chair. Trying to find a weapon, Teen Ashley looked around the room and noticed a heavy candlestick on the bookshelf.

"Not this time!" Teen Ashley said. She attempted to grab it, but her hands reached through it as though she was a ghost. "No," she cried. Adrenaline ran through her as she ran to attack Tom before he could remove his pants, but like the candlestick, she glided through him. "No!" she screamed again as Tom approached her younger self.

"Do you want to make Uncle Thomas happy?" Tom said.

Teen Ashley attempted to run out of the room, out of the doorless entryway, but a force field blocked her from escape. She suddenly felt claustrophobic, despite the large size of the room.

Realizing there was no hope, she curled up in the corner, shielding her eyes. She didn't want to watch what was to happen next.

"Ashley?" a male voice said.

She heard the voice, but she chose to ignore it. She wanted to ignore all sounds that were within this room of horror, and the young Ashton underneath the desk acted the same way. Even as a child, he knew what he was hearing was wrong.

Ashley closed her eyes and began to hum to herself the song she had known when she was a child. *"I'll take care of you, until the end of the time. I'll always love you, but I can't make you mine..."*

"Ashley?" the voice repeated.

Ashley forced herself to look up and saw her teenaged brother hovering above her. He wore a black sweater and dark jeans, the same outfit he had worn the day he had shot himself.

"Ashton?" Jake asked.

"Is that really you?" Ashley asked. Even if his appearance was only a trick of The Game, she still wanted him to be there.

Ashton nodded. There was something in his eyes that made her realize it was really him.

"Is this your Hell too?" she asked.

He nodded. She could see that his eyes were also watering.

"You're trapped in this room until the scene is over," he said. "When it's over, we and Tom disappear until the next show."

"I want to go home," Ashley said, rubbing at her eyes.

"Then we've got to find the white horse," her brother replied.

CHAPTER TWENTY-ONE

Ashton remembered when the Gemini family moved from their house near the Graces to their giant estate in the country. He was ten years old, and he remembered how the family drove up to the house in their new car, and how he had watched the movers bring in the furniture that Heather and Benedict had recently purchased at a fancy department store.

"It's so beautiful," Heather said as she stared at the house. Benedict wrapped his arm around his wife and he kissed her on the cheek. "Thank you," she added.

"I told you one day I'd give us everything we wanted," Benedict said. He looked down at his sullen daughter Ashley, who hung back by the car.

Ashton remembered standing next to his parents, glaring up at them, glaring up at the house. Benedict had told his children that all of the new things were to make up for what had happened to the twins when they were nine years old. He had told them that they were being rewarded for their silence, and that with their new money no one would be able to hurt them again.

"Did the man go to jail?" Ashley had asked her father.

Benedict looked into her eyes and nodded. "Ashley, everything has been taken care of," he said. "I don't want us to ever speak of what happened ever again. Don't talk about it with Ashton. Don't talk about it with your Mommy. Don't talk about it with anybody. Understand me?"

"Yes, Daddy," Ashley said.

Benedict stared down at his son. "Understand me, Ashton?"

Ashton did not want to keep quiet the way Ashley did, but he did not know how to refuse his father either. He stared up at the man, a man he feared more than God, and mustered up all of the courage inside of him to say, "I'll tell."

Ashton winced when Benedict slammed his fist into his jaw, and Ashley stared in horror as Benedict removed his belt. Her father's eyes flashed with crazy, the sweat dripping from his forehead.

"God punishes the wicked," Benedict said, going into preacher mode. "My son will not disobey his father." Benedict proceeded to give Ashton twenty lashes, though the number had no meaning. He just whipped his son until he cowered on the floor. "My son will listen when his father speaks!" Benedict screamed.

Ashley shut her eyes, tears flowing down her cheeks. In her head, she hummed the song she knew.

"I'll take care of you, until the end of the time. I'll always love you, but I can't make you mine...

"I'm sorry we can't be together, pretty girl, but I promise through the darkness that I will guide you to the light..."

**

Since the incident with Tom Ryder, Ashton and Ashley avoided Benedict's office at church. They took his warning to never speak about what had happened—not to their mother, not to strangers, not even to each other.

But one morning before church service, when Ashton was twelve years old, his mother asked him for a favor. Ashton was dressed in a crisp white shirt and black slacks, and stared at his beautiful mother, who was preparing take-away packets for new members.

"Honey," Heather said, "Could you go upstairs and get more Wednesday Night Brochures? I'm all out."

"Sure, Mom," Ashton replied. "Are they in the supply closet?"

"No, I ordered some last week. I think the box is still in your dad's office."

Ashton's face paled, and his mother cocked an eyebrow, confused.

"Is something wrong, honey?" she asked.

"No, Mom," he said. "I'll go get them."

He knocked on his father's office's door, and when there was no response, he entered. He saw that in three years, his father had not made any changes to the room. The floors were just as shiny as he had remembered, the furniture still austere and uninviting. The giant desk remained in its same place, and Ashton couldn't believe that he had once felt safe hiding underneath it.

Ashton scanned the room in search of the brochures. He had hoped that the box would be out in the open, where he could find it and leave as quickly as possible, but neither the box nor the brochures were anywhere to be found.

At that moment, he had two choices. He could leave, go back to his mother and make her find the brochures herself; or he could spend a few agonizing minutes combing through his father's drawers and closets.

Not wanting to disappoint his mother, Ashton sighed and searched through the office's closet. No brochures.

He searched through the shelves. No brochures.

He searched through the desk drawers, knowing they were large enough to fit a large box, but to his dismay, no brochure could be found.

Feeling satisfied that he had tried, he was ready to leave the room when he noticed a small pull-out shelf underneath the top of the table. Ashton knew that the shelf couldn't hold the brochures, but curiosity got the best of him and he wanted to know what was inside.

He glanced from side to side, worried that someone would see him. He hadn't been nervous when he had opened the other drawers, but something about this shelf felt mysterious and secretive. He had a feeling that he wasn't supposed to see what was inside.

Still, he pulled the shelf towards him, revealing bank statements and other bills. Ashton's shoulders slumped with disappointment when he realized there was nothing juicy to be found.

Ashton rose from the desk and was about to leave when he stumbled over the waste basket next to the desk. "Shit!" he said to himself, noticing the chunks of torn cream-colored paper in the wastebasket. The papers were of little interest to him until he saw the blue inked signature of Tom Ryder.

"Tom Ryder?" Ashton muttered to himself as he pulled out the chunks. Working at a rapid pace, he put the tattered pieces together. When he read the message, his jaw trembled with anger.

Dear old friend,
Thank you for adhering to our agreement. Enclosed you will find your yearly payment of $250,000.
Best,
Tom Ryder.

"What agreement?" Ashton seethed. Hearing a noise in the hallway behind him, he quickly swept the pieces back into the trash.

"What are you doing?" he heard a deep voice ask.

Ashton jumped and turned to see his father staring at him with his arms crossed. Ashton stiffened and stood up straight, like a soldier would to a commanding officer who had entered the room.

"Nothing, sir," Ashton replied as Benedict approached him. He stared hard at his son, trying to gauge whether or not he was telling the truth. Ashton tensed, still terrified of his father after all of these years, praying that his father wouldn't guess what he had been looking at.

"Your mother told me you were looking for the Wednesday Night Brochures," Benedict said.

"I couldn't find them in here…"

"That's because they're in the supply closet."

"Oh," Ashton said, his face reddening at his father's scrutiny.

"Well, are you going to get them?" Benedict asked.

Ashton exhaled, happy to escape. He ran towards the door, not giving his father a moment to stop him.

Benedict shook his head at his imbecile son. Ashton would never know what it was to be a man. To have to make decisions. To have to stand up for what he wanted.

Benedict heard the door to the supply closet open and shut. He pulled out his leather chair from underneath the desk, and as he sat down, he noticed the waste basket, the fragments of his letter from Tom Ryder clearly in view. He looked to the door as he heard the sound of Ashton's shoes pounding downstairs. At that moment, he knew that his only son had known about the bargain that he had made with the devil.

**

The Holy Church of Christ's main room was vast. Its wooden pews polished and shiny. Its carpet clean and royal purple-red. Its ceiling high, and its windows large and made of stained glass. Everything looked the way Ashley had remembered it, except for the lack of doors.

Eighteen-year-old Ashton entered and saw the large cross behind the pulpit. Watching his sister, he stood in the doorway. She sat in the front pew by herself, frozen in horror.

He walked up to her, but she avoided his eyes.

"You need to find the horse…" he said gently.

She looked up at him, thankful that he looked like himself, not like a zombie with a gunshot in his head.

"Where's Jake?" Ashley asked.

"He's looking for the horse," Ashton replied. "As you should be."

"Is this what you've seen for the last year?" she asked.

Although the answer was yes, he didn't want to upset her. He could have added that he also had to relive the days that led up to his suicide, how all he could surround himself with was the misery from that time, the guilt he felt. But because he only wanted to get his sister out of the game, he remained silent.

She looked forward at the cross as her brother sat beside her. "How can this exist in Hell?" she asked, pointing at the cross.

Ashton looked at it, shaking his head. "Because the sanctity of this church was destroyed years ago," he asked. "What you see there has meaning for others, but for us, it is only decoration in a house of ungodliness."

Ashley stared harder at the cross, wondering if she could make it have meaning for her. Wondering that if she made it represent in her mind what it was meant to represent, it would disappear. She furrowed her brow, trying to believe, but the cross remained and her heart remained closed as well. She sighed and began to play with her hair as if she was going to tie it into a ponytail. That is when Ashton noticed her mark.

"What's this?" He reached over and touched the *666* branded onto the back of his sister's neck. She winced, thinking his fingers on her tattoo would sting somehow, but instead, it felt nice to feel the warmth of her brother's fingers on her skin.

"They wanted me to know that The Game was real," she replied.

"I can't believe They put this on you," he whispered. "It's disgusting."

Ashley agreed with him, but she didn't have to say it.

Although the minutes were ticking down until the level was over, neither of them could make themselves get up and help Jake find the horse. There was still too much to say.

"Where's Kristin?" Ashton asked.

She looked into his eyes. The sadness within them gave him his answer.

He stood up. "I'm going to look for the horse," he said, his voice choking. "Are you coming with me?"

"I'll do it in a second," she said.

He left the room, and Ashley resumed angrily staring at the cross behind the pulpit. The scene in her father's office replayed in her mind, making her sick and causing her body to turn to stone. She knew she needed to get up and fight for her life, but she was too tired. Too sad.

"You're running out of time," a voice said.

Ashley jumped in alarm, and she turned to see Eric Whitehorse sitting beside her. He wore a white suit with a striped white and gray tie, as dressed for Sunday sermon. Ashley gazed at the host of the game, surprised by how angelic he appeared up close. His perfect complexion radiated, and he really had the most beautiful eyes.

"Are you here to gloat?" Ashley said.

"Do you really want to stay here forever?" he asked.

"Of course not, but I can't find the horse."

"You've given up. You've given up the way Ashton gave up on his life. That's why he ended up here, you know. All suicides, no matter how good the soul, end up in Hell."

"So I've heard," Ashley replied sarcastically.

Eric examined her, the passionate girl who had tried to break through the mirrors in Level Two was no longer before him. The girl next to him was a quitter, and Eric didn't like quitters.

"You could use your lifeline," Eric said before he opened his closed fist to reveal a sparkling white horse token. Ashley stared at him, wondering why he was always making things so easy for them.

"What are you getting out of this, Eric?" She bore into his eyes, trying to find the truth. Was he helping them only to hurt them at the very last level? After all, he had helped Kristin only to turn the group against her in Level Three. And now she was dead.

Eric broke free from her gaze and he stared at the cross.

"Do you believe in God, Ashley?" he asked.

Without delay, she replied, "No."

"And why is that?"

Ashley cocked an eyebrow. Was he unaware of the scene that had occurred upstairs? Was he unaware of the deal her father made with Tom Ryder to keep his family silent? Was he unaware of the pain she had felt when her brother shot himself or when her best friends, her only true family, abandoned her?

Of course, he wasn't.

He knew what Ashley had gone through. He knew she wasn't the nicest person, but he also knew why she was the way she was. Of course she wouldn't believe in a Higher Power because if one existed, it had let a child lose her innocence and it had let that child grow up into a monster.

"Would you believe if you were me?" she asked.

He looked at her with kind eyes. "Sometimes faith is the only thing that can get a person through hard times, and you must understand this, Ashley. No matter who you are, no matter where you are, life will never be perfect. One must be able to fight the darkness if they want to find the light."

"You're sounding more like an angel than a demon," Ashley said.

Eric stared at Ashley, and she blushed. She shouldn't have insulted him, especially since he was still capable of keeping her or releasing her from Hell.

"I never told you the history of Hell's Game," Eric said. Ashley stared at him, unsure where this was leading, and he looked at the cross in front of him, unsure if he should reveal to her his ancient secrets. He then gazed at Ashley, whose beauty had always taken his breath away, whose beauty made him wish that he was born human.

"I thought Hell's Game was just for us," Ashley said, and Eric shook his head.

"Since the beginning, God and the Devil have been at war with one another, one side trying to save souls, the other side trying to damn them. The war has been played on Earth, and humans have been given free will to decide which side they want to be on. But in some cases, such as yours, those who are damned were damned by circumstances not entirely resulting from free will. That was why The Game was created. To give souls a chance to save themselves."

Ashley stared at Eric, whose handsome face made her want to trust him, but how could she? When he had appeared to be a small-town policeman, that had been a lie, so why wouldn't he pretend to be trustworthy at this point in the game? After all, if she were to let down her guard, then he could trap her in Hell and with him forever.

"Has anyone ever won the game?" Ashley asked.

"The Devil has a way of playing dirty," Eric replied.

Ashley took a deep breath, letting it compute in her mind that no one had ever won Hell's Game before. What made her and her friends any different?

"I'm going to make a deal with you," Eric finally said. "Just like God and the Devil made a deal to create this game."

"What kind of deal?" Ashley asked.

"What if I were to release your brother to play the end of the game with you?"

Her jaw dropped. Was he serious?

He was, but there was a catch.

"In exchange for your brother, I want you to make a promise to me."

"What's that?" Ashley asked.

"If you get out of The Game," Eric said. "Then I want you to promise that when I'm ready, you'll marry me."

She stared at him, shocked. In her wildest dreams, she never would have thought that would be the promise he would want her to make.

"You want me to be your wife?" Ashley asked. Her mind flashed to the future, where she saw herself and Eric, married, at their baby shower with all of Eric's gorgeous friends. In Ashley's lap, she held their baby, a demonic child with red skin and golden, snake-like eyes, while around them, Eric's friends cooed before revealing their fangs.

Eric watched as Ashley shuddered.

"You don't have much time to decide. What is it?" Eric asked.

"For a wedding proposal, this isn't very romantic."

"Would you like me to get down on one knee?"

There was a puff of smoke and suddenly a black band with a gigantic diamond appeared in his hand. Ashley gasped as he got out of his seat and kneeled beside her. His offer was real, but she only had seconds to decide whether or not to save her brother or just herself.

"So this is happening?" Ashley asked, still not totally believing it, even as Eric held her left hand.

He gazed into her eyes.

"I will keep my word if you keep yours. You may give your brother the chance to get out of Hell, and in return, you promise that when I am ready, you will be my wife. Swear that you will wait for me, no matter how long it takes."

"What are you doing?" Ashton asked.

Ashley turned to see that Ashton and Jake had entered, and they were staring at the scene in disbelief.

Eric ignored Ashton as he gazed up at Ashley. She stared at her brother, knowing right away that there was only one choice.

"I will marry you," she whispered.

Eric smiled. He slid the ring on her left hand's ring finger, and when it was in place, both Eric and the ring disappeared in a puff of smoke.

"What did you do?" Ashton asked as he stormed towards his sister. Meanwhile, Jake noticed the door that appeared in the once empty doorway.

Ashley stared at her hand, and even though there was no jewelry there, she could still feel the ring's weight on her finger.

"You didn't make a deal with him, did you?" Ashton asked.

She closed her fingers, wanting to make the ring's sensation go away, and when she opened her palm, she saw the white horse token resting in her hand.

"You're coming with us," Ashley said.

Ashton shook his head in horror. "No…" he said. "Ashley, what did you do?"

She walked over to her brother and without a word, she extended her hand. He took it. They looked at each other, understanding that they were to never mention to another person what they had seen on this level, the deal Ashley had made to save her brother. The only thing that mattered was that the bond between them was strong. The bond between them was real.

"I love you," Ashley said.

With tears in his eyes, Ashton replied, "I love you too."

She reached for the handle and pulled the door open. As she, her brother, and Jake crossed through to the other side, the sixes on the back of her neck disappeared.

CHAPTER TWENTY-TWO

Jake, Ashley, and Ashton found themselves in a garden, a vast land with plush grass and a wall of well-trimmed hedges that stood eight feet tall.

"It's like *Alice in Wonderful* or something," Jake said.

Ashley walked close to the wall, where she found an entrance, which of course did not have a door.

"I think I know what this level is," Ashley said, turning towards her brother and her former lover.

"You found a clue?" Ashton asked.

Ashley shook her head. "It's obvious. We're in a maze."

Behind her, she heard someone clapping. She turned to see Eric Whitehorse in a white suit reminiscent of something Colonel Sanders would wear. She glared at her future husband, still feeling the invisible ring around her finger.

Next to her, Ashton glared at Eric, his jaw trembling with rage. His love for Kristin, his anger and sadness at the loss of her in Hell caused his body to shake.

"What's wrong with you, Ashton?" Eric asked before Ashton completely lost it. He ran towards Eric, ready to tackle him, when Eric suddenly raised his hand, stopping him in his tracks.

"I wouldn't do that if I were you," Eric said. Ashton felt his breath stop and his body stiffen like it was made of wood. Without moving his paralyzed head, he gazed below and saw that Eric had used magic to levitate him off the ground.

"Eric, put him down!" Ashley cried as though she had any authority over their host.

"All I came to do was inform you about the level. Was it really necessary to attack me?" Eric asked Ashton, who was unable to nod or shake his head. "Especially after I gave you a second chance?" Eric then turned to Ashley. "The rules of the maze are simple. You can always move forward, but if you backtrack, there will be consequences."

"What kinds of consequences?" Jake asked.

Ashley knew that she wouldn't like the answer. Eric smiled, pleased. It was as though the person who had expressed his desire for her earlier had completely disappeared.

"For every step that you retrace, a being that is both a man and an animal with a horn and two hands will appear. He is not clever, but he is hungry, and his brothers are just as ferocious," Eric said.

Ashley glared at her future husband. "Can't you ever just speak like a normal person?" she snapped.

He stared at her hard, and she worried for a second that she had offended him. Suddenly, he pulled his arm back and she winced, afraid that he would strike her. Instead, a timepiece flew from his hands. As she caught it, Ashton was released to the ground.

She gawked at the timepiece and saw it was covered with sand and blood.

Ashley knew the blood was Kristin's.

"You monster," Ashley said, tearing up.

"In the maze, you may also want this," he said, and suddenly a large knife in a sheath appeared in both Jake and Ashton's hands.

"What? I don't get one?" Ashley asked.

Eric forced a smile at her before he disappeared, but she swore she saw sadness lingering behind his eyes.

"That guy really knows how to make an exit," Jake said as Ashley ignored him, her gaze fixed on the clock. Jake noticed the bits of blood caked onto its gold exterior.

Ashley opened its cover and saw that the minutes were ticking by. "We don't have much time," she said.

**

Tired and now hungry, Jake walked ahead of Ashley and Ashton. On the outside, the wall of thick bushes did not seem high, but inside the maze, they rose up high enough to block out the sun, making it hard to see for the three players. The space was quiet, and the strange scent of raw meat permeated the air.

"Make sure you don't step backwards," Jake advised.

"We heard him, too," Ashley retorted.

"This isn't time to fight," Ashton said as the three of them turned left. They had been walking through the maze for ten minutes now, and everything looked the same—just green walls and green corners. Ashley attempted to check the time using her timepiece, but the lack of light hurt her eyes as she squinted to read the clock.

"Eric didn't tell us where to find the white horse," Jake said. "He just gave us a riddle about what we would see if we backtracked."

"You could use your lifeline to get us out of here," Ashley said to Jake.

"But we have one level left after this," he replied.

"Your point?"

"I don't want to waste my lifeline the way Kristin did early on."

At the mention of Kristin's name, Ashton's eyes narrowed, and the fury inside of him boiled once again.

"So are you saying it was Kristin's fault she died?" he snapped.

Appalled that he would suggest that, Jake stared at him.

"That's not what I'm saying..." Jake said.

"Well, I don't like you talking shit about Kristin."

"That's not what I was doing..."

"That's what I heard."

"Stop blaming me for what happened!" Jake said.

"Guys, stop it!" Ashley squealed. She looked at Ashton and Jake and saw that they were inches away from each other, about to fight.

"You saved yourself, and you let her die. You deserve to be in Hell!" Ashton then attacked Jake, punching him in the eye.

Jake's body jerked back in surprise, while Ashley could only watch the fight, horrified.

"Stop it! What's wrong you two?" she screamed.

Once Jake got over his initial surprise, he swung back, punching Ashton in the stomach. Ashton toppled over and coughed, the blow causing him to lose wind.

As Ashley watched them wrestle to the floor, she felt a bag fly over her head and encapsulate her entire body.

**

Trapped inside of the bag, Ashley touched the fabric in front of her and discovered it was made of velvet. She then rubbed her face against the fabric, lost in its luxurious comfort.

"Hello?" she called out. "Hello, is anyone out there?"

Suddenly the fabric flew upwards—so quickly that her hair fluttered in the wind. She blinked rapidly, trying to help her eyes adjust from the darkness to the light. She found herself sitting in a bright, white room with lots of frameless windows, and when she saw who was her captor, she was annoyed but not surprised.

"What's happening?" Ashley asked Eric Whitehorse, who sat in front of a window. He stared below, like a watchman.

"Come sit beside me," he said.

She knew she had no choice. She joined him in a large white chair that appeared to disappear amidst the white of the room. Once she sat down, he reached for her hand. To her own surprise, she didn't feel like moving it away.

"Why did you remove me from the game?" Ashley asked, and Eric ignored her as he stared down at the gigantic maze made of tall green bush. To her horror, she saw Jake and Ashton fighting near the entrance.

"Your brother and your ex-boyfriend are really not being productive with their time," Eric said, still not looking at his future wife.

"We weren't even close to the end. Were we?" Ashley asked.

Eric didn't respond.

"How can we find the white horse?"

"I already gave you your clue."

Ashley glared at him. Why wouldn't he look at her?

"How can we find the white horse?" she repeated, angrier. Stronger.

"I already told you. For every step that you retrace, a being that is both a man and an animal with a horn and two hands will appear. He is not clever, but he is hungry, and his brothers are just as ferocious."

"So the being has the horse?"

"The being will kill everyone before he or she can find the white horse," Eric replied. "That's the clue. I told you all how you were going to die."

**

"Where's Ashley?" Ashton asked in a panic. He ran forward, leaving Jake behind. "Ashley! Ashley!" he called out.

Jake ran after him, following him with every zigzag and turn. "Ashton, where are you going? We have to be careful because we can't retrace our steps!"

"Ashley! Ashley!" Ashton called.

"Ashton, you need to be more careful!"

At a crossroads, Ashton gazed in every direction. He felt dizzy with worry. He had gotten a second chance at redemption, only to discover that the love of his life and his sister would not see him on the other side. It was too much for him.

"Ashley!" Ashton yelled, picking a path at random.

Jake knew that he was running down a path that they had already traveled, and his eyes widened with worry.

"Ashton! Don't go down there!"

Ashton continued to run, shouting his sister's name, and below him, a thick red line appeared in the grass with each step. Jake called after his friend, but he wouldn't stop.

"Fuck it," Jake said as he ran after Ashton, the line beneath him growing thicker. In the distance the boys heard a guttural moan and stopped.

"What was that?" Ashton asked.

"It's the being that Eric talked about."

"He said there'd be a being with each step. Do you think it's true?"

"I don't want to know. We've got to take another path."

Jake looked to his right and then to his left. He couldn't tell where they had come from, and Ashton had the same reaction.

"It all looks the same to me," Ashton said.

Jake gazed around. Each corner. Each direction. There was nothing distinguishable about anything in this maze.

"Why don't you use your lifeline?" Ashton asked.

"Because we have one more level to go!" Jake said. "Why don't you use your lifeline?"

"I don't have one, stupid!" Ashton said. "Get over your pride, Jake. We can't defeat this maze, and it's stupid to think otherwise!"

"We can figure it out," Jake said, and he made the executive decision to go down the path to his right. He ran, not consulting with Ashton, who was resigned to follow him. They looked underneath their feet and saw the red line appear. "Shit," Jake said before turning again. They looked at the grass and thankfully, saw that they were not backtracking.

"I told you," Jake said.

"You should've used your lifeline to save Kristin," Ashton said.

Jake stopped. He couldn't believe that Ashton wouldn't let up on this fight. Ashton and he had another face-off, but this time, there were to be no blows.

"I'm done fighting with you. Say everything you want to say and then never speak of it again," Jake commanded.

"We're not on the football field. You're not the captain anymore giving orders."

"Just talk, Ashton!"

Ashton took a deep breath, trying to compose his thoughts. It was easy for him to fight, but it was harder to express in words what he was feeling.

"Why didn't you use your lifeline to save Kristin?" Ashton asked.

"You weren't there. Things happened so fast, and when it got crazy, I just…I didn't use my head. If I could go back and do it again, I'd have saved her. I promise you I would've."

Ashton stared at him, still unconvinced.

"I don't believe you," Ashton said, and Jake threw up his hands in frustration.

"I know you don't, and I'm sorry, but we've got to find the white horse or we're stuck here. Does that give you reason enough to shut up?"

"You let Kristin die! I loved her, and you didn't protect her. What would you have done if it was someone you had loved? How would you feel?"

Hearing Ashton's words shook Jake to his core. He loved Kristin just as much as Ashton did, and he fought himself not to say that aloud.

"What? The big bad Jake has nothing to say? You know I'm right. You're a…"

"I loved her, too!"

The words exploded out of Jake's mouth, and he immediately regretted them.

Ashton stared at him. Did he hear what he had thought he heard?

"What did you say?" Ashton asked.

"Don't tell me I don't know how you feel. I loved her too. And don't act like you're a better man than me. You left her first."

Jake began to walk away as Ashton stood paralyzed with the news. Once he understood what had happened, he screamed out, "Then why didn't you use your lifeline?"

Jake ignored him as he ran forward. He ran so hard that he wasn't paying any attention to where he was going. It just felt good to feel his body exert energy, to focus on running and not the thoughts churning through his head. He was so out of his head that he didn't see the eight-foot-tall beast blocking his path until the beast roared.

Jake and Ashton gasped.

The beast had the head of a bull and the body of a man. A giant ring hung from his nostrils, and he foamed at the mouth as he smiled. He was hungry, and he had finally found his dinner.

CHAPTER TWENTY-THREE

The minotaur stared down at Jake, his harsh breath causing Jake's lip to curl. Jake looked away from the minotaur's face, and his hand slowly reached for the handle of the knife attached to the sheath clipped to his pants. Ashton watched from behind as Jake jerked the knife out and plunged it into the minotaur's chest.

The beast howled, and Jake pulled the knife out and stepped back. As the blade dripped with dark blood, the beast seemed to freeze, but Jake could still hear him breathing.

"What do we do?" Ashton asked.

Jake stepped back slowly, a red line forming underneath his feet.

"Run," Jake said, and he and Ashton took off.

The minotaur roared to life and lumbered after them, drool dripping off of its teeth.

"Where should I go?" Ashton called.

"Turn left!" Jake replied.

"I think we've been there before."

"Screw it. Just go!"

Ashton turned right, dismissing Jake's order, and to his dismay, he saw more red lines form underneath his feet. In the distance, they heard another roar.

"Is that another minotaur?" Ashton asked.

"They must show up whenever we backtrack!" Jake replied.

"I'm sorry," Ashton said, turning around. "I should've listened to you."

"Just keep going!" Jake said.

They continued running, and as the first minotaur began to close in, Jake lapped Ashton and led him down another corner. He glanced down and saw that no red lines underneath him. They had found fresh territory.

Suddenly, a white horse dashed past them before disappearing.

"What was that?" Ashton asked.

"It was a horse," Jake said, confused.

"Do you think that's the white horse we need?"

"I don't know. I thought we were supposed to find a token…"

As Jake and Ashton passed an opening, they saw a second beast appear. A being that was half man and half goat—a satyr. Unlike the minotaur, the satyr looked non-menacing, except for the bow and arrow he had pointed at the boys.

The arrow flew towards them, but they ran fast, avoiding being hit. The thought of searching for the horse, not the token, escaped their mind.

"Where's this white horse?" Ashton asked as they ran. The satyr hurried towards them, launching arrows as he moved, his hooves stomping in the grass.

"I don't know," Jake said. "But at least we've only got two monsters."

"For now," Ashton said. He looked behind him and saw that the minotaur was slowing down. The beast clutched at his chest, where Jake had wounded him, and then he fell to his knees.

An arrow whizzed past Ashton's face, and he panicked as the satyr got closer.

"For a little guy, he sure is fast!" Ashton said.

"Just keep going!" Jake said.

Another arrow shot past them, only this time, it nicked Jake in the arm.

"Ow!" Jake screamed.

"Why don't you use your lifeline?" Ashton asked.

"There's only one beast. I'm not going to waste it now!"

Ashton glared at the back of Jake's neck, at the sixes burning on his flesh. This was not the time to believe one was invincible, and Ashton was amazed at how much pride Jake possessed in himself.

Jake arrived at another crossroads and stopped. He only had seconds to decide which direction to turn.

Ashton pulled up beside him. "I think we should go there," he said, pointing to his right. The path that lay ahead was full of roses along the walls. He was certain that they hadn't taken that way yet.

"Are you sure?" Jake asked.

"I'm sure."

Jake looked at Ashton, who appeared resolute. He glanced down at the path Ashton had chosen before he turned and bolted in the opposite direction.

Ashton felt hurt, but followed Jake nonetheless. To their dismay, a red line appeared underneath their feet, and another monster roared.

"Oh, God," Ashton said. "What's next?"

An arrow flew towards them and landed in Ashton's shoulder blade.

"Argh!" he screamed in pain, and as Jake stared at him, he had a terrible feeling of déjà vu. It was like watching Kristin perish all over again, only this time Jake wasn't going to make another mistake.

"Eric!" Jake screamed to the sky as he ran with Ashton limped behind him. To his wonderment, the white horse stomped away in the distance. "Eric, I want to use my lifeline!"

Ashton was thankful, happy to receive a free pass to the next level, but after several seconds of slogging along in pain, he realized that Eric wasn't coming.

"Where is he?" Ashton asked in alarm. Shooting pains roared from the arrow's tip, and he started to feel light-headed. The arrow must have been filled with poison.

"Eric, I use my lifeline!" Jake repeated as he saw his friend black out. His own arm felt a sharp tingle where the arrow had nicked him. "Eric!"

Another arrow soared past as a horned centaur appeared on the other side of the wall. It stood twelve feet tall, so Jake and Ashton could only see its face and horn. It glared down at the boys with coal-dark eyes and whinnied like a horse. Its face was hard, angry, and when it opened its mouth, fire flew outwards.

Jake felt his body break out into a sweat. "Eric, where are you?" he screamed again into the air, but no matter how many times he screamed, Eric was not going to come.

**

Ashley stared down at the game. One of her hands was on the glass while the other hand's fingers remained on her lips. She saw when the arrow struck Ashton, saw when Jake hoisted her brother on his back and tried feebly to run with him. Meanwhile, the white horse galloped on the other side of the maze, and there was no way that they would find it in the allotted amount of time.

"Why don't you help him?" Ashley asked Eric, who brooded in the corner.

"Did you know I wasn't supposed to give any lifelines?" Eric asked.

Ashley stared at him. "What?"

"I wasn't supposed to give you lifelines or help in any way. All I was supposed to do was introduce you to the rules and leave. I don't have the power to help anymore."

"You had the power to give me the horse in the last level. You had the power to take me here. You *have* to have the power to save them."

"I wasn't supposed to do that. I can help you in subtle ways, but completely rescuing everyone during the second to last level? I can't get away with that."

"That doesn't explain you helping me now."

"I didn't want the monsters to destroy you."

"What are you talking about?" Ashley asked, disgusted.

Eric looked at her sadly. "No one has ever gotten past this level," he said.

"How can that be? I thought this game was created by God and the Devil to win back souls?"

"It was, but that doesn't mean The Gamemakers didn't create a game that while not impossible to win, is nearly impossible to win."

Ashley watched as her brother and Jake battled the centaur with their knives. Ashton feebly stuck his blade into the centaur's side, but it lashed back at them, kicking Jake in the stomach and causing him to fly.

"They're going to die!" Ashley yelled.

"Yes," Eric said, true remorse on his face.

"You said if I would agree to marry you that you'd let Ashton go!"

"I said you can take him to the next round of the game. I didn't promise you he'd win."

Ashley was crying now. She hated how unfair this game was. She hated being manipulated and tricked. She hated feeling helpless.

It dawned on her that this was how she often made people feel, and she didn't like it.

"What if we made another deal?" Ashley asked.

"I shouldn't have made the deal with you in the first place. I'm no better than a demon now."

She cocked an eyebrow. She thought he *was* a demon.

"What are you?" she asked, but he looked away. She approached him and placed her hand on his cheek, forcing him to look at her.

"I can't give your brother and Jake a lifeline. They won't let me. I'm sorry."

Her eyes bore into him. "Don't say that. What if I made another deal?"

"Angels don't do deals."

"You're not an angel…"

He stared back into her beautiful blue eyes, and to her surprise, he kissed her, pulling her close. She first wanted to pull herself away, but she loved the urgency of his kiss, the feel of his mouth. The energy between them sent chills throughout her body. No man had ever made her feel this wanted.

He pulled her onto his lap and kissed her again, harder, hungrier. She wrapped her arms around him and let herself fall into the moment. Everything was so wrong that it felt right.

"We can't keep doing this," Eric whispered into her ear, and it was like the spell had broken. She remembered what was happening below.

"Stop the game," Ashley replied.

"I don't have that power."

"What power do you have?" she asked.

He avoided her eyes. "The only thing I can do…"

"What can you do?" she asked as he trailed off. He didn't want to tell her, but she was running out of time.

"The only thing I can do," Eric said with great sadness, "is send you back."

She stared at him, knowing that she needed to save Jake and her brother.

"Then send me back," she said.

He looked away because he didn't want to.

"You have to send me back, Eric," Ashley said. She squeezed his hand and gazed into his beautiful eyes, finding herself lost in their depth. "If you love me, then you'll send me back."

"Please," he said, begging her not to make him, but no amount of pleading would change her mind.

"Send me back in," Ashley said. With his jaw trembling, Eric raised his hand. He moved his finger swiftly, and she disappeared.

He bowed his head, praying that his love would be safe. He walked to the window and gazed out into the maze, pressing his forehead to the glass. He then sang a song, the one he sang to Ashley when she was a little girl. The song that he had sung to her so that she would feel protected when the people in her life harmed her.

"*I'll take care of you, until the end of the time. I'll always love you, but I can't make you mine…*"

He touched the glass as though able to reach Ashley through it, but he knew that he was limited to help.

"*I'm sorry we can't be together, pretty girl,*" Eric sang, "*But I promise through the darkness that I will guide you to the light…*"

**

There was a crack of lightning, and Ashley opened her eyes to find herself in the middle of the maze. In her hand, she held a sword, which she had never used before, and around her wrist was a small shield. Nearby, behind various walls, she could hear her brother and Jake fight to the death with a beast from Hell.

Ashley squeezed the handle of her sword as she looked to the dark gray sky where she knew Eric was watching.

"Thank you," she said, though she knew she wasn't going to receive a response. Then she stood up and ran.

CHAPTER TWENTY-FOUR

"The horse," Ashley whispered when she saw the white horse gallop past. Holding her sword to her side, she ran, the desire for freedom fueling her body. "Stop!" she screamed. Her feet pounded onto the hard dirt, and as she pushed herself to go faster, she found that the horse was getting farther away in the maze.

"Ashley!" Ashton said. Ashley whipped her head to discover her brother and Jake huddled in a dark corner. Ashton was shivering, his skin pale. He had removed his shirt, and Ashley gasped when she saw the gash on his shoulder where the poisoned arrow had entered.

"I can't let you die again," Ashley said, her eyes filling with tears.

"Eric won't help us," Jake said, eying the sword she held.

"Then we've got to help ourselves," Ashley replied. "Jake, you've got to carry Ashton on your shoulders. The white horse is nearby. We've just got to catch him."

Jake held up his right arm, which was singed black.

"I don't know if I can. We just ran into a centaur who breathed fire," Jake said. "My arm's pretty messed up."

"Enough for you to give up?" Ashley asked, staring into Jake's eyes. "We didn't come this far and we didn't lose Kristin so that you could wuss out because of a singed arm. Get up!"

Jake stared back at her, and then looked at the wounded Ashton, who spent two years in Hell only to be given a chance to escape. Jake looked at Ashley again, and it dawned on him that he was finally thankful for her bossiness.

"You're right," he said. He carefully moved to Ashton and took his arm, wrapping it around his neck. "I'm going to carry you, buddy."

Ashton, who had been coming in and out of consciousness, laughed. "Are you going to carry me across the threshold?"

"I'm going to carry you until the end," Jake said.

Ashton smiled as Jake lifted him up before closing his eyes again.

Jake turned to Ashley. "What's the plan, boss?"

Ashley's ears perked as she listened for the sounds of the horse's galloping. She heard nothing, but Jake spotted a bright green line forming underneath her feet.

"What's that?" Jake asked.

Ashley looked down. "Eric," she whispered.

Jake looked at her quizzically, but said nothing as she followed the green path. Carrying Ashton, Jake walked behind her, and she held up her sword as she turned left. The green line lengthened, and Ashley couldn't believe it when she heard the horse whinny behind a green wall.

After another turn, Ashley saw the white horse in the middle of a clearing. She watched as it stooped to drink water from an ornate fountain, and she couldn't believe how close they were to reaching the next level, the last level of Hell's Game.

Ashley stepped into the clearing while Jake struggled to carry Ashton. He stood next to her, as transfixed by the sight of the white horse as she was. It seemed to shine in the light, just as the token did.

Because of the horse, however, Ashley and Jake didn't seem to notice the army of minotaurs, satyrs, and centaurs who stood at attention around the walls of the clearing. The minotaurs stomped in place, the satyrs had their poisoned bow and arrows ready to shoot, and the centaurs blew smoke from their nostrils, ready to shoot fire out of their mouths.

Ashley looked to Jake, who shared her expression of terror. Ashton's jaw hung open as he slept, his breathing quiet and short as though his body was fighting to live.

"We don't need to kill these monsters," Ashley said. We just have to get to the white horse."

"You're going to have to fight them if you want me to carry your brother," Jake said.

Ashley nodded and took a deep breath. "Okay," she said. She held up her sword like a baseball bat, her face even more serious than before. "Ready," she said. She took a deep breath to compose herself.

Jake tensed, ready to sprint. "Set," he said as he looked forward.

"Go!" Ashley screamed before running towards the white horse. As she got closer to it, she noticed the token woven into its hair.

The satyrs released their arrows towards the sprinting Ashley and the slower Jake, who jogged while carrying Ashton, his tongue hanging out of his mouth. Ashley held up her shield to cover her face, but it wasn't able to protect her sides or Jake and Ashton's exposed bodies.

The centaurs rushed towards them, fire flying out of their mouths.

The minotaurs rushed towards the trio, their heavy steps causing the earth to rumble. Jake lost his footing because of the quake, and groaned in pain as an arrow punctured him in the back. He dropped Ashton, who rolled onto the grass before he himself fell to the ground.

"Jake!" Ashley watched as he writhed in pain. "Are you okay?" she asked as she bent to shield Jake.

"Get the white horse," Jake whispered as his entire vision clouded red. "Win the game. Save Ronnie."

Ashley teared up before she looked at her brother and gasped.

"No," she said. "No!"

Ashton laid in the grass, his eyes wide open but lifeless. Ashley couldn't believe that she had offered herself to a demon to save her brother from Hell, only to lose him less than an hour later.

Angry, she looked to the white horse, still drinking from the fountain. Ashley gazed at it and then back at Jake, who was starting to pale like her brother had just before he died.

"Don't leave me, Jake," Ashley whispered before she heard a loud roar above her. She looked up to see an angry minotaur bringing his arm down ready to strike. Ashley rolled out of the way, and to her horror, she watched as the minotaur smashed Jake's head. She cringed when she heard the sound of his skull crack.

"Oh my God," she said, crying.

She scurried away and ran towards the horse, towards the token in its hair. More satyr arrows flew past her head, and Ashley put up her shield to block her face. She winced as she felt the arrows ram into her shield, and with her free hand she swung her sword, slicing the arrows before they had a chance to come to her.

The white horse saw Ashley approaching and galloped away. But Ashley was quicker. She dropped her sword to the ground and grabbed the horse's hair, using it to hoist herself on its back. The token fell into her hand.

Suddenly, a white door appeared, and she held on tightly to the horse's mane as she guided it through the threshold. Ashley took one last look behind her at the chaotic scene of the centaurs, minotaurs, and satyrs attacking the dead bodies of Jake and Ashton. She closed her eyes tight, trying to fight the tears as the white light flashed and transported her to the other side.

CHAPTER TWENTY-FIVE

In a white room so bright that it was hard to tell where the walls began and ended, Eric sat on a bench with his head in his hands. He wore a white t-shirt and white linen pants.

"She survived," Chair White said as he approached.

Eric turned, revealing to the old man his red, teary eyes. "What about the others?" he asked.

Chair White shook his head. "I'm sorry," he said.

Eric only nodded. He had hosted many games in the past century, and he had seen many players meet their ends in Hell. He had learned to remove his emotions, to distance himself from caring, but he had come to care about the group from Deer Creek. He had also made the fatal mistake of falling in love with one of them.

Chair White sat next to Eric, and both of them looked ahead, avoiding the others' gazes.

"What if she fails the last level?" Eric asked.

"Then that is her fault and no longer your concern," Chair White said.

Eric looked away, angry, while Chair White continued to examine him. "I know that you helped the girl even after we forbid you from doing so," Chair White added. "I am afraid that I will be stripping you of your title, your responsibilities, and your powers. You cannot be trusted, and we cannot have you meddling in the affairs of humans when it is not your job to do so."

Eric looked at Chair White, unsure of what else he was going to say.

"Does Chair Black know?" Eric asked, and Chair White nodded.

"The Council has been fully aware of your actions, even since the beginning of the game."

"Then why did they allow me to cheat?"

"Because to them, it is more fun to punish an angel than three humans."

"I should have protected her better," Eric whispered.

"We can only give them help, Eric. We cannot interfere with the actions brought upon by man's free will. You knew that, yet you disobeyed the rules set."

"The Gamemakers are going to punish me. Aren't they?"

Chair White nodded. Then quietly, he stood, and Eric avoided his eyes.

"Goodbye, Eric," Chair White said, but Eric continued to look ahead, not giving his usual respects. After all, this goodbye would be his last.

CHAPTER TWENTY-SIX

"No way," Ashley muttered.

Using the tombstone next to her as an aid, she helped herself stand. After she got to her feet, her eyes darted back and forth, taking in the familiar surroundings. She took a deep breath, trying to brace herself for the final level of Hell's Game, the door disappearing behind her.

"So this is it," she said as she stared at the Deer Creek Cemetery. Just like on Halloween night two years ago, it was eerily quiet. No crickets were out. No creatures were stirring. The sky was clear and cloudless. The air smelled like dry grass and evergreens, and the only sound Ashley heard was her footsteps against the grass as she limped closer to the church. Without any new instructions, she knew what she was going to see and knew that this round would not be about finding a white horse.

"Oww," Ashley groaned as she took another step. Tears escaped her eyes as her face contorted with pain. She looked down at her calf as she moved and saw that two arrows had found their way into her calf. The poison within the arrowheads slowly shot up her leg, but she wouldn't stop.

"You don't have to do anything you don't want to do," she heard sixteen-year-old Jake say while Ronnie looked at him, knowing that he was lying. Ashley approached the scene, and to her astonishment, she saw Ronnie, Jake, Ashton, and Kristin, alive and healthy. They wore the same clothing they wore on that life-altering night two years ago, and Ashley herself was there, wearing her angel costume. As dirty, bloody, eighteen-year-old Ashley stared at her former self, she realized how silly she had appeared.

Ashley looked at the church that was now missing its iron door.

"Can we go now?" Kristin asked. "My mom's probably realized I'm not in my room by now."

Ashton and Angel Ashley stared coldly at Ronnie, who looked so frustrated that he was about to cry. Eighteen-year-old Ashley watched, surprised at how cruel she had once been, how cruel Ashton had been because of her.

"No one can be a part of this group without being initiated," Angel Ashley said. "And this is your initiation. If you don't do everything I say tonight, then you're not in the group."

Older Ashley shook her head. She couldn't take it anymore. "Shut up!" she cried. "Shut up! Do you know what you're saying?"

Unlike the level in her father's church, however, the characters in this game could hear her.

"What?" Angel Ashley asked as she and the rest of the party turned around. She was about to ask, "Who are you?" when she recognized herself and became tongue-tied.

Ashley stared at Ronnie, who stared back at her as he scratched his scalp. Specks of dandruff flew out and onto his shoulder.

"Ronnie," Older Ashley said, "You don't have to go in there."

Ronnie stared at her, wondering if his mind was playing a trick on him. He looked up at the church, which seemed to stare back at him with sad eyes.

"See, this is stupid," Jake said, holding up his keys. "Let's go."

Jake started to walk away, but Ronnie didn't follow him. He seemed to be harboring rage from years of being talked down to.

"Ronnie?" Jake asked.

Ronnie glared at him, but remained silent.

"Oh, come on…" Jake said. He had had enough of this nonsense and was ready to go.

Older Ashley couldn't believe that despite her interference, the scene was replaying nearly exactly the way it had two years ago.

"We all were initiated," Angel Ashley lied. She looked to Ashton for confirmation. "Tell him, Ashton." Ashton shrugged his shoulders, and Ashley smiled before looking at Kristin. "Kristin agrees too," Ashley said. "Right, Kristin?"

Kristin looked at her, not knowing what to say. Older Ashley stared at her beautiful friend, who was once so sweet and innocent. Older Ashley felt horrible for the way she used to manipulate her.

"I'm going!" Jake yelled as he held up his car keys, but he had only taken three steps before he had stopped.

"It's almost eleven," Ashton informed.

"Make a decision already, *Pencil Dick,*" Angel Ashley said.

"What did you call me?" Ronnie asked, his cheeks flushed red.

"No…" Older Ashley said, shutting her eyes and covering her ears. She couldn't believe it was happening again.

"Nothing," Angel Ashley said. "All I'm saying is that if you don't go into the church after eleven, then you can return to your old status and kiss being our friend goodbye. I don't need your stinking pictures. I'll take them myself."

She walked right up to him and snatched his camera, hanging on a breakable cord around his neck. She made sure to make a big show of taking photos of everything around her.

"What's wrong with you?" Older Ashley yelled at her younger self, but Ashley being Ashley, she ignored her.

With his jaw hanging, Ronnie stared at the twins before glancing at the church.

"Go into the church," Angel Ashley said as she bore into Ronnie, "and I promise you that no one will ever call you Pencil Dick again." She returned the camera to him and gently clasped the strap back around his neck.

"That church is The Gateway to Hell, Ronnie!" Older Ashley screamed. "Who cares who calls you Pencil Dick? Don't give up everything because a high school bitch asks you to!"

Everyone stared at her now, but she only focused on Ronnie.

"Please," she said. "Don't go in there."

Ronnie felt torn as he looked from Ashley to the mysterious person who had just arrived. Angel Ashley promised the one thing that he had wanted more than anything— acceptance, yet the stranger seemed so adamant about the danger he would face.

Older Ashley stared at him, praying silently that he would listen. She watched as his eyes darted from her to her younger self, but to her dismay, Ronnie marched up to the metal door of the church.

"Ronnie! No!" Older Ashley cried. She watched as the lights came on inside the building. Ashley attempted to run towards the church, but she ran into an invisible force field. She groaned as her body impacted it.

Jake stared at her, stunned, but Kristin, Angel Ashley, and Ashton were too busy watching Ronnie, who had his hands on what would have been the door's handle.

"Are you going to go in or what?" Angel Ashley asked.

Ronnie let go of the invisible handle, looking at the sinister-looking building in front of him. His initial courage had vanished, and he felt his palms sweat. He wiped them against the sides of his jeans.

"So what's it going to be, Smalls?" Angel Ashley called out.

"Ronnie, don't go in there!" Older Ashley said. Jake stared at her. Why did this stranger care so much?

Ronnie turned his back to the group before putting his hands on the handle. The laughter inside roared, a fire erupting behind the windows.

"What's happening?" Kristin said.

"What's that smell?" Ashton asked before the group realized that Ronnie's hands were burning.

"Help me!" Ronnie begged. "Help me!" The sinister laughter erupted just as the doors flew open.

"Ronnie!" Older Ashley screamed. As the rest of the group watched, paralyzed, Ashley ran against the force field. She slapped her body against the field so hard that she thought she was going to black out. The pain in her calf was excruciating, but she fought through it, just like she fought through her hysterical tears.

"Don't take him!" Older Ashley screamed. "If you want someone, then take me!"

The force field dissolved, and Older Ashley flew forward, towards the church. Although scared, she was glad they were taking only her, but to her dismay, a gnarled hand grabbed Ronnie as the other one snatched her. The hands felt old and crusty, smelling like sulfur.

"Nooo!" Jake yelled as the hands retreated into the church, the doors slamming shut.

CHAPTER TWENTY-SEVEN

Compared to the interior of the Holy Church of Christ, the Deer Creek Cemetery church was vastly underdressed. It consisted of only one room made of stone pews and a stone pulpit, and there were only two glassless windows.

"Congratulations," the deep voice of Chair Black said.

A broken, bloody, and nearly dead Ashley laid on the floor. She raised her head to see Ronnie, wearing the clothes he had worn on Halloween night two years earlier. He was tied to a plain wooden chair, his mouth gagged. Behind him, Chair Black stood in front of the other Gamemakers in Black. Without knowing who they were, Ashley could sense how sinister they were.

"Why do I not feel like I've won?" Ashley asked.

Chair Black smirked. "Because you're a clever girl," he replied, and the council behind him smiled. "Would you like somewhere to sit?"

The pain in Ashley's leg was as good as amputated, so bad that she couldn't get up.

"I'll remain on the floor, thanks."

"Very well," Chair Black said. "Enough with the pleasantries."

Even in pain, Ashley cocked her eyebrow at his ridiculousness. Members of the council bristled, nervous about how the Chair would react.

However, venom and ice coursed through his veins, and he was impervious to emotion. He stared at Ashley coolly as he continued to speak.

"We commend you for making it this far and for removing your Mark. What you've accomplished is a rare occurrence."

Ashley stared at him. "But?" she asked.

"But we know how much you were helped," Chair Black said. The coldness of his voice filled her with dread, and when he smiled, she became gripped with fear. "The rules were clearly stated. If you win the game, you free Ronnie's soul from Hell as well as freeing yourself from eternal damnation when the time comes. However, that is only if the game is played fairly. Because you were given a timepiece, clues, and lifelines, we ruled that you are only partially due the grand prize."

Ashley stared at Ronnie, who pleaded at her with his eyes even though he couldn't speak.

"So this is your choice," Chair Black said. "You can either save Ronnie Smalls from eternal damnation or yourself."

Ashley glared at him.

With the flick of Chair Black's finger, the pain in her leg heightened until she couldn't help but howl. The Gamemakers in Black watched her with a glint of joy in their eyes, and as she contorted, she squeezed her eyes shut and thought about the journey it took for her to get there.

"The game and this feeling in your body is only a glimpse of what your eternity will be like if you free Ronnie," Chair Black said.

Ashley fought the pain as she glared at Chair Black. "Where's Eric?" she growled, wishing he were there to save her.

"You won't see him again," Chair Black said. "He broke a lot of rules to help you and your friends, and he had to be punished."

"What did you do to him?" Ashley asked, but Chair Black didn't answer. His cronies behind him smiled, and Ashley felt as though her heart was going to stop.

The thought of losing Eric filled her with sadness as her mind raced with what they possibly did to punish him for helping her. Were they torturing him at this very moment? Was he suffering in one of the levels of the Game or was he facing a different form of damnation? Was everything he did in vain?

Ashley looked at Ronnie and his sad eyes, and she thought about how her cruelty had landed him here. She had made the choices that led her to Hell's Game, but Ronnie's only weakness was that he had let her peer pressure him with the hope that one day people wouldn't bully him anymore. He was an innocent.

Kristin was an innocent.

Her brother was an innocent.

Jake was an innocent.

They were all innocent until she had affected their lives.

When she thought she had arrived at her final decision, the pain suddenly stopped. She looked down at her body and saw herself in a beautiful, sparkly black dress. Her hair done up. Her make-up flawless.

"Just to up the stakes," Chair Black said to Ashley as she slowly rose to her feet. She stared at her transformation utterly confused. "If you choose to leave Ronnie and free yourself, then we will give you everything you have ever dreamed of."

A circle fell out from the floor, like a fisherman's hole in a cabin in Alaska. However, instead of water, Ashley saw herself walking in Beverly Hills, holding designer shopping bags, smiling as paparazzi snapped her photo as she entered Chanel.

"We will give you fame. Money. A variety of lovers and people who worship you. Best of all, you will suffer no consequence. You will live a long life and when you die, you are guaranteed to never come back here."

Ashley continued to stare into the hole where she saw her mansion, the one she had imagined sharing with Jake one day. She ran playfully as her gorgeous brood of blonde children chased after her. They looked so happy, and so did she. Her children seemed to be given the childhood she had never had.

"There's no catch?" Ashley asked.

Chair Black shook his head before he placed his hands on Ronnie's shoulders. Ronnie squirmed, hating his touch, which burned like fire.

"You have finished the game. You have removed your Mark. There is no catch, besides the fact that you lose Ronnie here, but the world has lost him before... and didn't miss him."

Chair Black smiled as Ashley thought about his proposition. She continued to watch the images of the life she would have on earth, and it dawned on her that no matter how many things she owned, how many people she had, or how much fame she possessed—she would never truly be happy without her brother and her friends.

"So, what is your decision?" Chair Black said.

Ashley gazed up to look at him before giving him her answer.

CHAPTER TWENTY-EIGHT

The hole in the floor disappeared as Ashley stared at Chair Black. The council behind him gazed at her with intensity, and Ronnie closed his eyes, thinking for sure she would take the fame and fortune over his soul.

"What about my friends?" Ashley asked. Ronnie sighed, thankful she had not yet chosen.

"Your friends are stuck in the levels of the game. Those were the rules," Chair Black said.

"Yes, but we seem to be changing the rules now. Aren't we?"

Chair Black was interested.

"What do you have in mind?" he asked.

"Release all of them," Ashley said. "Forgive Eric. Free Ronnie. In exchange for me, the winner of Hell's Game. That seems like a fair deal."

The council gasped at her request, and in an instant, her beautiful black clothing disappeared, returning her to the way she was when she first entered the Deer Creek Cemetery Church. The pain in her leg returned and she dropped to the floor, unable to stand.

"Why would I agree to that?" Chair Black said with a smile. "The option I gave you was the release of Ronnie for your soul. I have no reason to bargain with you."

Ashley felt the pain return, but suffered through it as she spoke. "Yes, but you have no reason to give me up and keep the souls you have already damned. If you were to keep me and release them, who knows if they'll find their way back here anyway? You could end up with all five souls, instead of just four."

The council began to converse amongst themselves as Chair Black stared at her with thoughtful eyes.

"So you agree to stay?" Chair Black said.

"I want to know you will release the others."

As she waited for his response, Ashley inhaled, hoping he would come to her terms. She watched him tap his chin pensively, as if really contemplating her offer.

Finally, he spoke.

"No," he said. "Only Ronnie. That's it.

Ashley's shoulders sank.

"So what is your choice?"

Ronnie and the others stared at her, unsure of what she was going to say.

Ashley looked down, the images of her happy future burned in her mind as the poison in her leg swam through her body.

"Can I speak to Ronnie?" Ashley asked.

Chair Black nodded and removed Ronnie's gag.

Ronnie stared at Ashley.

"Ronnie?" she said tentatively.

"Get out while you can," he said.

Ashley teared up. No matter what she had done, no matter what he had been through, he still cared about other people more than himself. That moment solidified for Ashley how undeserving Ronnie was of being damned.

"Free Ronnie," she said to Chair Black without any hesitation.

The crowd behind her seemed to groan with disappointment.

Chair Black remained stoic as the earth began to shake.

"What's happening?" she asked.

Chair Black said nothing as he and his council walked out of the room and through the solid walls. Ashley ran to help Ronnie escape the chair, but he was bound too tightly.

"The ceiling's collapsing!" Ronnie cried.

"It doesn't matter," she said as a beam fell to the floor. "I've got to help you!"

The wooden planks of the wall fell forward, revealing the stone wall outside, and as Ashley raced to free Ronnie, she realized that the church was caving in on itself.

"They lied to me," she said. "We're both going to lose."

"I'm sorry, Ashley," Ronnie said as they both looked up to see the ceiling come crashing down on them.

PART FOUR: REDEMPTION

"Be strong and courageous. Do not be afraid or terrified because of them, for the Lord, your God, goes with you; he will never leave you nor forsake you."

Deuteronomy 31:6

CHAPTER TWENTY-NINE

Jake's vintage Mustang pulled into the cemetery's parking lot, and as Kristin, Ronnie, and Ashton began to remove their seatbelts, Ashley bolted up in alarm.

"What's happening?" she asked, her voice in a panic, vodka in her hand.

"We're at the cemetery, just like you asked," Ashton replied.

Ashley looked down and saw that she was wearing an angel costume. She glanced in the passenger mirror, recognizing herself at sixteen on Halloween night. Her hair, perfect and curled. Her makeup, sparkly and flawless. She was reliving that night for the third time of her life.

"We're here," she said softly, and Ronnie's jaw tightened. He tried to smile, but his awkward grin only amplified his fear. "Where are you guys going?" Ashley asked as the back doors slammed shut. She realized that she needed to join the rest of the group.

"So, we're really going to see the Gateway to Hell, huh?" Ashton said. He looked at his sister who teetered towards him, and it surprised him that she seemed to be in a panic. "Ashley, are you okay?" he asked.

"We have to go," Ashley said.

"I thought you wanted me to take pictures?" Ronnie asked as he held up his camera.

"We have to go," Ashley repeated.

Kristin scratched her head, confused. Was Ashley playing another game with them?

Ronnie seemed to think so.

"I want to see the church," he said, and he said it with such conviction that Jake was unsure of what to do.

"Um...?" Jake stalled, not knowing what to say.

"Why see it at all? Let's leave," Ashley said. She looked to Jake. "Jake, you don't want to be here. You don't want Ronnie to be here. Let's go home."

Jake looked relieved as he pulled out his car keys. Kristin and Ashton shrugged, losing interest in the church if Ashley no longer wanted to see it.

However, Ronnie wanted to stay.

"I thought the whole reason we were coming out tonight was to take pictures of the church," Ronnie said. "You guys tricked me. You got me all scared and the minute we show up, you change your mind."

Jake stared at Ronnie with sympathy. "That's not what happened. We just don't want to go to the church..."

"You guys are going to tell everyone that I chickened out," Ronnie said, "but I didn't. I want to go!"

Ashley stared at him. What was his problem? Did he want to die?

"We're not going, Ronnie," she said. "It's for your own good."

Ronnie glared at her, his lip quivering as if he were about to cry.

Ashton, feeling sorry for him, turned to Kristin and Jake. "Fine," Ashton said. "Let's just check it out for a second."

To Ashley's amazement, Ashton, Kristin, and Ronnie walked away towards the church without her.

"Are you guys serious?" Ashley screeched.

Jake walked over and put his arm around her shoulder.

"You scared?" he asked as he nuzzled her hair. Even though she was worried, she melted into him, missing his affection. She found it strange that this was what it was once like between them.

"You don't hate me?" Ashley asked.

Jake laughed. "You annoy me a lot, but why would I hate you?"

Though she smiled, she was confused. Were the past two years all a dream? Was Hell's Game not real?

"Are you okay?" Jake asked.

"Are they really going to the church?" Ashley asked.

"I think so. Ronnie seems like he really wants to prove he's tough."

"That's stupid."

"Which is why we should check on him."

Holding her hand, Jake led Ashley to the church. She moved tentatively as though her legs were made of lead, and Jake found it amusing and strange that his overly confident girlfriend had finally found fear.

When they made it to where Ashton and Kristin stood, Ashley gasped, covering her mouth with her hand.

"This is crazy," Ronnie said as he snapped a photo of the church, which had fallen in on itself. All that remained of it was rubble and stone.

"When did this happen?" Kristin asked.

"I have no idea," Ashton said.

Ashley shook her head in disbelief as Jake held her tight. "I can't believe it," she said, utterly dumfounded. Her ears perked up and she heard crickets, something that had not existed in her previous memories of this night. "Maybe it was never real…" she whispered to herself.

"Maybe it was always run down," Jake said. "After all, who else has come here…ever?"

There was another flash of light as Ronnie took more pictures. He couldn't wait until he got home and printed them out. All the kids at school would think he was so cool for being out that night.

CHAPTER THIRTY

Ashley woke up the next morning and walked to the kitchen. She retrieved orange juice from the refrigerator and poured herself a glass. As she yawned, her brother Ashton, seated at the kitchen table, looked up from his newspaper. He smiled at her.

"That was nice what you said to Ronnie yesterday," Ashton said. "You really made his year."

Ashley sat across from him and sipped her juice. "I'm glad," she said.

"Were you serious that he could hang out with us whenever he wanted?"

She nodded. "Of course," she said. She was done being a mean girl.

Ashton examined her, and she looked away, uncomfortable with the scrutiny. "Something's different about you," he said.

"What are you talking about?" she asked.

"I don't know how to describe it, but you're different."

"In a good way?"

He smiled. "Definitely."

Ashley smiled back, and even though she had already known it, she further realized how much she loved her brother.

"How much of this matters to you?" Ashley asked, pointing at their lavish surroundings. She gazed at their granite countertops, stainless steel appliances, and fancy furniture. Although everything was beautiful, it meant little to her. She had seen even more beautiful things in Hell, and those things had come at a price.

"What are you talking about?" Ashton asked, confused by his new, nicer sister.

She stared at him, not wanting to be blunt, but since Hell's Game—or since her dream of it—she had been thinking a lot about her father and the deal he made with Tom Ryder all those years ago.

"Are you sure you really don't remember what happened?" Ashley asked. What if Ashton, Kristin, Jake and Ronnie did remember, but they were too scared to talk about it?

"Are you talking about the cemetery?" Ashton asked.

Ashley stared at him with excitement and disbelief. So she wasn't the only one after all. "So you remember?"

"Of course, I remember," he replied. "It happened yesterday. The church was gone. We broke curfew. You're acting really weird, Ash."

Ashley gawked at her brother, her shoulders slumping in disbelief. This would be the last time she would talk about her memories, which she now realized were nothing more than dreams.

"I'm going to tell Mom what happened to me when I was nine," Ashley said.

"Are you sure?" Ashton asked. He had wanted Ashley to say something since they were children, but he wasn't sure what had changed her mind.

Ashley nodded. "And after I tell her I'm going to report what happened to the police."

"So this is happening?" Ashton asked. Just as Ashley had, Ashton looked around at their environment, their life, and he knew it was all going to change.

**

Ashley sat in the passenger seat of her car, gazing out the window as she rode past the beautiful Victorian house of Mayor Hercules, its yard full of raked leaves. Ashley watched as Mayor Hercules sat on the front porch with his pretty redheaded wife Myra. Their adult daughter Brytani pulled up in a Mercedes and parked it in the driveway, her own kids happy in the backseat.

"Joseph," Heather said into her cell phone, pulling Ashley away from watching the Hercules family. "I want those divorce papers processed as soon as possible."

Heather parked her car in front of the Deer Creek Police Station. Ashley stared at the station's sign, a simple white sign with blue lettering, and took a deep breath. The gravity of what she was about to do filled her body with anxiety.

"Are you ready?" Heather asked as she reached for her daughter's hand.

"I'm ready," Ashley said.

**

That evening, Ashley prepared for bed as if it were any other evening, even though only two hours ago, she had watched as Captain Nickels had two police officers drag her father into a police car. She remembered avoiding her father's eyes and the feeling of relief knowing that she had finally broken her silence.

"He's not going to hurt any of us. I promise you that," her mother had said, and Ashley wondered why she had never said anything to her mother earlier. After Ashley had finally confessed what had happened, she felt as though the wall that had existed between them had finally disappeared.

"I'll take care of you, until the end of the time. I'll always love you, but I can't make you mine…"

Ashley hummed the song to herself as she put on her pink silk pajamas. She walked to her vanity and she stared at her reflection.

"I wonder..." she said as she lifted up her hair. She turned to the mirror to see the back of her neck, and saw that it was clear. "Maybe I'm crazy," Ashley murmured.

She climbed into bed, and after her head hit the pillow, she closed her eyes. Though she loved Jake, she could not stop thinking about her kiss with Eric Whitehorse. Even if it was only a dream, the memory still sent tingles throughout her body. How could an imaginary occurrence still do that to her?

She put her hand underneath the pillow to get comfortable, and to her surprise, felt something sharp, almost like a tooth that one would leave for the fairy.

"What the...?" Ashley said as she turned on the light. She sat upwards and pulled out the item underneath her pillow. It was a black engagement ring with a giant diamond, the one that Eric had offered her in Hell's Game.

She looked up and saw her shocked reflection in the vanity mirror. Above, written on the glass in fog was the word, "Someday."

THE END.

ABOUT THE AUTHOR

Teresa Lo is a writer living in Los Angeles. In addition to *Hell's Game*, *she* has published *Realities*, *The Other Side*, and *The Red Lantern Scandals*. For more information, please see her website **www.tloclub.com**.